THEATER –

RED PLUSH & ELUSIVE HOPES

Stephen P. E. Lees. LL. B.

This book published in 2017 by SPEL Publications
prodev@globalnet.co.uk

Copyright © Stephen Lees 2017

ISBN No. 978-1-9996817-1-5

A CIP catalogue record of this book is available
from the British Library.

Book and Cover design by SPEL

Typeset in Garamond

Printed and bound in the United States

SPEL Publication acknowledges kind permission from Bloomsbury
Publishers to reproduce some images from '*Visions of Architecture*' also by
Stephen Lees ISBN 978-1-4081-2881-7.

SPEL Publication further acknowledges kind permission from the
Calderdale Museums to reproduce the painting entitled, '*Briggate*' by
John Atkinson Grimshaw on this book cover.

Contents

Introduction

This series of five books on Music Halls starts with 'Royal Aq. - Queen of Music Halls' and then 'Music Hall - The Saga Goes On.' Followed by 'Vaudeville - The Struggle Continues,' then, 'Burlesque - The Endless Attempts,' and finally, 'Theater - Red Plush & Elusive Hopes.' All five books chronicle the hilarious exploits of two Vaudeville artistes out of New York, Jack Mitchell and Theo Houston, who accompany an impresario, Michael Lodge, back to England to perform in various London Music Halls.

By now after several weeks in London, both Jack and Theo have gotten into their stride and begin to understand the peculiarities of well appointed red plush Music Halls in London. This appreciation, however, does not prevent them from still falling into awkward situations. Or embarrassing moments, both on and off the stage, with more drama, making 'Theater – Red Plush & Elusive Hopes' even more humorous, enjoyable and informative. Complete with an extensive index, the book, chronicles the on-going saga of Music Halls and their intrepid performing artistes. All five books contain original line drawings of Music Halls and other buildings drawn by the author.

The book is

dedicated to

Soho

in which

Music Hall

is a daily event.

Chapter 1

The St Pancras Hospital

The next morning during our break-fast, Jack and I were discussing the previous day's events. This included our encounter with the eminent members of a loose confederation of Music Hall and theater impresarios, all of whom were attending a soirée in a town house in Harley Street. More importantly, however, was our performance on stage, earlier in the evening, at the Philharmonic Music Hall at Islington. And in particular Marmeduke's interpretation, as a Ventriloquist's Dummy, of the venal character of the Commissioner of the Metropolitan Board of Works. As usual, the newspapers hailed Marmeduke's act as a resounding *tour de force* as he swept all before him. Of course, it is to be remembered that Marmeduke is Cinderella masquerading as Marmeduke in addition to other characters including Little Bo Peep and a Ventriloquist's Dummy! All of which she has made her own and to great critical acclaim.

"Read this article Theo," said Jack, my stage partner of over thirty years, as he handed to me the morning edition of, *'The Globe'* newspaper.

I soon found the article which was generous in its praise of Marmeduke and his innovative act. Having read it, I looked up at Jack to express my thoughts on the article.

House in Harley Street

"Marmeduke never ceases to amaze me," I offered, up as Jack handed to me the, '*London Chronicle.*'

'Members of the public who were fortunate enough to patronize the newly rebuilt Philharmonic Music Hall at Islington yesterday evening, were treated to a series of spectacular acts including the evergreen Little Bo Peep and Cinderella. And, a new act in town performed by an accomplished artiste name of Marmeduke. His mimicry of the Commissioner of the Metropolitan Board of Work was convincing as it was compelling. And well worth watching.'

I still find it amusing to note that members of the public, including theater critics, still do not realize that

Philharmonic Music Hall

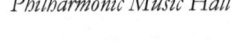

Cinderella, Little Bo Peep and Marmeduke are all one and the same person! This deception is a testament to Cinderella's artistic abilities.

I was just about to hand the newspaper back to Jack when something caught my eye. I focused in on the note, embedded in the Stop Press section of the, *'London Chronicle'* newspaper. I read the précised report.

'Music Hall artiste, miss Mabel Green was late last night admitted to the St. Pancras Asylum for the incurably deranged for her own protection and that of society's. A stipend magistrate sitting at Bow Street Police Court took only a few moments to grant the order confining miss Green to the asylum. Evidence was offered up that miss Mabel Green was observed wandering around the back streets of Covent Garden in a dishevelled state causing a commotion with members of the public with whom she came across and indulging liberally in coprolalia[1] in in addition to repeated overt acts of copropraxia.[2] And apparently with no shame or remorse. It was these acts & confident behavior by Green that first alerted the police to this breach of the peace. Later when she was being asked to give an account of herself the police were unable to determine whether Green was either drunk or suffering from some form of mental collapse. When taken in to custody, Green did not appear to understand where she was or why she had been arrested. When Green attempted to speak, it was insensible and incomprehensible. She also acted in a wild and erratic manner. claiming emphatically she was being fated by indifference and persons who wish her misfortune. Miss Green also claimed that she could hear continually very loud voices in her head urging her to perform her mission and certain acts.'

I paused and thought for a moment about the enormity of this report in the newspaper. It occurred to me that Mabel may in fact be only now re-acting to the audience's dismal response to her energetic choreographic endeavors on the stage at the Tivoli Theater of Variety, the other evening, which resulted in her dramatic mental collapse later in the Crush Bar. But obviously, it would seem that she is now retaliating to that adverse criticism or at least indifferent response of her performance by those seated in the auditorium on that fateful evening. And, whilst I do like Mabel and consider her to be very talented, she does however display innate symptoms of mental instability.

I handed the newspaper to Jack, pointing with my fork at the report in the Stop Press.

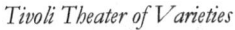

Tivoli Theater of Varieties

Jack's response was unexpected. Having read the report with a serious expression upon his face; he then burst into fits of laughter.

"Jack, I cannot see that a friend of ours being committed to the St. Pancras Asylum to be a cause for hilarity, as stated in that report which is of great moment. Mabel may be seriously distraught or upset or worse in a fit of pique. Surely this should be of concern to us? Perhaps I should wire Lodge and make inquiries to figure out what we can do to relieve her condition. If not effect a release from her incarceration," I remonstrated with Jack.

"Theo, I am not laughing at Mabel being admitted to the mad house. The situation is funny to me, simply because I can just imagine Mabel wandering around Covent Garden in this fog. Arguing with all and sundry whilst walking the streets and causing one commotion after another. But yes, you are perfectly correct. We should cable Loge and get him to use his undoubted contacts to help Mabel.

A cable-gram was duly dispatched to Lodge, or *Loge*, as Jack will refer to him as. Later in the day Lodge did arrive at the St. Pancras Hotel. He found us in the main salon. And having exchanged anxious concerns stated that not a moment should be lost in locating Mabel and endeavoring to effect a release from her confinement.

"If for no other reason," continued Lodge, "she is supposed to be doing a guest appearance on the stage in, *'Puss in Boots,'* at the Alhambra Music Hall in two days time."

Lodge thought for a moment.

"Though I do wish," he continued, "that Mabel would desist from her predilection for perambulating around the Metropolis. Most unbecoming for a lady of the stage; one might think her a flâneuse!" [3]

"Well we know she is holed up at the St Pancras Facility for the Criminally Insane. Say did we not drive past that place in a Char à Banc on our way back from Belle Elmore's botched funeral at Highgate Cemetery?" inquired Jack.

"That place is up the road behind this St Pancras Hotel. I suggest gentlemen that we avail ourselves of a carriage and travel to effect Mabel's rescue" announced Lodge, in tones of concern.

Whether that apparent concern was based on a genuine regard for Mabel's enforced confinement or her inability to perform under contract in a guest appearance on the stage in, 'Puss in Boots,' I simply could not determine. But knowing Lodge, I suspect the latter.

Irrespective of my thoughts, Jack and I followed Lodge through the foyer illuminated by chandeliers tinkling with

Alhambra Music Hall

cut glass and out in to the clammy acrid fog still present outside. We did not have long to wait before a Barouche four-wheeler carriage, driven by a liveried coachman, came clattering into the stone Port Cochère in front of the St. Pancras Hotel, in which Jack and I are holed up.

We climbed aboard the Barouche carriage and made ourselves comfortable on the green buttoned down leather upholstered seats. As we did so Lodge pointed, with his gold capped ebony cane, to a small brass plaque embedded in the highly varnished elm headboard immediately beneath the coach driver's bench.

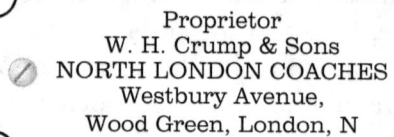

Proprietor
W. H. Crump & Sons
NORTH LONDON COACHES
Westbury Avenue,
Wood Green, London, N

"This Barouche carriage gentlemen, is part of a fleet of coaches operated, as you can read, by W. H. Crump & Sons. Crump. Crump of course, is our old friend Harry Champion, the acclaimed Music Hall artiste," advised Lodge.

At the same time, our coachman whipped up his Yorkshire Grey horses which then pulled us out of the vestibule, built of stone and decorated with ornate raised reliefs and carvings. A few moments later we turned into the Euston Road filled with lumbering carriages and pantechnicons.

"So tell me. What is it with this proprietor being called W. H. Crump & Sons?" inquired Jack, with his characteristic Jersey City blunt mannerism.

"Crump, William Henry Crump," responded Lodge, "as I mentioned earlier, is the real name of Harry Champion. Aside of his stage abilities he is also active in business. In fact he runs a business, as a successful entrepreneur, hiring out horse drawn Barouches, such as this one that we are riding in. Often he does so to fellow Music Hall artistes who wish to arrive in style at some place or other!"

"Do you hire the Barouche that you have from W. H. Crump & Sons?" asked Jack, innocently.

Lodge deigned not to have heard, but instead looked through his monocle into the fog laden aëther swirling around the Euston Road.

Eventually, after a complicated manœuvre, we turned off the Euston Road and into the Midland Road en-route to our destiny at the St. Pancras Asylum for the incurably deranged. That or come to Mabel's aid. The journey was not particularly long and in a short period of time we were entering the main gate of the establishment. A uniformed guard approached our W. H. Crump & Sons operated Barouche carriage. It was Lodge who answered his inquiry.

From what I could make out in the fog, the place had a minatory, even ominous look about it. Made even more so, by the sound of muffled screams drifting through the yellow fog swirling about us. Both the sounds and gloom of the place combined to create a sense of foreboding, manifested by a sensation of a vacuüm within my chest. The building type was Victorian and built of polychromatic brickwork and looked very much like a secured institution for the mentally impaired, including I suppose, our Mabel.

Whilst Lodge and Jack were arguing over the fare the Barouche carriage driver was attempting to exact from them. I began reading a stone plaque embedded into the dreary polychromatic brickwork to the façade of the main building dominating the entrance court yard.

SAINT PANCRAS
GUARDIANS OF THE POOR

This stone was laid on the 25th day of July, 1890
In the year of Our Lord

By

MAJOR GENERAL AUGUSTUS E. WARREN
CHAIRMAN OF THE BOARD OF GUARDIANS
ASSISTED BY Mr. CHURCHWARDEN A. BODEN
CHAIRMAN OF THE WORKHOUSE BUILDING
COMMITTEE
Mr. ALFRED A. MILLWARD
CLERK TO THE GUARDIANS

KIRK & RANDALL & Co. Ltd	A & C MARSTON
BUILDERS	ARCHITECTS
147 Grosvenor Road, SW	35 Agar Grove, NW

"So this place, I figured out, started as a work house to accommodate the *Undeserving Poor*, no doubt. Could Mabel be a secret member of the *Undeserving Poor*, occasionally seeking refuge with them in places such as this? Before I could answer my own question, Lodge dismissed our carriage and beckoned me over to where he was standing. We all of us then followed the guard. And possessing our souls we entered this place of mental torment and anguish as evidenced by the audible screams still racing through the fog laden aëther. Would they keep us here, I asked myself.

"You will need to sign in as guests at the main reception at the end of this corridor," informed the guard.

"Given who I am," retorted Lodge, "I was at least

hoping to meet with the director of the place, in order to secure Mabel's release."

The guard simply ignored Lodge's remark.

Walking down the corridor was a bleak experience and the walls of which were painted in brown paint up to the dado level. Thereafter the upper walls, progressing up to a high barrel vaulted ceiling, were finished in a dull creamed colored paint. From this high ceiling were suspended opaque white light globes. No decoration or fixtures of any type adorned the walls of this bleak corridor.

Having made our way down the corridor, with trepidation into the depths of the asylum, we reached the end and marched into a large room filled with a variety of people, the majority of whom were in some capacity or other clearly mentally unbalanced. I instinctively looked around for Mabel. Lodge in the meantime had made his way through the assembled inmates and was now arguing with a fellow wearing a white jacket and monocle in front of one eye.

"Do you not know who I am? Does the name Lodge, Michael W, impresario mean nothing to you?" demanded Lodge of the monocle wearing attendant.

"No sir, it does not. With respect this is an establishment to house the imbecile and the criminally insane, including your Mabel Green, whom you seek. As you can see, we are neither a Music Hall nor even Vaudeville, despite appearances to the contrary," replied the attendant.

I merely wish to be taken to the Superintendent, a Mr. Nathan Robinson" [4] said Lodge, in more conciliatory tones, "in order that I might be of benefit to the incarcerated Mabel. And relieve this worthy institution of the financial burden of caring for her."

Trust Lodge to work in a monetary implication into his plea, I thought. Based no doubt on his overt reverence for and infatuation with Box Office receipts! However, his stratagem worked, for at that very moment, the attendant started to write a note on a piece of paper. Presently he handed it to Lodge whilst at the same time beckoning an inmate standing nearby.

"This is Fortesque, a trustee, he will take you to Superintendant Robinson," informed the attendant.

Lodge thanked the attendant and then turned to face our guide, Fortesque.

"Lead on Forteque! Not a moment should be lost in obtaining Mabel's emancipation from this, this place of eternal damnation," insisted Lodge.

"If you say so sir," replied Fortesque, "please follow me."

We did. And whilst we followed Lodge and Fortesque walking down one white washed walled corridor after another. Jack and I exchanged glances. Fortesque looked exactly like Lodge's truculent ex man-servant Aloysius! The resemblance was astounding as it was remarkable.

"Could this flunky, this Fortesque be Aloysius' twin brother?" Jack whispered in my ear.

We pulled back from walking immediately behind Lodge and Fortesque, in order that they should not overhear our conversation.

"He walks with that pronounced shuffling gait which Aloysius always did. And his face looks exactly like that of Aloysius's; pocked-marked and sallow. Even his smile is sad. And, his black hair is lank and greasy as is Aloysius' hair!"

"But Jack, it is that twitch he has afflicting his hands and eye. He has the St. Vitus's Dance, [5] and is obviously an accomplished St. Vitus's Dancer!" I offered.

"I should like to engage this Fortesque in conversation. Just to see if our discussion would lead rapidly to an argument. As inevitably it would with Aloysius and to figure out if this Fortesque has a razor sharp and facetious wit, similar to that of Aloysius's. A wit, as we both know, Aloysius has perfected and vented on Lodge mercilessly on numerous occasions especially in our presence," said Jack.

Whilst walking down the corridors, the floors of which were paved with York flagstones. We came across several inmates tethered together. Some of whom were clearly severely mentally imbalanced. As they shuffled past us, a few looked at Jack and me, though with vacant expressions and eyes seemingly staring into oblivion.

We continued walking down the bleak corridor. Often we caught glimpses, through open doors, of the inside of cells and other holding rooms. There was a feeling of utter desperation which pervaded the place. And I began to regret being here and thought more about quitting our mission and abandoning Mabel to her fate.

Suddenly Fortesque stopped outside a heavy oak cruciform door, reënforced with iron bands across the front. He lowered his head and thought for a moment.

"This is the office of the Superintendant Robinson," he said, whilst knocking on the door with his knuckles.

I was not sure what to expect when entering the Superintendant's office; but an irrational feeling of apprehension attended my thoughts.

Within seconds of Fortesque knocking on the door; it was flung open.

"Yes, yes what do you want?" asked a voice from a person who was out of sight from where I was standing. "Why do you disturb me at this hour? Oh, it is you Fortesque!"

"These gentlemen have come to see you and plead for the release of that Mabel woman," answered Fortesque.

"Which gentlemen?" came the reply.

These gentlemen standing here," said Fortesque, pointing with his shaking right hand to where Lodge, Jack and I were standing.

At length a bald head emerged from within the door frame and a face peered out into the corridor. Its owner then turned to view us. And did so through the gold colored pince-nez he was wearing.

Lodge took a deep breath and was about to take the initiative, but was prevented from doing so.

"Yes, yes what is it? What do you want?" asked the bald headed superintendant.

Lodge breathed out and answered the inquiry.

"My name is Michael Loge, sorry Lodge, impresario..."

"What of it?" interrupted the superintendant, "and why are you confused about your own surname? Are you schizophrenic? Are you an inmate here?"

Lodge viewed the superintendant with a seasoned eye.

"No, certainly not," replied Lodge, categorically, "we have come to talk with you about as recent admission to your fine establishment of a friend of ours, name of Green, Mabel Green.

The superintendant did not answer Lodge, but viewed him, and for that matter, Jack and I with an equal distain for quite some time.

"You had better step inside, I suppose," he deigned to offer.

We all of us stepped into the superintendant's office, including Fortesque!

Not having been in an office of the governor of an institution housing the insane or the imbecile, I was uncertain just what one might expect. The décor of

Superintendant Robinson's office came as a surprise not only to Jack and me; but also to Lodge too, judging by the expression upon his face. Fortesque, who had clearly been in the room before, made his way to an ornately carved eighteenth century escritoire writing bureau upon which was a impressive selection of drink. Without asking, either the superintendant or us, Fortesque proceeded to pour out five decent measures of whisky.

Whilst he did so I looked about Superintendant Robinson's office. In comparison to the dull, if dreary corridors we had just marched down. Robinson's office was extremely well-appointed, with expensive items of furniture ranged around a large airy room. Complete with a high ceiling decorated with raised filigree designs in the plaster work and from which three intricately fashioned chandeliers, tinkling with cut glass and crystals, were suspended.

On the walls, covered in Regency yellow and white striped wallpaper, were affixed large gilt-framed paintings of sylvan scenes of classical buildings and landscapes. One of which, a drawing called *'Visions of Architecture,'* I recognised immediately. For this same image exists in Sir Augustus Harris' country house and in Lodge's town house in the Bergen Avenue. I should be interested to learn who possesses the original image. Since first seeing it, I have been fascinated by this intricate drawing of a collection of ancient classical structures and temples.

I suppose my being entranced by the drawing, is grounded upon my instinctive appreciation of the inherent beauty of an ancient classical building, such as a Greek temple. Though I think, or rather suspect, that beauty is not necessarily based on æstheticism; but founded more on Pythagoras's trigonometry as mathematical proportions expressed in elegant masonry.

Visions of Architecture

I continued to look around the room and noticed set into one wall were three ceiling high French windows, leading out on to a balcony, fenced with iron railings and overlooking a manicured garden. Against each window and pulled back and secured with gold colored twisted cords were curtains of fine brocade. Against the opposite wall was constructed an extensive library filled with reference books of philosophical treatise or of an æsthetic persuasion. The floor of the office, uncarpeted and bare, was made up of polished elm floorboards which created a soft warm appearance.

This was clearly the office of a dilettante, who took his interior décor and comfortable appointment of his surrounds seriously, and from which, he ran a madhouse for the criminally insane!

In the corner of the room was a substantial mahogany desk the top of which was covered in a red tooled leather finish. On each corner of the front of the desk was an ornate and exquisitely designed brass lamp stand supporting an opaque white globe from which radiated a soft warm light. It was behind this desk that Superintendant Robinson now sat viewing us, still with a cultivated distain in his eyes.

However, eventually he motioned us to join him around his elegantly fashioned desk, which we did by sitting on the Chippendale chairs, the seats of which were upholstered in white and yellow striped moiré silk. Presently Fortesque joined us with five glasses filled with neat whisky. At the same time, the Superintendent offered us cigars from his red velvet covered cigar box.

"Right," said Lodge, looking at his whisky glass, "let us do this thing. Superintendant Robinson, we have to thank you for your time and hospitality. And fully appreciate the challenging demands made upon you in running this asylum, even from the opulent and comfortable appointment of your office."

"We address the St. Pancras Asylum simply as, No. 4 King's Road, St. Pancras," [6] said Robinson, inspecting his glass of whisky with a questioning look in his eyes.

"They have come to plea for the release of the Mabel woman from the clutches of our overbearing care," offered Fortesque.

"Why?" inquired Robinson .

"Oh for such inconvenient reasons as those incorporated into the Bill of Rights or Habeas Corpus or other less significant rights appertaining to the individual," answered Jack, pensively.

"And for several more important reasons," interjected Lodge, "not least that she is scheduled to make a guest appearance in a production called, '*Puss in Boots*,' at the Alhambra Music Hall in two days time. I would personally deem it a great service to Music Hall if she could be released, if only for that reason, in order that she might fulfil her contractual obligations to appear on the evening."

"And avoid those dreaded cancellation fees, which inevitably arise from such calamitous circumstances, as failure to turn up and fulfil the contract," interposed Jack, much to the amusement of Robinson.

"And their devastating impact on Box Office receipts. For let us dare not underestimate that terrible and most debilitating and cruel state of desperation," added Lodge, passionately, whilst looking at Robinson with moist eyes.

"Is not the Mabel woman of the drag?" asked Fortesque, with a glint in his eye, "and does she not sometimes sing lascivious songs for her supper in Public Houses, especially in the Whitechapel district, of an evening? And did she not cavort with a disreputable and highly suspect dance troupe, all of whom, even now, take perverse pleasure in calling themselves the, *Inexhaustible Cremorne Belles*, before she was ignominiously dismissed? Dismissed I add, for outrageous behavior in public unbecoming of a so called lady, or at least so defined by her sartorial preference on that particular occasion?"

"Do not be ridiculous!" answered Lodge to the first question, "Her desire to sing in Public Houses, whether in the Whitechapel or indeed in St. James's is immaterial. But if she does, one could only imagine it is to keep her tessitura as wide open as possible. And as for her association with the renowned *Inexhaustible Cremorne Belles*; I understand that she deliberately decided to pursue a soloist career as a singer. And accordingly, joined, after much competition, my illustrious trio of sopranos called the *Three Graces*."

I could see that Lodge, was working himself in to a state of indignation, as indicated by his relapse into his monomania affliction of looking over both his shoulders for no apparent reason. An irrational act which I noted was also noticed by the superintendant with furrowed brows.

"The *Three Graces,* of which Mabel is one," continued Lodge, "regularly perform the sacred oratorio called The Choral Anthem Symphony and, do so to great acclaim. Mabel is the sweetest of creatures and the sort which would burst into tears at the sight of crushed red rose, for such are her feminine sensibilities. She conducts herself with the greatest of bearing and deportment and these two gentlemen would readily testify accordingly as to her real character."

I wondered. Were Jack or I to be invited to give an account of Mabel's real character. Then it is conceivable that we would not see Mabel performing on the public stage for quite some years.

"As to this unfounded and scurrilous attack upon her character," continued Lodge, "one could only imagine that it is a fabrication design by her detractors in order to discredit her. For every successful artiste, such as Mabel, there are legions which comprise the jealous and venal and let me assure..."

"She was apprehended walking the streets of Covent Garden in a state which did not quite reflect her so called, *femimine sensibilities*, shall we say regarding crushed red roses. But that she was caught wearing men's clothes accompanied by very audible profanity of coprolaliac proportions, and in the fog-bound street, being uttered from her mouth. It was that fact which attracted the three constables' attention. All three of whom were needed desperately in order to affect an arrest on this Mabel," interrupted Fortesque.

Lodge continued his unflinching and gallant defense of Mabel's unimpeachable character. No doubt motivated, by her incarceration and the consequential frightening prospects of the specter of reduction on his Box Office receipts.

"The fact that Mabel was wearing men's clothing is surely irrelevant; for I too wear such clothes," said Lodge, unaware of his faux pas.

Superintendent Robinson's response was unexpected. He looked up at the ceiling, decorated with raised filigree designs in the plaster work, and then eased himself out of his chair. Having done so, he walked over to one of the French windows overlooking the manicured garden area. He stood there for quite some time with hands clasped behind his back. At length it was Fortesque who broke the silence. He walked up to the superintendent and stood next to him. Moments later both fell into a deep muffled conversation.

Very well," said Robinson, "we have other inmates with whom to deal. And I have more urgent consideration with which to occupy my time. Fortesque will take you to her. But be warned, she is unpredictable in her current mental state and disposition. Be advised, you may become distressed when meeting with her. However, you are more than welcome to try and reason with the woman."

1 Involuntary swearing and utterances of obscene words or inappropriate derogatory remarks
2 Performing obscene gestures
3 A female idler who walks the streets observing all and sundry
4 Robinson was in fact the chairman of the Board of Guardians
5 A nervous affliction causing twitching to the eyes or hands
6 To protect inmates from the stigma of having been incarcerated there

Chapter 2

The Imprisoned Soul

As a result of a commotion in the streets of Covent Garden, of which Mabel, was the cause and main instigator, we now found ourselves, as visitors to her, within the confines of the St. Pancras Asylum for the mentally deranged. Or more colloquially known as, so we have been told, No. 4 King's Road, St. Pancras and at present, home to Mabel Green, the third member of the *Three Graces*. The times Jack and I have driven past the St. Pancras Asylum are too numerous to mention. But, never in my wildest dreams did I expect to find ourselves within its walls on a mercy dash to relieve Mabel from her incarceration. Our guide to Mabel's location within the asylum was Fortesque, an inmate, but clearly with a hold over the superintendant of the asylum, name of Robinson. More alarmingly, was Fortesque's remarkable resemblance to Lodge's former man-servant, Aloysius. Both individuals were afflicted with the St. Vitus's Dance and twitches to their eyes. Each had sallow skin that was severely pock-marked. Both retained a lethal turn of wit and an inordinate arrogance, given their respective menial or subservient rôles.

As the four of us made our way down one corridor after another, we past several groups of shackled inmates being escorted by guards. Some would try to break away from the confinement in a forlorn bid for freedom. One inmate of the asylum, wearing a robust straight jacket was being escorted by two guards down a corridor towards us. When suddenly he broke away from his guards and came shuffling up to Lodge jabbering interminable nonsense in Lodge's face.

This unexpected action somewhat unnerved Lodge and for a moment he lost that cultivated image of a suave, but decisive, tough businessman, if you will. The inmate, whose reason had been clearly stricken from his mind, was brought back under control. But continued to shout loudly, whilst gesticulating wildly at Lodge and indulging in an impromptu bout of concerted copropraxiac gestures. [1]

Lodge tried to maintain a posture of nonchalant indifference to this outburst.

However, irrespective of this incident, I began to harbor great fears for the state of Mabel's mind and hoped to God she had not totally lost her reason too.

We continued through more corridors all of which combined to create quite an elaborate Labyrinth from which escape seemed an impossibility. Even if one were predispose to attempt such a venture, as Theseus did back in ancient Greece times, albeit from a Minatour infested Labyrinth of tunnels and not a mad house in London.

At last Fortesque led us to a set of white painted double doors which opened up into a Nightingale ward.

"This is where that Mabel woman is held," he announced, as he approached the ward supervisor.

After a few moments of hushed talking between the two during which the supervisor nodded his head in agreement several times. Fortesque beckon us to follow him into the depths of the ward.

Mabel's ward was located within a three storey brick built Nightingale Ward Block. This building, according to another plaque cemented into the brickwork, was designed by the architectural firm of Messrs. John Giles & Biven. To each floor of the block was allocated a ward. Mabel's ward was typical and comprised a series of iron framed beds, set in front of elongated windows which provided light and aëther into the ward.

We were escorted to Mabel's bed. The bed was surrounded by a group of inmates. As we approached the bed, my heart began to pound within the walls of my chest, such was my presentiment of what; I did not know. Would our Mabel simply be a mental wreck jabbering incoherently? Or worse, lost to the world and staring out at us with blank unrecognising eyes set a tortured face reflecting a vacant expression. The expectation was unbearable. Especially since the ward was filled with manic screams drifting up from various beds.

"Get me some quail's eggs and a flagon of porter, now," came an injunction from within the group surrounding Mabel's bed.

The sound of this voice had an astonishing effect on Lodge. He immediately stopped dead in his tracks and looked at both Jack and me.

The voice was that of Mabel's and did not seem in any way diminished in its sanity or indeed clarity. We all pushed our way through the crowd and came face to face with Mabel.

Mabel was sitting upright in an iron-framed bed wearing a pink colored bed bonnet trimmed with white frills and a voluminous pale green padded bed coat adorned with floral patterns. Mabel did not seem in the least bit surprised at seeing us, but merely said as she looked up.

"I knew you would come," she uttered, "and would you like some quails' eggs? They are very fresh. We keep a few quails in the back yard of the ward. Come to think of it, where are my eggs?" Mabel demanded of nobody in particular. Although, at that moment, two persons immediately broke away from the entourage gathered around the bed, presumably in search of quails' eggs.

"Supervisor can you open the window as it is a trifle stuffy in this ward," instructed Mabel.

The ward supervisor obeyed Mabel's instruction without hesitation or demure.

"A little something from the superintendant of the asylum," said Fortesque, as he handed a flat half bottle of whisky to Mabel.

"Now, now Fortesque," admonished Mabel, "we do not say asylum here, but simply, No. 4 King's Road, St. Pancras."

"Quite possibly, but we do remain a place in which to house the incurably deranged." retorted Fortesque.

Whilst we were standing there a continuous procession of inmates came to Mabel's bed side and beseeched her with questions and advice. Did Mabel like the dress that a particular inmate was wearing? Or, from another, was her hair fetching and alluring? Mabel replied in the positive to both supplicants.

I looked at Jack who returned my questioning gaze. We had both witnessed Fortesque's obsequious behavior to Mabel. According her a deference, as though she were an Eminence Gris,[2] ordering the ward supervisor and other inmates around. Whilst holding court from her bed side, as it were.

It was Lodge who burst in to this delusion.

"Mabel," said Lodge, "we have come to take you away from this place of torment, of insanity and hopeless causes."

"Why?" Mabel responded,

"Because..." replied Lodge.

"My work is not finished here," interrupted Mabel, "so much to do and so little time in which to do it!"

"What can you talking about?" continued Lodge, "you are holed up in the middle of madhouse surrounded by the insane and the mentally unbalanced and condemned. What is this nonsense about so much to do and so little time with which to do it?"

"My people," responded Mabel, "you see around you here, need me. To them, I remain a beacon of hope in a sea of lost hopes and uncertainties. I am the conduit through which they can find eventual salvation from their misery and dashed hopes. I could never abandon them to their fates."

I was beginning to think that perhaps Mabel had lost her reason after all and had finally succumbed to her fragile state of mind brought on by her brain fever. That even the properties extolled in that patented preparation called Phospherine was unable to relieve.

I contemplated the advertisement I has seen recently somewhere.

Lodge on the other hand had not quite abandoned Mabel to her mental plight real or imaginary, motivated, no doubt by other, less altruistic, reasons. Not least the contractual obligation he has to the Alhambra Music Hall. And accordingly, continued to exhort Mabel into seeing reason.

"If the people you see around you here, need you Mabel as you say," continued Lodge, "because to them, you remain a beacon of hope in a sea of lost hopes. Then I too need you Mabel to perform your guest rôle in, '*Puss in Boots,*' at the Alhambra Music Hall in two days time. And bring hope to me. By carrying out the terms of your

Brain Fag?
Nervous Exhaustion ?

That's me!

Miss Lily Elsie writes:
'Phosferine is invaluable for nervous exhaustion and helps me support the strain of two performances, and I think it makes the voice stronger. It is indispensible for anyone engaged in public work, and I shall always recommend it to my friends for brain-fag. You are at liberty to make use of my remarks if you desire.'

CAUTION !
There is only one Phosferine –
beware of illegal imitation –
do not be misled by
PHOSPH THIS or PHOSPH THAT,
but get
PHOSFERINE
THE REMEDY OF KINGS
Phosferine has been supplied by Royal
Commands to

The Royal Family,
H.M. the Queen of Spain,
H.I.M. the Empress of Russia,
H.M. the King of Greece,
H.M. the King of Spain,
H.M. the Queen of Roumania
&c.

The 2/9 s size contains nearly four times the
1/1½ s sizes

contract and provide albeit hope against hope of gaining reasonable Box Office receipts or at least avoiding crippling cancellation fees."

"The decision must be Mabel's. And, she cannot be coerced in to quitting this place," said Fortesque, with a discernible affection in his voice.

"Rubbish," countered Lodge, becoming increasing vexed by the absurdity of the situation. "Mabel's obligation to me, takes precedence over this bunch of unfortunates living at No. 4 King's Road, St. Pancras, or in the local asylum whichever. We are living in a real world. Well at least some of us are beyond the walls of this madhouse. It is about time you came down to earth Mabel, gather what possessions you have and accompany Jack, Theo and me out of this place of perpetual misery and perdition."

These words brought an unexpected re-action from the inmates assembled around Mabel's bed. It was spontaneous as it was unanimous. All of a sudden the inmates started to laugh manically at Lodge and point at him with their shaking fingers. Some even began to move around the bed towards him with a look of manic intensity in their eyes. For a moment, I felt as though we were going to be in for a rough time. I even noticed that Jack take a deep intake of breath in preparation for what looked like a confrontation with the inmates, who numbered about twenty surrounding Mabel's bed.

It was the manic laughter together with the wild staring eyes which created a real anxiety within me. I have witnessed this behavior before and the unpredictable is the one predictable thing in such circumstances. However, our concerns were soon allayed as Mabel got up from her bed and walked up to Lodge.

"You say that I should abandon my people here and

fulfil my contract in the guest rôle in, '*Puss in Boots,*' at the Alhambra Music Hall in two days time. And, bring hope to you by carrying out the terms of my contract and provide that hope against hope of gaining reasonable Box Office receipts for you. Do tell me, why should I be obligated to you? You saw how that audience, at the Tivoli Theater of Variety treated me. An audience which comprised nothing more than a confederation of ingrates and philistines and not one of them was capable of appreciating my artistic abilities. That terrible audience was cruel, simply to be cruel to me," said Mabel.

"Mabel, I know nothing from nothing. But from what I have seen of your performing skills. You have nothing to fear from any audience. I have seen you perform now on numerous occasions and even during Lodge's reception given at his town house in the Bergen Avenue some time ago. Mabel you are a treat to watch. I speak not only for myself but for Theo here and Lodge. And, even the inmates of this here asylum. I speak also for the Music Hall going public who do enjoy your turns on stage. Sure we all of us get that odd night where it simply does not pan out. But they are few and far between," said Jack, with a sincerity and affection in his voice.

"What Jack has just said I endorse entirely. I have nothing to add except your audience awaits you, especially in two days time in your acclaimed rôle in, '*Puss in Boots,*' at the Alhambra Music Hall. Do not Mabel, let them and us down; or indeed, yourself down!" I offered.

The re-action from the inmates gathered around the bed was again unexpected. Slowly at first but becoming unanimous and louder was clapping from the inmates.

"Perhaps we should move our act to the madhouse instead of working the Music Halls or Vaudeville," I whispered to Jack.

Irrespective of that prospect, Jack and my entreaties to Mabel appeared to have succeeded and accordingly, Mabel announced that she would return to the Music Hall stage forthwith. And that not a moment should be lost in her doing so.

What then followed was as touching, as it was affectionate. Mabel hugged several of the inmates as she bade them farewell. I noticed tears in the eyes of some of them, including Fortesque's. Some were unable to control their anguish and loss at the prospect at Mabel's imminent departure. A few of the inmates were even moved to kiss Mabel's hand as though she were a venerated person. Mabel spoke to her admirers. After which she issued a few final instructions to some of the inmates, regarding the quails' eggs and indeed how to look after quails by keeping them happy so that they laid more eggs. Mabel then gathered up her possessions, including a not inconsiderable size jar of Beetham's Glycerine & Cucumber Skin Preparation, from the small metal bed side cupboard. We then all followed Fortesque out of the Nightingale ward. Mabel did so, holding her head up high and with a dignified and measured step.

"I find that I can rejuvenate my soul in this place of tranquillity and inner reflection," Mabel later related to us, as we made our way out of the asylum and back in to a saner, if a not altogether forgiving world.

The prospect of Mabel being in temporary command of the asylum fills me with conflicting thoughts. Even though I still remain uncertain as to exactly who was running the asylum; Superintendant Robinson and his staff or Mabel and the inmates.

I related this dilemma to Jack who replied, as usual, incisively.

"If it is a question of the Superintendant and Fortesque

running the asylum; that or Mabel aided and abetted by those incarcerated in that secure establishment. Then I suspect, it is Mabel who would prevail!" informed Jack.

"Indubitably," I replied.

1 Performing obscene gestures
2 One who secretly wields power and influence behind the scene.

Chapter 3

The Patagonian Theater

Our trials and tribulation at the St Pancras Facility for the Criminally Insane, in which Mabel was but recently an inmate, were thankfully resolved when she was released and her dignity restored. Mabel was effectively given her freedom in order that she might fulfil her contractual obligations as guest rôle in the new acclaimed version of, *'Puss in Boots,'* at the Alhambra Music Hall in Leicester Square. From the glowing revues we have read in various newspapers. It would seem that Mabel has now recovered her self esteem and regained that crucial self confidence and is willing to face the world with a renewed optimism. In the meantime Jack and I are to make our long overdue début this evening at the Patagonian Theater in the Strand.

"I am pleased that Mabel has found herself again," I said to Jack pensively, whilst drinking whisky at the bar in the salon at the St. Pancras Hotel in the late afternoon.

"It just goes to show how a bad night on the stage, whether deserved or not or for whatever reason can unhinge one," replied Jack, "but what surprised me. Was Mabel's re-action to the audience's indifference to her performance at the Tivoli Theater of Variety. I would have though Mabel's character was a bit tougher and more resilient to adverse criticism from an audience. I

31

sure did not expect her to collapse in the way she did. But, let it be a lesson to us all."

"I was bemused by her matriarchal rôle in that Nightingale ward. Bossing the inmates and staff around, including Fortesque, with a confidence which seemed at variance with her mental condition and the very reason of her being incarcerated there. It really was as though she were some kind of Eminence Gris," I offered.

"Well what about that Fortesque feller? Just what is his story, was he an inmate, a member of staff or what?" inquired Jack.

"I do though now recall that the attendant in the main reception referred to Fortesque as this trustee," I replied.

"True," replied Jack, looking at his nearly depleted glass of whisky.

"At the time I was convinced that if we ever were fail at Vaudeville or on the Music Hall stage. We could always try our luck at the St. Pancras Asylum and build up a loyal following there. Think about it Jack, we could even make this venture peculiarly ours with exclusivity to perform there regularly!" I joked.

"Joking aside Theo, we had better make a move for we do now have our turn to perform at the Patagonian Theater. And, hope to God we do not suffer the same fate as Mabel did at the Tivoli Theater of Variety. Remember, both theaters are in the Strand," said Jack, as he drained the last dregs of his whisky.

Moments later we made our way to the stone Port Cochère addressing the front of our hotel and availed our selves of a Stanhope carriage. After giving our instruction to the coachman, we clattered off into the fog headed for the Strand in which the Patagonian Theater is located. Our journey was uneventful and in a surprisingly short period of time we arrive at our destination. On doing so, I stood on the side walk to view the front of the building. Of all the theaters and Music Halls in London, the Patagonian Theater in the Strand stands out as one of the most strikingly elegant and beautiful.

I suspect that this is because of its uncluttered classical façade, dominated by two Corinthian columns, each off set immediately in front of a smooth faced pilaster crowned with a Corinthian capital. Both the columns and pilasters frame the entrance doorway, rising up to support an architrave bearing an impressive masonry parapet structure on to which the word *Oideion* had been carved.

After Jack had settled our fare with the Stanhope carriage driver, we made our way into the foyer of the theater. It was Jack who intercepted an usher, resplendent in his dark blue tail-coat, and asked for directions to the manager's office.

"Ah that will be a Mr. Thomas Clark," said the red faced usher, "his office is on the *piano-nobile* up that flight of stairs and third door on the right."

We took the usher at his word and made our way to the manager's office. The third door on the right was in fact a rather plain looking door with little or no raised decorative features upon its surface. Irrespective of this utilitarian approach to ornamentation, Jack tapped lightly on the door.

It was opened by Lodge and he stood there for a few moments. I noticed he was wearing his favorite mid-night blue colored tail-coat. With matching trousers and a silver-toned finely woven silk waist-coat and a rather ostentatious large gold Albert chain connected to each pocket. His white shirt was fronted by material creating a ruched, ripple effect and finished with a stiff collar secured by a gold stud. In the center of which was a brilliant orchidaceous purple stone of amethyst.

The Patagonian Theater

His shoes were black and covered in a highly varnished finish, which gleamed beneath the corridor gas lights. On his head he wore a shiny black silk top hat at a jaunty angle and a monocle in front of one eye. His sartorial assemblage was covered by his flamboyant black silk cape with the blazing red silk lining lending him an aura more akin to the Count of Monte Cristo than a Music Hall impresario.

"Are we performing tonight on the stage Loge?" inquired Jack, in response to Lodge's impeccable sartorial ensemble.

"No, but you are, and you had better meet the manager of this here theater, name of Clark" he replied, beckoning us both into the manager's office.

We all shook hands and then made ourselves comfortable on the only seating in the office which happened to be an inordinately large Biedermeier sofa positioned immediately in front of Clark's not insubstantial desk. Having taken our place on the sofa, we found ourselves looking up at the manager. It was as though we were in the front seats of the stall looking up at the stage. Also one got the distinct impression that this manager liked to address several people at once sitting attentively in front of his desk.

After he had offered us Trichinopoly cigars from his red velvet covered cigar box, he started in.

"Let me give you the run down on this theater," Clark commenced without even offering us a drink, "the name Patagonian Theater is really a misnomer. That theater was created in a space above what was known as the Exeter Exchange. The *'Morning Chronicle'* at the time has the Patagonian Theater opening its doors for the first time way back in 1776, your year of the Declaration of Independence.

"The Patagonian Theater was effectively replaced in 1831 with an auditorium called the Exeter Exchange,[1] which could hold upwards of four thousand persons. The Exchange building, sometimes called the Exeter 'Change, was designed by John Gandy, the brother of the more famous architect Joseph Gandy, if that means anything to you."

"Why is the word *Oideion* carved into the upper section of the façade to the theater?" I asked in an attempt to show that I was an acute observer of such details.

Clark looked at me with a questioning expression upon his face. After a few moments he leaned back into his chair, drew several times on his Trichinopoly cigar and finally answered me.

"I have not got a clue," he said with confidence and, conviction.

At length it was Lodge who responded with a cough.

"Gentlemen," he said, relishing the situation, "the word *Oideion* is carved in to the stone work which comprises the entablature immediately above the decorative projecting architrave addressing on the upper sections of the front of the building. It does so simply to reflect the ideals of ancient Greek theater. We associate the word *Odeon* with buildings constructed for the performance of music or singing. The word *Oideion* comes from the ancient Greek which means 'singing place,' based upon the root word, *oide* which we today recognise as meaning ode."

"Really?" was Clark's only response to Lodge's illuminating discourse, as he rose up from his chair to shake our hands and wish us good luck as we treaded the boards this evening.

I was more impressed with Lodge's knowledge of ancient Greek and architectural description, than clearly Clark was.

Presently we found ourselves on the other side of the utilitarian-designed door to the manager's office.

"Follow me, "invited Lodge.

We did and followed him along white washed brick lined corridors into the very depths of the theater. At the end of one particular corridor was a button down red leather covered door. On reaching it Lodge flung it open to reveal Marmeduke sitting nonchalantly on a sideboard eating an apple and reading the latest edition of, *The Actor's Bible*, called '**THE ERA**' journal.

Lodge bowed and offered his excuses to leave us.

"I must away to my private red plush box to enable those who matter to see me this evening. As I have stated before gentlemen, as an impresario," Lodge announced, looking at Marmeduke, "I have to be seen to be omnipotent. It is not enough that I am here you understand; rather I have to be *seen* to be here!"

After he had abandoned us, we all burst out laughing.

"'It is not enough that I am here, you understand; rather I have to be *seen* to be here.' Do tell me, what interminable nonsense is that I ask you? Does not even make grammatical sense and his propensity for catachreses [2] is still very much in evidence; omnipotent? Surely he meant omnipresent,'" said Jack, whilst accepting a bottle of beer from Marmeduke.

"How are you doing Cinderella," I asked looking furtively at the door to make sure it was closed and our secret not revealed as to Marmeduke's real identity. "I still find it amusing to realise that Lodge has still not figured out that you Marmeduke are in fact you Cinderella. As indeed you are also Little Bo Peep as well. I must confess, it would not surprise me Cinderella, to learn that you are also Vesta Tilley or even Vesta Victoria!"

"I see we are following a double act, name of Fred &

Tom Mc' Naughton. I have never heard of them. Do they mean anything to you Cinderella and what are the goods on them?" asked Jack.

"Not really, except I think that Tom might be a Water Rat, [3] or something like that," replied Cinderella, "but aside of that. It is just as well that we are doing our Ventriloquist's Dummy act here at the Patagonian. For it was in this very theater that the concept of the Ventriloquist's Dummy was invented, as it were. Though the dummies started out as wooden dolls, albeit being manipulate with hidden wires."

"Do not let our former Ventriloquist's Dummy, name of Judd, hear you say that. He would be very upset to learn that he could have been controlled by hidden wire, at any stage of his existence!" responded Jack, with a rue smile on his face.

Suddenly the door to our dressing room opened and a call boy announced that we are up in ten minutes. We accordingly gathered our things and filed out of the room and up to the back of stage area to await our call on to the boards.

Jack and Marmeduke were on first doing their *Vent* act. I waited in the wings. Whilst doing so, my attention was caught by another yet blatant advertisement poster plastered to a brick wall, a feature of central London, so it seemed to me. I wondered just how these posters appeared. Does a shadowy figure, at the dead of night, plaster them on to unsuspecting walls? I began to read its spurious claims whilst waiting for the act to finish.

By the time I had read it extravagant boasts. Including quite how a Doctor Scott's daily use of his electric flesh brush could remove lameness, was beyond my comprehension.

I looked on to the stage to see Marmeduke regaling

Every Man and Women in England
& Empire should Use

DR SCOTT'S ELECTRIC 'FLESH' BRUSH

WHY ?
Because it quickens the circulation,
opens the pores, & enables the system to throw off those
impurities which cause disease. It instantly acts upon the
blood, nerves and tissues.

Imparting
A Beautiful Clear Skin
New Energy and New Life,
TO ALL WHO DAILY USE IT
AND IS WARRANTED TO CURE

Rheumatism and Diseases of the Blood, Nervous Complaints,
Neuralgia, Toothache, Malaria, Lameness, Palpitations,
Paralysis & All pains caused by impaired circulation.
It promptly alleviates Indigestion, Liver and Kidney
Troubles, Quickly removes those "Back Aches" peculiar to
Ladies, & Imparts wonderful vigor to the whole body.

**ALL DEALERS WILL REFUND PRICE
IF NOT AS REPRESENTED.**

All Checks, Drafts or Post Office Orders made payable to

**Dr. Geo. A. Scott, 42 Broadway,
Victoria, London, SW**

the audience with songs and a series of witty remarks to the brilliant accompaniment of Jack's superb mastery at playing the pianoforte. But, it is also to be remembered that Jack is an accomplished pianist. And he trained at the prestigious Julliard School of Music in New York City. It is quite possible that if Jack were to abandon the stage, he would find no difficulty in working as an accomplished classical concert pianist.

Their act came to an end and the velvet curtain came trundling down from the attic. This interval was only to allow a change of act to occur. Within moments the curtain was ascending back in to the attic from whence it came. I was grateful to hear our names being called out by the resident Compière. And, accordingly I marched out into a brilliantly illuminated stage and met Jack in the middle of the stage. We shook hands, and then took up our places in readiness to perform. On this occasion our song and dance routine involved a new song. It is called, '*A Walk Down Lake Shore Drive*,' with lyrics and music by the acclaimed composer, Edward Plesse. Jack and I are confident that the song will be a great success with audiences here in London. As it was in America, where we first performed it, and hopefully and will sweep all before it here in London.

Jack started off caressing the ivory keys on the piano forte. And in so doing, he created such a sound of serene harmony involving triple fifths and arpeggios. The effects of which sounded as though diamonds were ricocheting off slabs of marble. Such was my entrancement with Jack's producing this sublime music by his skilful playing of the piano forte that I nearly lost my place and only just came in on cue with the lyrics.

A Walk Down Lake Shore Drive [4]

On a dark December evening,
Just as it was snowing,
I looked up into the sky,
And saw a light beacon glowing.

I had never seen it before,
And therefore wondered why,
Then I saw the reason,
It was to illuminate the sky.

The beacon atop a tower,
That rose high in to the sky,
A tower on Lake Shore Drive,
It could not evade the eye.

Held high in the sky by that tower,
Was that bright beacon of light,
With its light of such a power,
It easily caught the one's sight.

The light was so reassuring,
As it reflected upon the lake,
That as I walked towards it,
Others followed in my wake.

We all looked up in wonderment,
At the beam of light in the sky,
And too my utter amazement,
I saw that people began to cry.

These were not tears of sadness,
But rather the tears of glee,
For the glowing light of the beacon,
Was there for all to see!

For such is our pride in Chicago,
We want to share it with friends,
And that bright beacon in the sky,
Shows where their wandering ends.

Our applause was sustained as it was enthusiastic. But then, with Jack playing the pianoforte sonorously, it was not difficult to create sublime and serene music. Even if the lyrics did not reflect the inherent beauty of the music.

After a couple of more songs and dance routines during which I shook my straw sennit hat with my left hand whilst twirling my cane in my right and doing so with uncharacteristic gay abandon. We vacated the stage as the purple velvet curtain came hurtling down from the attic above the stage indicating an interval. The decent of the curtain also triggered off a uncontrolled stampede out of the stalls and into the various Crush Bars ranged around the Patagonian Theater. We made our way to a particular Crush Bar in which, Lodge had suggested, we could meet. We got there just propitiously, as Lodge was ordering drinks.

"Ah Jack, Theo, just in time," said Lodge, with aspersion in his voice, "what can I get you?"

"Champagne," answered Jack.

"That new song you sang out there appeared to go down well with the audience. Who composed it?" inquired Lodge.

"A friend of ours from way back," replied Jack, "name of Plesse, Edward Plesse."

"I know the name," replied Lodge, handing us a fluted glass each. And into which he then poured chilled champagne.

"What do you know about Lake Shore Drive Loge?" asked Jack.

"Absolutely zilch Jack," responded Lodge, in a mock Lower East Side accent, "clue me in."

"Lake Shore Drive," Jack obliged, "is a fashionable tree-lined avenue running alongside the shore of Lake Michigan in east Chicago. It might be considered the equivalent of upper Fifth Avenue, filled with mansions, in New York City. The avenue was laid out originally in 1882 by a business Titan, name of Palmer, Potter Palmer, the owner of the Marshall Field departmental and notions store.

"In 1871, several buildings in Chicago, owned by Palmer, were destroyed as a result of the devastating Chicago Fire of the same year. Only the stone built Federal Building and the Gothic Water Tower survived the conflagration. Despite that disaster, Palmer went ahead with his grandiose scheme to construct a large fire proof mansion, in the style of a fantasy Gothic castle on that newly laid out tree lined avenue.

"He was inspired by the construction of the Neo-Gothic Water Tower on North Michigan Avenue in the Near North Side neighborhood of the city. Whilst the tower is Gothic Revival in terms of architectural style, it was constructed in 1869 using a steel infrastructure which was then clad in Indiana limestone blocks. This form of fire proof structure ensured its survival in that major conflagration which consumed Chicago two years later in 1871.

"You can well imagine why Palmer, having had all his real estate go up in flames, was anxious to construct his

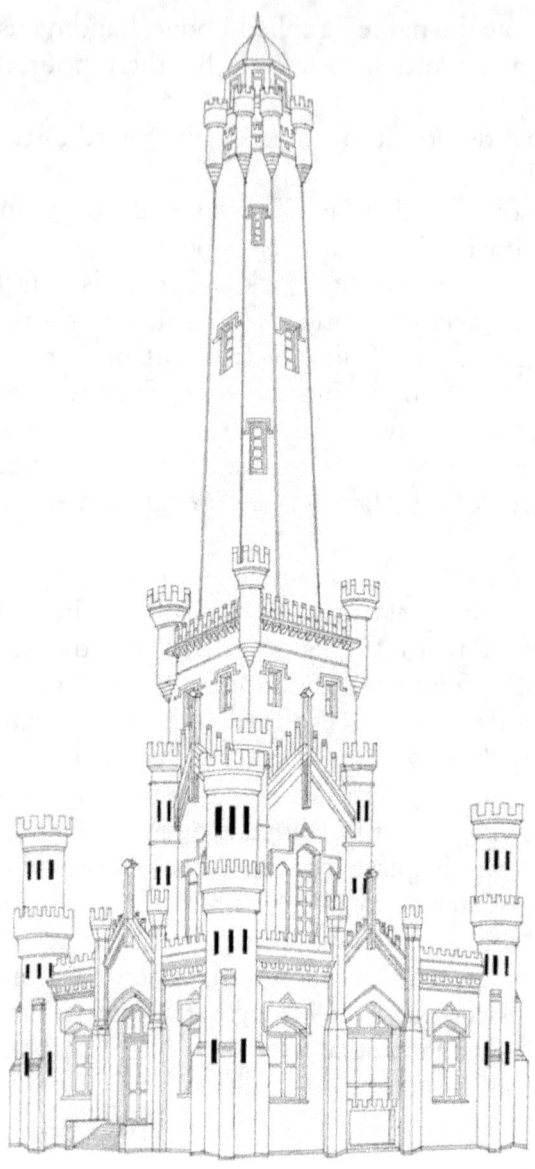

Gothic Water Tower

family mansion using the same method of fire proof construction which saved the Gothic Water Tower from destruction..." said Jack.

"You are a font of knowledge," interrupted Lodge.

"Other people also built large very beautiful and substantial mansions," continued Jack, "which line each side of the avenue. Eventually, the avenue, now called Lake Shore Drive, became a thriving prosperous neighborhood of Chicago, attracting the wealthy and famous," completed Jack.

"The song by Plesse," I added, "pays tribute to that fine and elegant avenue and in particular to Palmer's Gothic mansion, which is remarkable for another peculiar reason. Potter Palmer designed the doors leading into the mansion without handles or locks; so the only way to get into the house was to be admitted by someone from inside!"

It did not seem that much time had gone by, before we became aware of a bell ringing, signalling the return to the auditorium. Jack and I decided to buy tickets and watch Cinderella from the Dress Circle rather than from the wings of the stage. We found our seats and waited in anticipation for the curtain to rise. We did not have long to wait before it did so.

Having been introduced by the Compière, Cinderella marched on to the stage wearing outsized pit boots with iron studs on the soles. The first thing she did was to verbally insult the costermongers seated in the front rows for no apparent or discernable reason. After their stunned surprise, they re-acted in customary fashion by hissing and booing. This mild display of antagonism by Cinderella towards the costermongers continued for a few minutes with vitriolic remarks being mutually exchanged freely between them.

Cinderella, as usual, seemed to be in her element strutting around the stage in her outsized pit boots which she wore beneath a bellowing white cotton layered dress of the type favored by *Southern Belles* back home in the southern states of America. At length she removed her black silk top hat, revealing that her short auburn hair had been cropped lending her a rather severe look.

"Praise God," she said, "this is an awful place." [5]

But before the costermongers could respond to this outrageous observation the footlights were dimmed throwing the stage into twilight. In this subdued lighting a rumbling noise could be heard above the hush of expectation in the auditorium. We were disappointed as nothing manifested itself on the stage and the rumbling noise subsided. Then a single shaft of weak yellow limelight shone down from the upper tiers of the auditorium.

The beam focused on a solitary person who in the process of quietly executing an elegant and tasteful dance in her outsized pit boots. It was Cinderella. On seeing her dancing across the stage the audience spontaneously and unanimously erupted into thunderous applause.

Cinderella continued dancing in the limelight which followed her around the stage. Then the beam of yellow light began to fade until there was no illumination. Assuming this to be part of her act, the audience remained quiet. The lighting on the stage was again returned to that of twilight.

Imperceptibly a first, but becoming more visible, were shadows fleeting across the wide stage. I could see members of the audience straining their necks forward to see what was happening on the stage. They need not have bothered for in the next moment, an explosion of light illuminated the stage. In an instance we all recognised the presence of the *Inexhaustible Cremorne Belles,* carrying out a series of precisely coördinated choreographic manœuvres and singing, *"It is the limelight for us or nothing."* The audience actually staggered up from their plush red velvet upholstered seats and applauded both enthusiastically and loudly for this popular Corp de Ballet.

In an instant, the *Cremorne Belles* divided in to two halves creating a central aisle down which Cinderella strutted noisily in her heavy iron studded pit boots. As she did so, members of the Corp de Ballet curtsied in turn. When Cinderella had finally made her way to the front of the stage, she paused immediately above the footlight blazing out their illumination.

She then launched herself into a series of intricate dance manœuvres with such intensity as to defy belief. It was as though she was trying to induce herself into a delirious trance. She may well have succeeded. Because all of a sudden she leapt into the aëther above the stage with such a vigorous display of balletic skill and in so doing created an impressively wide arc. At the end of which she landed perfectly and then curtsied to the admiring audience. The mere fact of the appearance of Cinderella in her dancing rôle, meant the audience would be treated to a grand spectacle. And they knew it!

In the next instant, Cinderella was surrounded by the Corp de Ballet, the *Cremorne Belles.* When they departed from Cinderella, she was kneeling on the floor of the stage. At the same time the *Cremorne Belles* executed a series of intricate and precise coördinated choreographic movements for which they have an enviable proud reputation and justly so. Their balletic dance involved swirling around Cinderella at an increasingly frenzied rate of speed. Eventually, Cinderella, in the middle, executed an impressive Pas de Deux with one of the *Cremorne Belles.*

Then it happened. As Cinderella spun around something fell from her embrace and rolled around the stage floor. I assumed it was a stage prop come loose and rolled on to the stage. It was probably those members of the audience sitting in the front rows that realised what the object was. Because it was from those red plush velvet upholstered seats that gasps of horror were heard. I looked at the object which now had ceased rolling about the stage and immediately took in a sharp intake of breath through my teeth.

I was looking at a severed head. I noticed too that Cinderella, had one hand clasped over her mouth and with the other, pointing at the decapitated head.

In the next instant the purple velvet curtain descended down from the attic with indecent haste in order to shield the audience from the grotesque spectacle of the severed head.

1 The Exeter Exchange Hall was demolished in 1907 to make way for the Strand Palace Hotel
2 Incorrect use of words
3 The Grand Order of Water Rats founded in 1889 by Joe Elvin and Jack Lotto is a charity for Music Hall artistes
4 Refers to a tree lined avenue in an affluent neighborhood of Chicago next to Lake Michigan
5 Uttered by Captain Scott recently on reaching the desolation of the South Pole, after Amundsen had gotten there first.

Chapter 4

The Dance of Salomé

We were appearing at the Patagonian Theater located in the Strand. Jack and I, having performed earlier on stage had taken our seats in the Dress Circle in order to watch Cinderella's stage act. That turn was apparently terminated prematurely due to the appearance of a severed head rolling about on the stage floor. Throughout the auditorium, hushed conversations were taking place about the appearance of the decapitated head, and from whence it came. Moments later the purple velvet curtain ascended back in to the attic space above the proscenium arch in front of the stage.

The stage scenery presented to the audience, was one of the interior of an ancient palace constructed of purple white veined *Rosso Levanto* marble columns and red pennants swaying in a breeze. The opulent appointment of the place suggested we were looking into a palatial residence of a wealthy king or emperor. I assumed we were looking at the stage set for the next act. I then realized that we were in fact looking into King Herod's throne room, in the middle of which, was Cinderella in her rôle as Salomé performing a series of macabre dances for Herod. It was if course, Cinderella's adaptation of the, *'Tanz der Sieben Schleier,'* [1] based on Rickard Strauss's choreographic ballet scene from his opera *Salomé*.

The decapitated head that we saw rolling around the stage floor previously, was supposedly to be that of John the Baptist's. And, if I remembered correctly, the teachings from the Synoptic gospels, it involved a minor king, name of Herod. It was he, who as Tetrarch of Galilee, a minor province of the Roman Empire, had imprisoned John the Baptist. Herod did so because John had criticised Herod for divorcing his wife Phasaelis. Salomé, Herod's step daughter, agreed to dance for the Tetrarch on the occasion of his birthday celebrations.

Her dancing impressed Herod to such an extent that, in a drunken state, he foolishly granted her any wish she desired. Ultimately Salomé's asked her mother, Herodias, what she should ask for. Her mother advised her to demand the severed head of imprisoned and troublesome John the Baptist. The wish was granted. And Salomé performed a macabre *'Tanz der Sieben Schleier'* around the decapitated head.

We were now watching an interpretation of this biblical story as Cinderella executed those dances on the stage floor. And, she was being ably assisted by the *Inexhaustible Cremorne Belles*. Some of whom were playing Japanese fiddles.[2] As they executed their complex and precisely coördinated choreographic manœuvres around Cinderella and the decapitated head.

I have noticed that when Cinderella appears on stage in whatever Music Hall. She is billed simply as 'Cinderella.' What she does on the stage, invariably is a surprise for the audience. She plays any rôle that takes her fancy. Be it singing, dancing or indeed indulging in offering ad lib abusive remarks to the costermongers, much to their secret delight.

What also intrigued me was the high moral tone of the

dances being performed on the stage in front of us. The dances, or rather the subject matter upon which they are based, that is biblical scripture, appeared to me to be somewhat incongruous with their performance in a Music Hall! But then of course, we had recently been regaled with a performance of a pantomime based on Rickard Wagner's comic opera called, *'Männerlist größer als Frauenlist oder Die Glückliche Bärenfamilie.'* [3]

However, any notion of these dances retaining an instructive reverence about them soon evaporated the moment Cinderella, leaned down to the floor and picked up the severed head. She looked intently into the face of the head during which there was a deathly hush throughout the auditorium.

What Cinderella did next surprised not only me but the audience too.

After looking at the head, Cinderella then threw it into the center of the Corp de Ballet, which comprised the *Inexhaustible Cremorne Belles.* They in turn tossed the head around to each other. As they did so they broke out spontaneously in to a song called, *'Heads You Win; Heads I Don't.'* During which Cinderella strutted up to the front of the stage and exhorted the costermongers to sing along with the *Cremorne Belles.* The costers duly obliged and staggered up out of their comfortable red velvet covered seats and sang in surprising harmonic unison and synchrony.

At the end of the singing Cinderella, who had now repossessed of the head, again looked intently at the face and then placed it on the floor of the stage facing the audience. Then the footlights were lowered plunging the stage into twilight, except a single shaft of limelight illuminating the head. I could just make out moving shadows on the stage. That indicated to the audience the *Cremorne Belles* were evacuating the stage. Eventually, the stage was deserted and only the head, still facing the audience, illuminated by a weak shaft of lime light, remained on the stage.

I did not realise it at first. Nor, I suspect, did members of the audience. But eventually, it seemed as though the head were levitating. And so it was and imperceptibly so, inch by inch the head rose above the deck of the stage. The decapitated head was ascending slowly into the space above the stage. And, in so doing created a ghostly apparition, which was eerily effective. At length the lime light illuminating the head petered out and we were left looking into total darkness.

Presently, the purple velvet curtain was lowered. An atmosphere of justifiable expectation descended upon the audience. A minute later the curtain was raised on a brightly lit stage. With the truly *Inexhaustible Cremorne Belles* lined up at the front of the stage with Cinderella at the center of them, holding nonchalantly the decapitated head under one arm. The curtain had barely risen when the audience, led by the costers in the stalls, erupted into thunderous and sustained applause. Some members of the audience were even moved to banging the floor with their boots in an attempt to induce themselves into deliria of pure ecstasy. For such was their delight at what they had enjoyed.

I looked at Jack whilst clapping wildly. We both knew how fortunate we were not to be following Cinderella's act on the stage.

"How could one go on the stage after what she had just performed?" I asked Jack.

"How indeed," he replied, "one simply cannot!"

1 *Dance of the Seven Veils*, from Rickard Strauss's opera Salomé Opus 54
2 A one-stringed instrument popular with street performers
3 *Men Are More Cunning Than Women, or The Happy Bear Family*

Chapter 5

The March to Charing Cross

Jack and I were waiting on Cinderella in the foyer of the Patagonian Theater in the Strand where we had performed that evening. There I had sung our new song, '*A Walk Down Lake Shore Drive,*' which appeared to have been well received by the audience. And even Lodge was predisposed to inquire as to the origin of the lyrics. But it was Cinderella, innovative interpretation of the rôle as Salomé in her adaptation of Rickard Strauss's, '*Tanz der Sieben Schleier,*' which had caught the audience's imagination and approbation on a monumental scale.

Presently, Cinderella joined us followed by Lodge looking very ostentatious in his favorite mid-night blue colored tail-coat with matching trousers. His stiff shirt collar was fastened with a stud in the center of which was a brilliant stone of orchidaceous purple amethyst. He looked quite the theatrical impresario to end all impresarios. Especially his wearing a silver-toned finely woven silk waist-coat and a large gold Albert chain connected to each pocket, which lent him an aura of gravitas.

He walked up to us twirling his gold capped ebony cane in his hand. As he did so, he placed on his head a black shiny silk top hat.

"Cinderella, gentlemen," Lodge started in, "please do

allow me to stand you dinner at the Gatti's Restaurant at Charing Cross! By the way where is that Marmeduke?"

"Oh he made his excuses," answered Jack, "something about his aged aunt. But do tell us. What is it with the reckless generosity in standing us dinner?"

Irrespective of Jack's facetious question, we all nodded our consent and followed Lodge, not out into the Strand and into the night, but rather back through the theater itself. Gradually, we followed Lodge down some stone steps which descended into the depths of the theater where the dressing rooms are located. We made our way through a very long white washed brick lined corridor that progressed beyond the confines of the Patagonian Theater. Presently, we came up to a heavy oak door, fronted by a metal push bar.

Lodge pushed against the bar but failed to open the door. Cinderella leant against it and immediately the door sprung open. Lodge pretended not to have noticed this feat by Cinderella. But we did follow him through the opening and found ourselves outside in a very busy thoroughfare, the Victoria Embankment. Lodge informed us. Whatever, the yellow fog laden aëther was stilled and heavier and made thicker by the presence of the nearby river Thames. Together with a pervasive pungent acridity that attacked one's senses. The sidewalk upon which we were standing was made up with York flagstones, made slippery by the acrid fog condensing on them.

I took Cinderella's arm.

"Right, Cinderella and gentlemen, if you will follow me," said Lodge, "it is but a few minutes down this road and the short walk will make our appetites all the more keener."

Accordingly, it was with great reluctance that we

followed Lodge down the Victoria Embankment, shrouded in dense fog, towards Charing Cross. Though undaunted by the swirling fog in the vicinity of the Thames, Lodge marched off in front of us with his black cape flapping like the wings of a giant bird of prey. Jack, Cinderella and I were not so confident and walked with a more cautious step in order to concentrate on where we were treading on the slippery York flagstone.

After a few moments of walking in silence, Lodge stopped.

"This is about right," said Lodge, as he prepared to cross the Victoria Embankment thoroughfare to reach the other side next to the Thames.

With trepidation, we started to cross and paused only to take refuge on the central island in the middle of the busy carriageway. Thereafter, we continued to the second stage of our crossing of this mighty thoroughfare of the Metropolis, teeming with lumbering wagons, including those of the pantechnicon type. When we did reach the other side of the road we found ourselves against a granite retaining wall of about four feet in height. I detached myself from Cinderella's and peered over the top of the parapet wall and beheld the vision of the murky swirling waters of the Thames.

I am not particularly fond of great expanses of water and often its presence, especially in the form of a dark murky river with its dangerous undercurrents and swirls, can unnerve me somewhat. And induce feelings of anxiety and vulnerability. This is a natural re-action to being in the presence of a life-threatening situation if one is not used to it; as I am in the presence of large expanse of water in the form of deep wide rivers. Much, one would imagine, as vertigo might equally affect the inexperienced climber. Or somebody not used to heights.

Accordingly, I pulled back from the vision of the river to rejoin the others. But found myself some distance behind Cinderella, Jack and Lodge who had continued walking on.

As I walked along the Victoria Embankment constructed to tame the waters of the Thames. I became aware that I was quite alone. Then, only just visible in the fog, I realized that I was in the presence of a large blue granite plinth. It was shaped, as a tomb might be fashioned, complete with funereal detailing to its masonry of at least fourteen feet in height and twenty feet in length.

The top three layers of granite blocks, of which the plinth was comprised, were recessed at each level suggesting a stepped apex structure reflecting a pyramid concept. This concept was reënforced by the presence at either side of two large bronze Sphinxes guarding the tomb. It was not, however, the plinth that caught my attention, but rather what was positioned above it, and rising into the fog-bound aëther. I could hardly believe my eyes as I took in detail after detail as the fog and its vortex allowed my vision to do so.

It appeared to me, as I looked at it, to be yet another edifice constructed of granite stone blocks. It was secured to the plinth by four interlocking bronze clamps to each corner creating a continuous bracket around the base of eight feet by eight feet. The bronze sleeve bracket was decorated with ancient Egyptian hieroglyphic symbols and raised designs incorporating representation of extended wings, the sacred scarab beetle and birds.

I stood there, transfixed by this monumental Mausoleum styled edifice and the feeling of stillness that radiated from its monolithic presence. As my eyes became accustomed to the fog surrounding it, I also noticed yet another structure rising even further into the fog-laden aëther. However, due to the swirling fog, obscuring the masonry, it was difficult for me to ascertain its structural details.

Then, my heart nearly failed me and my mouth became instantly dry, as I became aware of what this bronze clamped stone Mausoleum was supporting. As the fog swirled around it caused vortices making the fog thin out in places and in so doing created a brief vision that I observed with my eyes wide open. The vision came into my sight and then as quickly disappeared as the enshrouding fog reclaimed it and made it again invisible to me.

Then, as the fog receded the structure momentarily came back into view. It was a gigantic monumental solid stone tapering structure in the form of an Egyptian Obelisk at least forty-five feet or so in height. It was a sight to behold, especially when one came across it unexpectedly. I have mentioned to Jack and Lodge in the past that the all-pervasive fog can present one with peculiar experiences that would not necessarily be gained in the absence of the fog. Though ironically, I had glimpsed this structure before. On that occasion it was when Jack and I were making our way to then Charing Cross Hotel to bear witness to Lodge's heroic defense of Music Halls against the insipid encroachment of the Metropolitan Board of Works.

Of course, had I approached the Obelisk [1] in sunlight, then the spectre of the structure would perforce have been diminished as one would accept its structural propensity and presentment. Being subject to those two aspects of its monumentality in an instance of visual impact can affect one as an unexpected shock. Such concerns and feelings however did not affect Lodge, as

The Obelisk, Victoria Embankment

he chatted away amiably with Cinderella and Jack, who by now I had caught up with.

"I was just saying Theo, that when the venal and interfering Metropolitan Board of Works, constructed this fine Victoria Embankment with its retaining walls to confine the river Thames. Was one of the only undertakings it somehow managed to achieve with a modicum of success. And, as I have said before, the Metropolitan Board of Works really should confine its activities to constructing deep level sewers, such as the one beneath this Embankment. Rather than try to run our precious Music Halls. You will of course know that this actual Victoria Embankment road is constructed directly above on the arches that form the tunnels in which is laid the permanent way of the Metropolitan Rail Road's District Rail Road," informed Lodge, in an enthusiastic manner whilst describing this engineering feat as though it were one of the Seven Wonders of the World.

I re-took Cinderella's arm. And she smiled at me.

I enjoyed watching you perform this evening Cinderella," I said, "especially with the *Inexhaustible Cremorne Belles*. You and they together are an absolute joy to experience. Including those who were playing Japanese fiddles! And your accomplished performance of the '*Dance of the Seven Veils,*' along with the *Cremorne Belles* with such intricate and superbly coördinated and precise choreography, was spectacular!"

At length we came to bridge rising above the Victoria Embankment as it spanned over the river Thames. I recognised it as the Charing Cross Rail Road Bridge. And at Lodge's signal we re-crossed the Victoria Embankment and headed straight into Charing Cross Underground Station, located as it is on the Victoria Embankment thoroughfare.

Charing Cross Rail Road Bridge

It was at this urban rail road station that Jack and I had arrived by train a few weeks ago, en-route to that fateful meeting at the nearby Charing Cross Hotel. It was in that very hotel, that Lodge took on valiantly the Metropolitan Board of Works during an epic confrontation which also involved some members of the Fourth Estate! It would seem that this neighborhood of Charing Cross is punctuated with memories.

We made our way through the Charing Cross Underground Station and into Villiers Street which rises up to the Strand. A few moments later, having staggered up the fog-bound street, we entered Gatti's Restaurant. It was into the restaurant's brightly illuminated foyer that we walked quickly in our eagerness to secure the brightness and fog-less space of the restaurant. In so doing we stepped into a brilliance of incandescent light emanating from large lanterns of glass and chandeliers tinkling with cut glass suspended from the ornate ceiling which illuminated the plush crimson silk broadloom carpet upon which we were now standing.

"Ah Mr Lodge," exclaimed a red faced gentleman, wearing a morning-coat and striped trousers, "very pleased to welcome you to my restaurant; and the delectable Cinderella too. What indeed have we done to deserve such a distinguished company this evening?"

"Possibly because of the fact that we are hungry, Carlo" retorted Lodge, whilst shaking his hand.

"Please follow me. I am sure we can accommodate you and satisfy your appetites," replied Carlo.

As we made our way to a vacant table, I noticed Katie Meyrick and the loquacious Ellen Terry seated separately at other tables. Lodge deigned not to acknowledge them. However, Cinderella did with a wave of her hand to both.

When we had all made ourselves comfortable on Chippendale chairs, the seats of which were upholstered in blue and white stripped moiré silk, Lodge ordered inordinately expensive vintage champagne. He did so loudly so that others in the restaurant might hear, and thus bear witness to his reckless generosity.

"Are we not in the vicinity of the Hungerford Music Hall," I asked no one in particular, as we all perused our menu cards, "embedded in the depths of the arches supporting the Charing Cross Rail Road Station? Yes, that very same Music Hall in which Jack and I first encountered that dreadful rather diminutive and plump looking, woman, the danseuse, Flora Miller? At the time she was attempting to do a rendition of the, '*Lost Chord*,' in a very lewd and very suggestive manner. Aided and augmented by her ornately engraved brass-plated Aëolian Pianola on to which intricate raised designs had been etched in to its metallic surface?"

"Absolutely Theo," answered Lodge, "and Carlo Gatti there is the owner of that august Music Hall."

"Having wound up her brass-plated Aëolian Pianola to its limit," I continued, "she turned and faced the audience. Then with a flourish and a bow, she immediately launched off into bouts of singing in the irritating key of C # minor. She sang in the most appalling voice, whilst waving her head from side to side, which I remembered, got the audience going in sympathetic response. She spent her entire act singing verses of such a blatant nature exhorting the audience, especially the costermongers, very evident in the stalls, to join in with her, which they did, enthusiastically chanting out their repulsive and indecent responses."

"The costermongers adore her; for she knows how to get them going in an extended sing song," said Cinderella, after which resorted to her fluted glass of champagne from which she drank deeply.

"Have you ever worked the Hungerford Music Hall Cinderella," I inquired of Cinderella.

"All too often," came her reply, "I played the rôle of the Captain of the Guard in the serenely melodic pantomime, '*Humpty Dumpty,*' opposite Dan Leno, Daisy James and George Lashwood."

We all of us considered Cinderella's reply.

"Please do tell us Lodge?" Jack started in. "Why did you make us walk along the Victoria Embankment when we could have quite easily have strolled down the Strand which is at the top of the street we are now in. We appeared to have come around the long way, why?"

Lodge thought for a moment then drew on his Trichinopoly cigar.

"The time is now five and twenty minutes after ten o'clock at night. The Strand may be fashionable in broad day light, but at night time it changes in to a less than salubrious place. It can be full of foot pads, dog stealers, pick pockets and gangs of youths, rich or poor, hell bent on drinking and causing a mischief or commotion for any cause. And most of whom come from the Rookery, that notorious hive located only just north of the Strand. I should not wish to expose you to such behavior extant in the Strand of an evening!" said Lodge, in tones of seriousness.

Jack looked at me then at Cinderella.

"Loge, Theo here is from the Lower East Side in New York City. I myself am from Jersey City. Never mind!" said Jack, with a dismissive wave of his hand.

Lodge merely looked at Jack with a perplexed expression upon his face.

"However, I did ask in the foyer of the Patagonian

Theater" continued Jack, "what is it with such reckless generosity in one so dapper. And the question still stands; why are we here, irrespective of how we have gotten here?"

"Ah I did not tell you," responded Lodge, as he pulled a buff colored envelope out of his breast pocket. "We have been given an evening at the Albert Hall to perform the Choral Anthem Symphony. And it will be performed tomorrow.

"Which hall?" I asked.

"The Royal Albert Music Hall of course..." replied Lodge.

"You mean the one located in Canning Town in the depths of the East End amongst the docks," interrupted Jack.

"The very same one Jack," replied Lodge, whilst handing over to me a playbill with the words 'Royal Albert Music Hall' embossed in bold letters across the top.

I could not help thinking if this was a wise decision and had grave misgivings as to the venture. One hoped it would not end in a débâcle similar to the one which attended the Titanic Benefit Concert at the Queen's Hall recently. But with characters as the Rat Catcher's Daughter and acrobat Jules Léotard appearing on the same bill. My misgivings were well founded. Especially when I noticed that they had listed Lodge's work as the *Cholera* Anthem Symphony instead of the *Choral* Anthem Symphony.

But then I remembered that Lodge had departed with two thousands guineas, as a deposit, to Relf, the Mercurial manager of the Royal Albert Music Hall. Also, I realized, Lodge has evidently suspended his threat to revenge himself upon the person of Relf. As he assured Jack and me outside the Charing Cross Hotel that he would do so.

ROYAL ALBERT
MUSIC HALL

Victoria Dock Road, Canning Town

Licensed by the Lord Chamberlain to
Mr. Charles Relf, Manager

GRANDEST NIGHT OF THE
SEASON TO GUARANTEE
DELECTATION AND
UNSURPASSED ENJOYMENT!
& POSITIVELY THE LAST
NIGHT BEING FOR THE
BENEFIT
OF THE ACCLAIMED
&
EVER POPULAR

Mr. H. Missouri

- 0 -

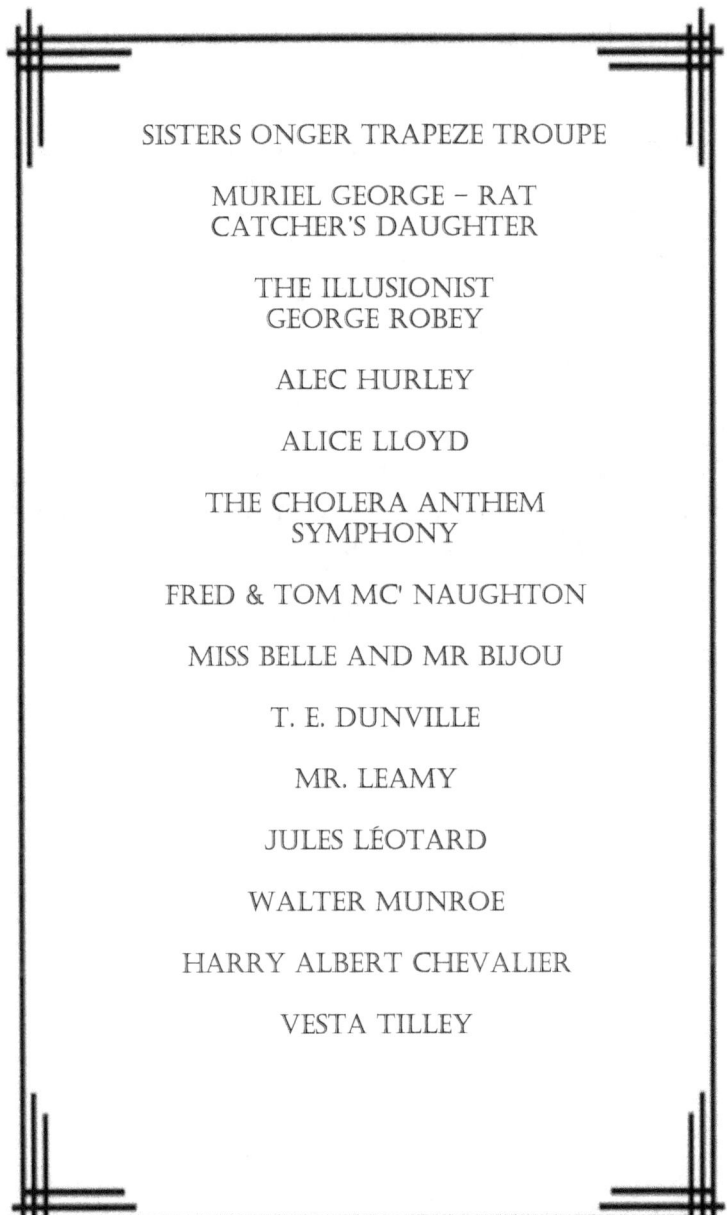

SISTERS ONGER TRAPEZE TROUPE

MURIEL GEORGE – RAT
CATCHER'S DAUGHTER

THE ILLUSIONIST
GEORGE ROBEY

ALEC HURLEY

ALICE LLOYD

THE CHOLERA ANTHEM
SYMPHONY

FRED & TOM MC' NAUGHTON

MISS BELLE AND MR BIJOU

T. E. DUNVILLE

MR. LEAMY

JULES LÉOTARD

WALTER MUNROE

HARRY ALBERT CHEVALIER

VESTA TILLEY

Presumably, Lodge has now concluded he may as well get his money's worth out of Relf.

What madness, I asked myself, drives Lodge to undertake such reckless ventures with his Choral Anthem Symphony? However, notwithstanding my misgivings about the Royal Albert Music Hall being a suitable place to perform Lodge's much vaunted Choral Anthem Symphony. We all of us enjoyed ourselves at Gatti's Restaurant fuelled by Lodge's ostentatious and inexhaustible generosity.

Later as we bade our repeated farewells to Gatti, I began to think about the Choral Anthem Symphony and Royal Albert Music Hall in a contemplative mood. Lodge, in comparison, appeared elated at the prospect of his symphony being performed there.

1 Commonly known as Cleopatra's Needle.

Chapter 6

The Royal Albert Music Hall

Whilst we were taking dinner yesterday evening at Gatti's Restaurant in Villiers Street, in the heart of Charing Cross. Lodge had informed us that he would after all be putting on a performance of the Choral Anthem Symphony involving the *Three Graces*. The concern that we had then and, still do, is not the actual performance of the choral work; but rather where it is to be performed. But apparently, it is now to be staged at the Royal Albert Musical Hall located in the depths of the East End of London amidst the docks, costermongers, tossers [1] and not least, contingents of the *Undeserving Poor* aided and abetted by the *Rough Trade!*

"Well Jack, the day has dawned. And before night claims this day, we will have experienced yet another performance of the Choral Anthem Symphony, sung by the *Three Graces* in the persons of Kate Lawrence, Dot Hetherington and of course insane Mabel Green," I said, perusing my bar tab, but undaunted, ordered another round of drinks.

Jack did not bother to reply but continued studying a cable-gram that he had just been given by our hotel Concièrge still wearing his black morning-coat.

"It is a rambling note from Loge," said Jack, "advising us to take the urban rail road to the Royal Albert Music

Hall. Were we to avail ourselves of a horse and carriage, he states, then we would never arrive, least not this side of eternity. He goes on to suggest that according to Bradshaw's Railway Guide, we should ride the Metropolitan urban rail road to Mark Lane Metropolitan Station.[2] Make our way to the nearby Fenchurch Street Rail Road Station, and board a train to a place called Canning Town in east London. Then get a carriage down to the Victoria Dock Road to the Music Hall."

"Seems straight forward enough," I responded, with memories flooding back into my mind of the time I rode a train out of the St. Pancras Rail Road Station. En-route to the New National Standard Music Hall in an east London neighborhood called Shoreditch. And in particular, I remember my staggering through fog-bound lanes and sordid back streets whilst searching for the Music Hall. An experience I did not care to repeat.

"Well let us do this thing," said Jack, as he drained the last dregs of his whisky with a dash of aërated water. I pondered my drink. Then gulped down the entire contents of the glass and having done so, breathed out noisily, as Marie Lloyd might.

I concurred with his suggestion and within a minute or two we were walking out of the St. Pancras Hotel and into the acrid yellow fog swirling around in the aëther. At length we entered King's Cross Metropolitan Station located conveniently beneath the St. Pancras Hotel. I walked up the acid etched glazed fronted ticket kiosk to purchase our tickets. Having purchased our tickets, we then made our way down to the platform to wait for our train. Whilst doing so, I amused myself by reading the spurious claims arising out of a nearby advertisement poster plastered to the wall opposite us on the other side of the permanent way.

New National Standard Music Hall

Again, being in London, I am conscious of the ungoverned liberality that attends the publication of advertisements, which extol quite shamelessly their elixirs, concoctions or preparations in order to aid or promote a sovereign remedy and in so doing achieve a miracle cure for the uninitiated or gullible.

Presently an engine of the Metropolitan Rail Road, painted in purple livery and hauling several carriages, came thundering down the side of the platform. As it passed us, it deposited black smuts of soot on to our jackets. As soon as the carriage doors were flung open, there was the usual stampede as passengers fought to alight from the carriages, whilst others battled to get into

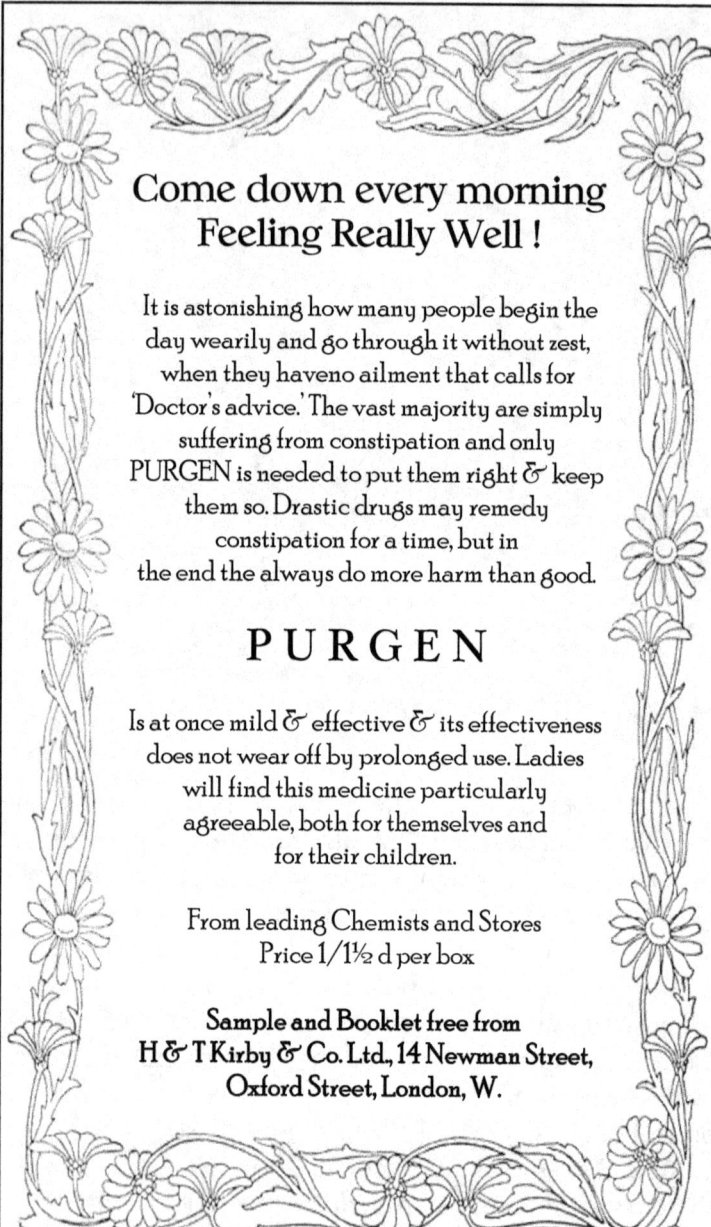

Come down every morning Feeling Really Well !

It is astonishing how many people begin the
day wearily and go through it without zest,
when they have no ailment that calls for
'Doctor's advice.' The vast majority are simply
suffering from constipation and only
PURGEN is needed to put them right & keep
them so. Drastic drugs may remedy
constipation for a time, but in
the end the always do more harm than good.

PURGEN

Is at once mild & effective & its effectiveness
does not wear off by prolonged use. Ladies
will find this medicine particularly
agreeable, both for themselves and
for their children.

From leading Chemists and Stores
Price 1/1½ d per box

**Sample and Booklet free from
H & T Kirby & Co. Ltd., 14 Newman Street,
Oxford Street, London, W.**

the train. Jack and I just stood there and waited for this undignified mêlée to subside. When it had we boarded the train.

Our journey to Mark Lane Metropolitan Station, near the Tower of London was uneventful. Our trying to locate Fenchurch Street Rail Road Station was. And we spent an inordinately amount of time asking total strangers for directions, some of which blatantly contradicted directions offered by other persons. Eventually we found the station and after a typical, if somewhat predictable 'misunderstanding' at the ticket window, we stepped on to the platform and awaited our train. Thankfully, we did not have long to wait.

Within minutes a train of the London & Blackwall Rail Road was backed into the station. When it came to a stop, we and other passengers boarded it. A minute or so later a whistle was heard. Immediately and with a sharp jolt the train then began to traverse along the edge of the platform and eventually blasted its way out of the station confines and into the fog outside. The predictable rocking and rolling action of the train carriage and the noise of the steel wheels pounding the iron rails below us, indicated to me that we were piling on the steam.

We then steamed into Shadwell Station. As soon as the train stopped, our carriage was invaded by a large contingent of costermongers. Two of them sat on the bench directly opposite Jack and me. Having done so, they immediately began talking with each other, but using an esoteric language, including a cryptic vocabulary, indecipherable to all, but themselves.

They spoke in this manner, in order to keep the meaning of their talk with each other secret and could involve speaking words backwards. They were successful, because their conversation was incomprehensible to me and, I suspect, probably to Jack as well.

Our train continued its journey east calling at stations as Stepney Junction, Limehouse and Poplar. On each occasion a bevy of costermongers climbed into our carriage. All of whom, of course, knew each other intimately. Most of the women were arguing with each other whilst their male 'companions' played cards or ate oranges, the peels from which they simply discarded on to the floor of the carriage. They looked a vital set of individuals wearing their silk neckerchiefs or King's Men, I have been told they are called. Together with ostentatious earrings hanging from infected earlobes.

The carriage was now quite full. And looking around me I observed readily that it did indeed comprise a large contingent of costermongers. The rest were either tossers or the generally *Undeserving Poor,* who were inordinately well represented. Some were even reading *Penny Dreadfuls.*[3]Most present in the carriage were smoking tobacco. And in so doing, their addiction to this cheap leaf added to the general unpleasant atmosphere extant in the rail road carriage. I desisted from smoking my Trichinopoly cigar for fear of attracting unwarranted attention.

It was as if we were being transported in cattle box wagons, such was the vicissitude of the thick and acrid smells which had developed since the costermongers had climbed into the carriage. The noise was deafening and their children squabbled. Their un-tethered dogs roamed around the carriage poking their long muzzles uninvited into private domains and recesses. The dogs, children and tobacco smoke, all of which contributed to the overall unpleasant cacophony, were pervasive throughout the carriage.

I now understood perfectly what Lodge had once mentioned in the bar at the Criterion some weeks back. It did not make sense to Jack or me at the time. It certainly was making sense to me now, unfortunately. Jack and I were in fact travelling in what was obviously a 3rd. Class carriage of the London & Blackwall Rail Road. Such trains as this train, so Lodge had advised us, were almost certainly what they call *Parliamentary Trains*. Typically, a train would be made up only of 3rd. Class carriages, with cheap fares, and were deliberately established by an overzealous Parliament, eager for popular votes. And, also to allow the teeming masses, travel around the realm, and unescorted too. A dangerous adventure, it was noted at the time. Jack and I were now obviously riding a Parliamentary Train, which comprised only 3rd. Class carriages.

"Next stop Blackwall, then Canning Town Theo," said Jack, looking at a rail road map of the London & Blackwall Rail Road fixed above our window.

Several minutes later we rolled into Blackwall Station. It was here that the two costermongers got up and left the train. I looked out of the carriage onto the platform and found myself gazing at yet another advertisement plastered to the platform wall.

A ghastly thought then struck me. Was not this R.M.S. *Olympic* boat, the very same boat when we took passage from New York to England also the sister to the ill-fated R.M.S. *Titanic*, which was lost only recently?

Moments later a dubious looking individual sat down opposite Jack and me. His dress was remarkable in that it resembled a loose collection of worn material in need of urgent reparation to avoid being relegated to that of the status of rag. He wore heavy boots, the name for the types of which I believe are prefaced with the word 'pit'.

The White Star Line **R.M.S. "*Olympic*"** the largest vessel in the world is well named for she stands for the highest skill and perfection yet reached in the art of ship building.

VINOLIA "OTTO" TOILET SOAP

Stands for all that is best in the art of soap making. It is fitting, therefore, that on board this magnificent vessel, with accommodation for nearly 3,000 persons, the Toilet Soap supplied to all first class passengers is **Vinolia "OTTO."**

The well known purity and emollient properties of Vinolia **"OTTO"** make it just the soap to counteract the effect of the salt sea breezes upon the skin, and also the whole range of Vinolia Toilet Specialities, ensures the maximum comfort and pleasure which absolute purity and scientific skill in manufacture can afford.

VINOLIA COMPANY LIMITED, LONDON & PARIS

His trousers were baggy and soiled and supported only by a length of twine around his waist that, I observed, he made no effort to conceal. The material of his jacket was of the type which resembled the skin of a dead animal of indeterminate specie. And, was no cleaner and fared even less than his trousers, save that it was of a tighter fitting. The shirt on his back was of grubby aspect and he wore no completing necktie!

This general assemblage of dirty clothes and ill-fitting attire was surmounted by a head the face of which was pocked-marked and of sallow complexion. The hair on his head though thick was greasy and unkempt. I looked at his hands and found to my surprise not only were they clean, but they showed no signs of rough or manual labour. I wondered what he could be. One who might be deployed on a building enterprise perhaps?

After all, one does see them in ever increasing numbers these days, employed as they are, in constructing dams, turnpikes, rail roads or bridges, but, surely not with those hands? I doubt they had ever handled anything harsher than a bar of Vinolia's "Otto" toilet soap. Probably an overseer of building workers or navigators,[4] I conjectured with confidence and a betting certainty.

At that moment our train screeched to a halt. This was followed by a general commotion which erupted spontaneously as the costers, tossers and the *Undeserving Poor* gathered up their dogs and what possessions they still retained which they had not gambled away. At this point, Jack and I also got up from our seats to leave the unpleasant confines of the carriage. And after some pushing and determined behavior, we all eventually piled out on to the platform. We then made our way, in a noisy fashion, down the stone steps to the street level.

On leaving the station with the noisy costermongers

and in particular the tossers, Jack and I were fortunate to find, standing in a nearby rank, a Hansom carriage without a fare. In order to secure this stoke of good fortune. I ran to it to ensure we engaged him before some other person did.

"Royal Albert Music Hall in the Victoria Dock Road, Canning Town; and step on it," I bellowed out to the carriage driver.

He took me at my word and within moments we were hell raising our way down a wide road headed south.

Our Hansom carriage ride did not take long. It would also appear that Lodge's instruction on how do get here were unerringly accurate. On arriving at the Royal Albert Music Hall I was immediately conscious of the fact that this was no ordinary London Music Hall of the standard variety. The outside of the building was plastered with a mass of advertisement posters, all of which were competing to gain any observer's attention. One particular advert did in fact catch mine.

I have said it before. Were such reckless claims made in New York City. Then they would certain land the advertiser in jail! And judging the blatant claims made in that advertisement. It would appear that Doctor Huber electrical devise in nothing short of a practice run for the electric chair!

At length Jack and I entered the foyer. It was organised chaos bordering on pandäemonium, with people attempting to find themselves let alone the way to their seats. I instinctively searched out the nearest Crush Bar. To my horror it was packed with people. To the extent that bitter experience, born of disappointments, told me that the chances of our being able to obtain a drink at that bar, were at best minimal; at worst, none existent.

I looked around foyer to occupy my mind in a vain

attempt to forget my crushing dilemma. The audience assembled in the foyer, still waiting to take their seats, resembled not so much a well behaved gathering of Thespians, than a loose confederation of rivals, intent on entertaining themselves at each other's expense.

Presently we progressed through the Music Hall. And, it was with some difficulty that we found our places. When we did find our seats in the Balcony, they were occupied by ruffian and his female companion. And it was only after a heated argument and Jack waving our tickets in their faces, that they relinquished our seats to us.

The woman was by far the more vocal of the two. And judging by their peculiar language and in particular remarks to me, I suspect they may have been costers, or possibly tossers, who were clearly well represented in the stalls below. Sitting next to them and looking decidedly uncomfortable was Lodge dressed in his mid night blue suit and top hat. We had of course previously arranged to meet with him here in these seats having booked them in advance with ticket agents, Keith, Prowse & Cº.

Eventually we settled down in our red plush velvet covered seats. And looking down into the stalls below, I could see quite clearly that elements of the grotesque were already in evidence, even before the curtain had even gone up. I also noticed that the large contingent of costermongers present in the stalls, were already picking arguments with total strangers as they entered the auditorium. Those who were not arguing with all and sundry, were overtly gambling with each other in a forlorn bid to enrich their purses.

At length the green velvet curtain ascended into the attic space above the stage. As it did so, a diminutive Harry Missouri stepped into the lime light and commenced his turn. It was not his act that caught my attention. Rather, I could not quite believe what we the audience were presented with in front of us. Even in my days working Vaudeville throughout the eastern United States, especially in West Virginia, I had never seen a stage, the walls of which were covered in so many garish advertisement posters. This stage set was obviously a permanent feature of the Royal Albert Music Hall.

The advertisement posters ranged in their deplorable and suspect claims from those promoting health enhancing devices; to miracle cures. One in particular, '*Koko for the Hair*' confined itself to women's hair. "A Woman's Crowning Glory is Her Hair." it boasted, whilst depicting a woman, with impossibly long luxuriant hair riding a white charger, as though on a quest.

'Will Positively Stop Hair From Falling Out!'

It went on to establish, in the absence of any concerted contradiction, the bold statement that their compound of Koko will categorically,

'Surely Increase The Growth Of Hair!'

Adjacent to that poster was one extolling the virtues of having the treat of the 'Seaside at Home' by the ingenious application of the 'Niagara' Wave & Rocking Bath. The poster depicted a gentleman wearing not only a striped bathing costume, but a look of smug contentment on his mustachioed face positioned inside what looked like an outsized curved rocking cot. Filled with water presumably, one rocks oneself back and forth. And in so doing, imitate the seaside surf! At a cost of only four guineas who could possible deny oneself such an unadulterated pleasure, I thought.

Eventually, Harry Missouri vacated the stage allowing the audience an unimpeded view of more advertisements for our delectation and enlightenment.

One poster in particular addressed the real concern of physical comfort and excellence. Including which established the irrefutable fact that C B Harness's electric corsets were the very thing for ladies.

Before I could take in the merits or make a mental note of the poster, the second act commenced in a vigorous manner with the arrival of aërial trapeze artistes. Within moments the aëther above the stage was filled with ladies swinging on their triangular trapezes. They were of course the Sisters Ongar Trapeze Troupe and confirmed to be so by the Compière. Their silent aërial complex manœuvres reflected a coördinated and precise choreography which had been well rehearsed.

Occasionally, one would fly out over the first few rows of the stalls, invariably occupied by the costermongers. Some of whom would duck each time one of the trapeze artistes swooned over them. They in turn vacated the stage to thunderous applause from the audience. This was not before the costermongers had settled down again in their cheap seats having been thoroughly entertained by the Sisters Ongar's impressive and their intricately coördinated aërial gymnastic display.

Again we had to wait for the next act to commence; affording the audience enough time to dwell on the stage advertisements. I consulted my handbill. The next act was the Illusionist followed by George Robey's Simple Pimple act, Then Muriel George doing her rendition of the Rat Catcher's Daughter. Alec Hurley would then follow in and finally Alice Lloyd's act bringing to a close the first half of the evening. After the interval the uplifting Choral Anthem Symphony would open up the second half in a stately and majestic manner befitting this solemn work of high moralistic propensity and benign glory.

THE 'VERY THING' FOR LADIES'
Health, Comfort and Appearance
Mr. C. B. Harness's

ELECTRIC CORSET

It makes the most awkward figure
become graceful and elegant, prevents
chills, gives perfect support, exercises a
most beneficial influence on the
respiratory and other internal organs, and
is thus an invaluable adjunct of attire for
DELICATE WOMEN.

It should be worn daily, in place of the
other one; it will always do good, and
never any harm.

There is no sensation whatever felt in
wearing it, while benefit quickly follows.

It soon INVIGORATES the entire
system, and assists nature in the healthy
development of the chest.

ONLY 5/6. Post Free.

SPINAL NEURALGIA.

Madame Lena Scheyer, 5, Walterton Road
West, St. Peter's Park, writes 7th.
December, -

**"I have much pleasure in recommending
the Electric Corsets invented by
Mr. C. B. Harness, to all suffering from
Spinal Neuralgia.
I have derived much relief and support
since wearing one."**

Cheques and postal Orders should be
crossed
"London and Country Bank.'

'FOR THAT 'WEAK BACK'
Light, Cool & Invigorating

NOTE ONLY ADDRESS

The MEDICAL BATTERY Co. Ltd
52, OXFORD STREET, LONDON, W.

I looked on to an empty stage and perused a few more advertisement. One of course understood the efficacy of these advertisements. During the intervals, between the various acts which might last for two or three minutes. One was compelled to read the advertisements whilst focusing on the stage waiting for the next act to begin. Similarly to waiting on a rail road platform or sitting in a train at a station. Often, one got the impression that trains waited regularly at rail road stations for some length of time in order that their passengers might be afforded ample opportunity to read the uplifting claims in platform advertisement posters displayed, of course, on rail road property.

Rather as I am now doing waiting for the next act, billed as the Illusionist to make his appearance on the stage.

A thought then occurred to me. It would be most unlikely that these advertisements would ever be removed. In order to display, say a sylvan back ground. One depicting a classical Greek pastoral scene of wood nymphs dancing gaily with each other with trailing ribbons intertwined about their hands. In which perhaps the *Inexhaustible Cremorne Belles* might dance or perform some other complex or intricately precise coördinated choreographic manœuvres.

The implication of this thought came rushing into my mind. Rather like a tidal flood of biblical proportions. This Music Hall, I conjectured, simply stages verbal presentations. No scenery was required to augment the acts on stage; as no act would require such scenery. The Royal Albert Music Hall was not so much a Music Hall. But rather was the nearest to real Vaudeville in London and therefore, not really a suitable place to have a recital of Lodge's much vaunted Choral Anthem Symphony.

The seeds of destruction had been sown. And Jack and I would now be witness their dramatic growth in to a monumental disaster.

"It will be just like the Titanic Benefit Concert, Loge put on at the Queen's Hall recently. Only this time, this concert will end with more tears," said Jack, reading astutely my thoughts as well as the ghastly expression which had developed upon my face.

Irrespective of this deep foreboding feeling that had gripped my heart. I consulted my playbill to confirm the appearance of the illusionist who would step imminently in to the limelight to entertain us. Though from what I had already witnessed the entertainment had already begun in the stalls below our Dress Circle.

Reading my dog-eared handbill, it informed me that the illusionist in question was fellow, name of Cordova, Colonel Cordova, out of Hackney, London. He had performed his illusionary acts recently to spectacular acclaim at the Town Hall, Stratford, where ever that is. But tonight be will be ably assisted by a certain Mademoiselle Odin, from the Conservatoire in Paris, France. On this occasion, she will appear in an act called the *Marvellous Flight* which will involve floating Mademoiselle Odin's body from the stage to the Balcony! The handbill went on to proclaim that no so called Conjuror or Illusionist in the world has ever been able to perform this *Marvellous Feat*!

Mademoiselle Odin, so the handbill informed me, will first be trussed up and then placed in a sack. She will then be lowered into a coffin, the lid of which will then be closed and locked down. This procedure will be done in full sight of a committee appointed by the audience to rule out any tomfoolery or concerted effort. After this elaborate procedure is completed, and within just a few minutes, Mademoiselle Odin's inert body will be seen to float from the coffin and up to the Balcony! [5]

I wondered what the assembled costermongers, or for that matter the *Undeserving Poor*, occupying the stalls would make of this illusionary feat of magic. Within moments of my doing so, sporadic applause erupted in the stalls as the Illusionist stepped into the limelight and marched up to the footlights fronting the stage.

"Ladies and gentlemen," the Illusionist started in, "please attend me as I galvanize such wondrous feats of illusion as to stun your minds!"

Not a very propitious statement to make to an audience, which in the main comprised costermongers, who might take exception to such a proud, if reckless boast involving their minds!

Immediately behind the Illusionist was an ornate highly varnished elm coffin with brass handles and fittings with its lid open. It had been placed on a catafalque, draped in black crushed velvet, adding further to the notion of a rising body that then would float in the aëther above the stage whilst making its way to the Balcony.

"Please bring your hands together," the Illusionist exhorted the audience, "for the delectable and resistant Mademoiselle Odin, whose body will miraculously leave the confined of her wooden box, coffin if you will, and become resurrected in the aëther above the stage and float to the Balcony over there."

"The costermonger character may be anything to anyone and have various aspects to it; but incredulity is not one of them," I said to Jack.

In the next second the Illusionist's protégée Mademoiselle Odin, a plump rather rotund woman stepped heavily on to the stage.

"I doubt if she could even clamber up to and fit inside

that coffin let alone have her body floating about above the audience. I should not like to be below her; in case the illusion or whatever failed and she then came tumbling down in to the stalls," said Jack.

"May I have four volunteers from the audience to form an impartial committee to guarantee that no tomfoolery is extant when we place Mademoiselle Odin's body in the sack and then lower her into the, the ...coffin!"

No sooner had the Illusionist invited members of the audience to *assist* him. Than at least half of the stalls erupted as members of the audience, including several costers, jostled with each other in order to be selected to carry out this highly responsible duty.

After some undignified pushing and visible aspects of determined behavior by some of the eager applicants, the Illusionist selected four reasonably sober looking individuals from the mêlée which had broken out on the steps leading up to the stage. The misunderstandings continued, but eventually attempts at reëstablishing order on the stage by Compière were marginally successful. Later a sack was produced into which Mademoiselle Odin was helped by the four committee members. The sack was suitably closed with a cord which was fastened in full sight of the committee. This was followed by the unenviable task of attempting to lift Mademoiselle Odin's inert, if embonpoint, [6] body from the stage deck and place it in the open coffin.

It took several minutes as four stout costermongers staggered around the stage holding this deadweight. Several more moment went by before they eventually managed to place the sack in to the coffin. It was with a look of satisfaction and relief upon the faces of the costermongers when one of them slammed the coffin lid closed and in so doing sealed the fate of Mademoiselle Odin encased inside, shrouded in a sack.

After the stage was cleared of people, the footlights were then dimmed. The only light came from a single shaft of weak limelight that illuminated the coffin placed on the catafalque draped in black crushed velvet. The Illusionist, was dressed in deepest black which made keeping him in sight difficult. Especially since he moved around the dimly lit stage, as a black shadow might pass over a darkened background.

Not only was the auditorium plunged into darkness; an uneasy silence also pervaded the place. The kind of silence no Music Hall or Vaudeville artiste wants to endure before their act. It is a quietude laced with a potential where anything could happen; and usually the least expected would.

Jack and I were sitting left of center in the Balcony. We naturally had an uninterrupted view of the stage and all that was happening upon it. The Balcony of course is where the body of Mademoiselle Odin is supposed to arrive having risen out of her coffin. Then I heard it. Almost imperceptible at first, but knew that I had heard something directly in front of me in a space that was about thirty feet above the stalls below us. I knew that my perception was confirmed when Jack looked at me with a furrowed brow above his eyes and then he too looked back out in to the dim oblivion in front of us.

Others in the Balcony held their heads at odd angles in order to detect the least sound. Again we heard it. This was no flight of the imagination, but rather a real thing out there in the twilight of the auditorium. I could not, despite the peculiar sensation running through my person, quite bring myself to expect to see Mademoiselle

Odin floating through the aëther past our very persons in order to take her seat in the Balcony.

Then all of a sudden one became aware of a commotion below us in the cheap seats, the ones normally occupied by the *Undeserving Poor*. Those of us seated in the front row of the Balcony peered over the red velvet covered parapet wall to see what the fuss was about. Jack and I both looked out into the dimness of where we supposed the commotion originated.

To our right appeared to be a feint shower of small bits of black paper half the size of a 10c mail stamp. The costermongers and a few of the *Undeserving Poor* upon whom this paper shower was falling were not impressed. Some were brushing their shoulders or hats clearly annoyed at what they considered an invasion of their dignity. The more vociferous of the costers were waving the clenched fist in to the aëther above where they were sitting.

I could understand very well their discomfort in being subject to small bit of virtually invisible black paper falling on them, creating an odd sensation to say the least.

Suddenly I became aware of Jack tugging my coat sleeve. At the same time I noticed people were staring into the space above the commotion. It was Jack who pointed it out to me. Indeed people had good cause to look into the space above the commotion and the indignant costermongers. I could, now that my eyes had adjusted to the gloominess of the auditorium, just make out a shimmering movement in the space between the stage and our Balcony, but further to my right. A hush returned to the auditorium and even the costermongers were moved to remain silent as people tried to make sense of this strange shimmering mirage seemingly suspended in the aëther within the auditorium.

I continued to look at the strange vision hovering in the near distance and from which a silent shower of black paper continued to fall on the hapless costermongers seated below.

"Are you there Mademoiselle Odin," inquired the Illusionist, "are you at your place of destiny?"

"I am here; but cannot make form. I, I am disintegrating," came a voice from the shimmering image.

Even Jack, a confirmed sceptic, if ever there was one, was mesmerised by what was unfolding before us and others too seated in the dimly lit auditorium.

"I cannot make form I am failing... it is beginning to..." continued the voice, before trailing out into silence.

Then at that very instant a whooshing sound assailed my ears accompanied by a sensation of something like soft fur brushing past my face, Jack felt the same sensation. Others in the Balcony also indicated they had done so too.

"Are you there?" asked the Illusionist, with an audible timbre in his voice which could indicate a real anxiety he was experiencing at this present moment. After all, his assistant, the plump Mademoiselle Odin had not answered his final call to her to where she was at; wherever that at, was. Was she in fact disintegrating on to the costermongers seated below us in the stalls, I wondered.

The Illusionist was standing there on the stage and seemed to be exhibiting further signs of becoming distraught. He kept staring into the auditorium and into the space where her voice had last been heard. Gradually the light from the footlights was increased illuminating the Illusionist and the coffin still resting on its catafalque draped in black crush velvet.

The Illusionist approached the coffin. But then he

hesitated uncertain what to do; or what to reveal. Presently he steeled himself into some activity. He began by unscrewing the brass brackets with which the coffin lid was locked shut. I noticed that some of the costermongers in the front row of the stalls stood up in order that nothing, including what the Illusionist might do, should elude them.

At length when all the brackets on the coffin had been released the Illusionist threw back the coffin lid in a manner one would not associate with the opening of a coffin. But having done so the Illusionist looked into the coffin, but then withdrew immediately gripping his chest with both hands and collapsed into a nearby chair with a look of absolute astonishment upon his face!

A few moments later the Compière got up from behind his desk and approached the distraught Illusionist who kept muttering, whilst pointing at the coffin, that he had lost her and that it has all gone wrong and what was he to do.

The Compière, left the Illusionist and approached the coffin. On arriving he too looked into the open coffin. But unlike the Illusionist, he reached inside the coffin. We all of us expected the rotund Mademoiselle Odin to jump up and with the help of the Compière ease herself out of the coffin and down to the stage floor.

Nothing of the like happened. Instead the Compière merely rummaged around for a few seconds with his hand and then lifted a sack out of the coffin. An empty sack, the one in which Mademoiselle Odin had been placed in and secured with a stout cord!

A general and very audible gasp went up in the auditorium as people realised what had happened in front of their very eyes. Some even stood up in order that they may gain a better view of the proceedings on the stage.

She had quite literally disappeared. That fact was confirmed when two inquisitive costermongers, without being invited, stepped up on to the stage and peered into the coffin themselves. One even looked beneath the black velvet draped catafalque to make sure no trap door was in evidence. Both of the costers were satisfied that Mademoiselle Odin had indeed left the coffin. They then indicated, with hand signs, to their fellow costermongers that the coffin was in fact empty.

At that moment the heavy green velvet curtain came thundering down with indecent haste bringing that act to a premature end. I was not sure what to think. Jack was in deep conversation with a fellow seated on his right, who too was confused about what had taken place in the auditorium of the Royal Albert Music Hall.

Jack then turned to me.

"What is it with this Mademoiselle Odin; where there hell has she gotten to?" Jack asked, looking about the Balcony, as though expecting to see her sitting comfortably in her plush red velvet seat.

Since the Illusionist's act had been somewhat brought to an end, I began to look around the well-appointed auditorium to see if I could detect any apparatus wires, tricks, noises or other distractions which might facilitate the disappearance act. I found no such devices visible. Eventually my gaze settled on the costers assembled below us in the stalls to see how they were re-acting. Apart from a low murmuring amongst them they were not. Though I did notice that they were now seeking to make the own entertainment in the absence of any activity on the stage.

I did so, more as an immediate source of impromptu entertainment than for any other reason. The costers, not so much as made up the general Thespian public. But rather, comprised the massed ranks of the London *monger* fraternity.[7] They were assembled, as though one might do so for a respectable joint stock company's annual general meeting.

The costermongers, of course, were in their element shouting at each other, and offering abuse to all and sundry. Including artistes who had previously performed their turns and were not immune to threats of their being thrown off the stage. In addition encouragement, advice or demands to leave the stage were freely bandied around, as were nut shells and orange peel. Most of the various mongers including the costers, were eating something or wiping the sweaty faces with playbills, acquired from someone or somewhere.

Irrespective of the general commotion extant all round, especially in the stalls, some costermongers were endeavoring to display themselves and their ostentatious sequined costumes in an overt manner. Indeed their women, if anything, were worse and even bolder in their outrageous conduct. Their exaggerated behavior did not in any way stop them from offering their opinions on anything to anyone.

One got the overriding impression that the women thought that it was perfectly reasonable to continuously insult the players on stage and even members of the audience too. And, that picking an argument with a total stranger was a perfectly acceptable way of behaving in public. And whilst indulging in this, *behavior,* some would fan themselves with their shabby feathers in an exaggerated, and perforce, suggestive manner.

It was not so much the antics or cavorting extant in the stalls that I found appalling. But it was against this background of disruption, that the artistes on stage had to contend with. And which made them resort to being even more outrageous and impudent, in order that they might gain the attention of the by now distracted audience. I dread to think how this audience would receive the Choral Anthem Symphony and its morally uplifting virtues embedded therein.

I consulted my handbill and saw that George Robey was on next followed by the Rat Catcher's Daughter. I and an expectant audience looked towards the stage. There was no movement or appearance. I then realised that despite the fact my playbill listed the order of appearance of various acts and turns. We seemed to have reached a point during to have descended in to general chaos on the stage.

That there was some sort of commotion back stage was evident and appeared to involve a number of artistes in a violent argument over the order of appearance of the acts. And as to who should be on the stage doing their turn. In fact a quite audible argument was developing between the competing groups of artistes. Much, I noticed, to the delight of a disconcerting audience, who revelled in this impromptu entertainment of the real variety.

And certainly, if the language being deployed by the arguing contestant artistes, was anything to gauge by. The arguing artistes clearly resented being relegated or who should take precedence in appearing before or after a rival artiste. Eventually, the Music Hall management stepped in and virtually escorted, not George Robey, but Muriel George into the limelight to do her turn as the Rat Catcher's Daughter.

The esoteric lyrics to this song were totally lost on both Jack and me. Probably, I figured, on account of their being overlain with Cockney lascivious innuendo and therefore unintelligible to us. And, I still found it hard to accept, that according to Lodge, the lyrics were actually written by a cleric, name of Bradley, Edward Bradley, And with help from a Sam Cowell with later additions by Charles Sloman.

Eventually Muriel George having done her turn, curtsied and left the stage and straight into another commotion as she did so. During this mêlée, the Compière banged his gavel for all to hear.

"Ladies and gentlemen," he said, "a slight change...a slight change to the printed order of acts. We will not be watching Mr. George Robey at this stage. He will be on later. Instead we are proud to present the delectable, incongruous and unimpeachable *Three Graces* to perform the Cholera Anthem Symphony! Please welcome the incomparable Dot Hetherington, the ever competent Kate Lawrence and not least Mabel Green, fresh from her recent incarceration in the mad house!"

I looked at Jack. Jack looked at Lodge and Lodge looked as if he was about to have apoplectic fit. For at that very moment he was thrown into a blind panic accompanied by his monomania affliction of constantly looking over his shoulders.

"This, this cannot be so, this is unendurable," Lodge spluttered out, in a blind panic, "the order of appearances, as I agreed with the manager Charles Relf should have been George Robey, followed by Muriel George then Alec Hurley finishing with Alice Lloyd's act then the interval. Then after a suitably long interval my noble and sublime Choral Anthem Symphony would open up the second half of the evening. My symphony cannot be performed with a sense *Noblesse oblige*, [8] or ethereal majesty immediately after Muriel George's bawdy rendition of the Rat Catcher's Daughter!"

"That may well be the case Loge," said Jack, with an

undisguised smile on his face, "just look down there. It is a bit late. The unendurable has begun!"

Sure enough as Jack uttered his observations of the stage the costermongers in the stalls began to applaud the arrival of the *Three Graces*. The usual off stage voice announcing the *Three Graces* began its lugubrious introducing of the sopranos.

"Ladies and gentlemen, imagine for a moment, those noble ideals we all of us continue to strive for," the voice invoked. "I refer to such ideals as *Hope, Aspiration,* or *Courage* especially when one has to deal with them in the face of continuing adversity in our short but tragic lives. Imagine if you will, a symphony, a symphony in which those noble ideals are encapsulated and given laudable expression. Ladies and gentlemen, the Royal Albert Music Hall is pleased to present, for your delectation, the *Three Graces*, who shall sing the rôles, especially composed for soprano, in espousing those noble ideals and promulgated in this magnificent Cholera Anthem Symphony.

"Ladies and gentlemen, please welcome the unimpeachable Mabel Green fresh from the mad house who will be singing the rôle of *Courage*. Our renowned and delectable Katie Lawrence will sing those sections devoted to *Aspiration*. And she will be followed by the incomparable but indomitable Dot Hetherington who will bring up the rear and sing those sentiments devoted to *Hope*!"

As each of the sopranos was called, the intensity of the applause increased accordingly. Culminating into a thunderous crescendo, where everybody in the auditorium rose from their seats and stood up, thus showing unequivocally their unadulterated approbation for their *Three Graces*. Also during this ecstatic welcome for the *Three Graces*, some members of the audience erupted with unbridled enthusiasm. Whilst others, deliberately ascended into an uncontrolled delirium, at the prospect of hearing their favorite sopranos sing in this symphonic choral extravaganza.

Though it must have been apparent, even to the musically bereft, that this performance could hardly be called symphonic, since nowhere in sight, was there a symphony orchestra, let alone a standard Music Hall pit orchestra! Instead, it looked as if the musical passages to the symphony were going to be paraphrased by two barrel organs and transcribed by three player pianos.

First to lead off was Mabel, looking all the better despite her recent sojourn at the St. Pancras Asylum for the Criminally Insane. Mable in the rôle of *Courage,* stepped forward up to the footlights and commenced her sustained attack on harmonic structure; augmented by the combined ethereal sound of two barrel organs and three player pianos. Even with her wide tessitura, she sang atrociously in *falsetto*. But this did not stop the costermongers from joining in. However they joined in with alternative lascivious lyrics, which in no way reflected the original intention of the sublime intensity of the lyrics composed by Gustav Mahler with a little help from Lodge.

I looked at Lodge. He just sat in his seat his head buried in between his hands.

Mabel completed her recitation and then withdrew to center stage, but not to the back. This made room for Katie Lawrence to occupy the front of the stage above the foot lights to gain the greatest visual presence. After the barrel organs had played out their introduction tunes, Katie commenced her recital in praise of *Hope*. And, despite the potential sublime lyrical intensity of the work,

Gustav Mahler

she stood there waving her arms about in an abandoned manner screeching out her words in and especially in the irritating key of C # minor. After fifteen minutes of this musical onslaught accompanied by the full throated costermongers, Lawrence curtsied and then raising her hands, finally withdrew to the rear of the stage.

We then had the so-called, *Symphonic Interlude,* played by the two barrel organs and the three player pianos. No sooner had this *Interlude* ceased, than Dot Hetherington glided to the very front of the stage. As near to the footlights as possible, in order that she too might be illuminated to the fullest intensity. She then launched into those lyrics devoted to the noble ideal of *Aspiration.*

All of a sudden Hetherington had the audience swaying from side to side in their seats, in response to her waving her head from side to side. Hetherington's achievement in getting the audience going and to re-act in sympathetic harmony, was to the very obvious annoyance of the other two sopranos Green and Lawrence there, standing somewhat redundant and powerless to intervene but wearing fixed grins on their faces. And especially, given the fact that both had somehow failed to move the public in the auditorium in quite such an enthusiastic way.

After twenty minutes of ecstatic re-action from the audience and calls for encore and bravo, Hetherington finally conceded the front of the stage. She then had the temerity to actually summon the two other sopranos to join with her in holding hands!

Neither Mabel Green nor Katie Lawrence could scarcely reject this overt magnanimous gesture by Hetherington and were somewhat compelled to comply with her invitation. Hetherington, standing in the middle of the sopranos holding hands, had without doubt, executed her very effective coup de grâce, upon her co-sopranos in establishing just who was *Prima inter pares*. [9]

Irrespective of what was supposed to happening on stage in terms of performing Lodge's precious Choral Anthem Symphony. This was not a rendition which would meet with Lodge's endorsement. And whilst, I knew there was more of the symphony to come. Including the finale, in which all three sopranos are supposed to sing together in perfect harmonic unison, representing, as it were, the three rôles of *Courage, Aspiration or Hope* combining in a resounding expression of an unbreakable faith in the future.

But on this occasion, all the signs were that this would not be the case and the symphony would disintegrate into pandäemonium at best or a débâcle at worst. This was a very evident possibility on account of the ad lib singing of alternative verses, by the combined mass ranks of costermongers and tossers supported over enthusiastically by the *Undeserving Poor*.

Lodge must have known this in his heart. For at that precise moment he got up and walked out of the Balcony. Jack bade me not to follow as I too rose from my seat to leave. So I resumed my plush scarlet velvet covered seat.

1 A person who searches the Thames shore for washed up valuables
2 Now called Tower Hill Underground Station.
3 A novel of a sensational nature usually read by the lower orders
4 Otherwise known as 'Navvies' as they navigate the building of roads
5 Based on a performance at the Stratford Town Hall in January 1878
6 A person of plump proportion
7 Monger as in, iron monger, fish monger or cheese monger &c.
8 Denotes a concept of a noble purpose to enlighten
9 First among equals

Chapter 7

The Inexplicable Co-incidence

Lodge, Jack and I had just witnessed a partial performance, or collapse, of Lodge's much vaunted Choral Anthem Symphony in the less than salubrious surrounds of the Royal Albert Music Hall in the depths of the East End, adjacent to the docks at Canning Town. However, Jack and I had decided to abandon the auditorium and seek refuge in a nearby Crush Bar. It was whilst we were drinking at the bar. That Jack decided to impart to me, some information of a peculiar nature.

"Do you remember some weeks ago Theo?" Jack asked, "Loge was talking incessantly about a Public House, called the Waterman's Arms [1] in the Limehouse neighborhood of the East End and owned by a friend of his, name of Farson, Daniel Farson. And the fact that this Farson had turned the Waterman's Arms into a small successful Music Hall in which turns and acts by the public are encouraged? Well Limehouse is not far from here. In fact we could make the place, I figure, inside of thirty minutes if we can secure a carriage."

"What are you suggesting Jack? Do you want that we should make our way to the Waterman's Arms in Limehouse? For whatever reason and why should we go this evening?" I inquired of Jack.

"Trust me on this Theo," replied Jack, as he motioned

me to finish my whisky. "Loge is not in the best of moods at the moment. He is unlikely to publicise the apparent débâcle which this evening's concert has degenerated in to. No, he will avoid another embarrassment of the type which attended his ill-fated Titanic Benefit Concert in the Queen's Hall. Therefore it is reasonable to suppose that he will not head into central London. Instead it is probable that he will seek refuge or solace in a place less conspicuous than his normal West End haunts."

"You have lost me Jack," I responded.

"My guess is he will head for the Waterman's Arms. If only because it is but a short ride in a carriage from here," replied Jack

"Do you really think Lodge will make for that place in this fog?" I asked.

"Indubitably and because I suspect Loge knows this part of the East End like the back of his hand," replied Jack. "Loge is almost certain to go to that Waterman's Arms, after this evening's débâcle. Rather as a top hat wearing toff might venture in to the East End of an evening in search of adventure! Though in Loge's case; he will be seeking solace. But think about it Theo. What did Lodge advise us to do earlier today by cable-gram?"

"Something along the lines of...we should ride the Metropolitan urban rail road to Mark Lane Metropolitan Station. Make our way to the nearby Fenchurch Street Rail Road Station, and board a train to a place called Canning Town in east London. Then get a carriage down to the Victoria Dock Road and to the Music Hall. And indeed come to think of it. Having gotten to Canning Town and secured a carriage it did not take us long to get here. You are correct Jack. It would appear that Lodge's instruction to us on how do get here were unerringly accurate. He does know his way around these parts!" I said.

Jack just smiled at me.

"Alright then, let us do this thing," I said to Jack, "though I cannot imagine for a moment how we are going to avail ourselves of a Barouche or Landau carriage. Let alone intercept a Hackney or Hansom carriage to Limehouse, wherever that is."

Accordingly, we left the comfortable confines of the Crush Bar and made our way through the Music Hall. A few minutes later we found ourselves outside in fog bound Victoria Dock Road where all was quiet, save for the sound of a distant out of tune barrel organ.

"I hope we are in luck in being able to intercept any passing carriage, even a dog cart will suffice. I do not relish the prospect of standing around here all night!" I remarked to Jack, whilst beginning to read an advertisement poster plastered to the front of the Music Hall.

I decided to read the advertisement, in an attempt to occupy my thoughts or at least divert my attention from our predicament of being yet again stranded in the depths of the East End.

I had no sooner read the advertisement, when Jack hailed a passing Hansom carriage. Eagerly we both climbed aboard and closed the double doors in front of us which then forms the protecting dashboard. At the same time Jack instructed the driver as to our destination.

"How many times will Lodge insist on having his Choral Anthem Symphony performed in less than desirable places," asked Jack, as we made our selves as comfortable as one could in such a carriage. "It seems that Lodge does not learn. Short of having the symphony performed in a Cathedral, or the musical equivalent, a plush Theater of Variety or at least an aspiring Music Hall, as we have witnessed in the past. But to stage it in

NEVER SWEEP CARPETS WITH A BROOM !!

Its strong brittles wear off the nap and throw up dust.

How different with the

'EWBANK'

Carpet Sweeper
(British Manufacture)

Like gentle rain, it penetrates without damage –the broom, like the raging flood, ravages the surface only.
The 'EWBANK' is quiet – easily worked to and fro – collects all dust – carpets always look fresh

SPECIAL FEATURES
Hand–made brush, – last 10 years.
Few working parts are outside case

SWEEPERS from 11/6 to 15/6

Refused any sweeper offered in place of the 'EWBANK'

From all dealers or write

ENTWHISTLE & KENYON LTD
Accrington
who will send nearest dealer's name

the Royal Albert Music Hall in the depths of the East End, amidst the teeming docks, could only inveigle catastrophe or court disaster."

"Probably, "I replied, "but my concern right now, is what do we intend doing were we to meet with Lodge in that Waterman's Arms, assuming that he will be there?"

"Well if he is there, and he will be. I suppose that we should buy him a drink," said Jack.

Our Hansom carriage driver seemed to know where he was headed and we were making good progress down the Victoria Dock Road.

Eventually we turned off the Victoria Dock Road and into another thoroughfare addressing the eastern aspect of the Isle of Dogs. I noticed in this part of London that the fog was denser with a pronounced pungent smell to it. This was probably due to our being in the close proximity of the river Thames.

"I also remember Lodge mentioning the fact that the Waterman's Arms Public House, was built in 1853 by William Cubitt, and formed part of his grandiose building scheme to be called Cubitt Town. Cubitt's modesty was not limited to naming a town for himself. His younger brother, Lewis, built King's Cross Rail Road Station too," said Jack.

"Lodge is a veritable depository of information, both relevant and, irrelevant," I responded.

"I agree Theo. One gets the distinct impression that Loge says things with impunity; but with no intention of carrying it through or being held accountable!" said Jack.

At length and within thirty minutes of having set off from the Royal Albert Music Hall, we actually arrived outside the Waterman's Arms, located in Limehouse on the corner, so the road plate informed us, of Newcastle Street and Wharf Road. Whilst Jack was occupied settling our fare with the coachman. I looked at the building.

King's Cross Rail Road Station

From what I could make out in the fog of the Waterman's Arms Public House, revealed to me that it was a handsome four square three storey building, the ground floor façade of which was finished in red glazed tiles. Above, on the *piano-nobile* were three elongated French windows, one of which was pedimented, set behind ornate balconies confined by metal balustrades. Above them on the second floor were three square window reveals one of which was bricked up. There was also, I noticed, a singled storey ground floor annex addressing the Newcastle Street elevation.

As we walked up to this Quality Wet Public House, we could see that there were several doors leading into the interior. We chose the most elaborately decorated door on the reasonable assumption, that what lay on the other side might be opulent or at least of sumptuous, if meretricious appointment. It was neither, as we soon learned on entering what was clearly the Saloon. Undaunted Jack led the way further into the interior of the establishment. I followed. The sound of singing accompanied by pianoforte could be heard. Jack and I instinctively made our way to the source of the music.

This act involved our having to negotiate our way past several patrons in various states of inebriation. At length we left the saloon and after a short walk down a corridor entered what looked like a Vault and Tap. No pianoforte was visible. So Jack continued in to the further recesses of the establishment where we finally ended up in a large room. It was in this large chamber that the pianoforte was located surrounded by revellers singing for their supper.

On one wall was a bar at which I distinctively heard a patron ask, "May I have a large absinthe and a dash of crushed lemon. And for my friend here a large whisky

Waterman's Arms Public House

with a dash of that chloral hydrate [2] concoction, to which he has become addicted."

Surely, I thought to myself, Lodge would never frequent such an establishment as this. Where persons at the bar were inclined to act in an ostentatious and reckless manner by demanding drinks such as those he had asked for. The bar-tender, to whom this order had been addressed, stood there with all the dumb aloofness of Greek god. The fact that he was dressed in chequered trousers, wore a white apron, sported a large handle bar moustache that matched his shiny black hair with a central parting and flattened down on to his skull was not of relevance here. Because he simply viewed the patron with a seasoned distain and then walked off into the back recesses of his bar!

In the meantime, my eyes were taking in the late Victorian appointment of this *Quality Wet* Public House. The place comprised several bars we had walked through; the Saloon, Vault and Tap, the Public and the 'Snug' and was divided by highly decorated glazed mahogany timber partition walls. Each room had a bar, which in turn formed a central horseshoe shaped bar in the middle. For the present we found ourselves in a well-appointed, almost opulent room with a stage at the far end. For all intent and purposes: it was a small auditorium, indeed resembling a Music Hall. Irrespective, the place was brimming with people singing and shouting or gesticulating wildly at each other To the extent their mannerisms would, without doubt, put the steering committee of the British Tourette Society to shame. [3]

This room, or whatever, was the more salubrious of the bars and by far the largest, which suited my purpose. I have always preferred the large bars with space than cramped little bars the size of a doll's house, but typical of Georgian corner Public Houses. For it is in these small claustrophobic bars that misunderstandings can all too readily lead to something else not conducive to having a refreshing drink. Typically, one may quite innocently turn around and in so doing inadvertently cause some adjacent person to spill or even drop their drink, with the resultant unfortunate and all too familiar consequences, which they may lead to.

Notwithstanding this potential, this small music hall had quite an ornate plaster ceiling, supporting several chandeliers tinkling with cut glass and giving out a myriad of light. They in turn illuminated an even more decorated deep squared cornice that terminated the ceiling at the wall, below which was a painted raised frieze with relief, leading down to an elaborate architrave. Below this white plaster architrave, the walls were covered in raised green velvet flock wallpaper, punctuated with gilt-framed paintings of sylvan or ethereal scenes which added an aura of Thespian respectability and theatrical to the establishment. The street side of the room was dominated by large red velvet curtains framing windows, the glazed panes of which displayed intricate designs acid-etched into the glass made more apparent by the opaqueness of the fog outside. These decorative appointments were of such lavish aspect, as to lend successfully, verisimilitude to the room.

Suddenly staggered applause erupted as someone completed their song accompanied by the pianoforte. In the meantime, Jack had caught the attention of a bartender and had, thankfully, ordered large whiskies for us both. Whilst accepting my drink from Jack. I was aware of a commotion at the far end of the room. I naturally assumed it was just high spirits fuelled by alcohol. Then the pianoforte started up and a voice, a distinctive voice became audible. It was an octave higher than normal. But this did not stop Jack or me from looking aghast in the direction from whence the voice came.

It was with a fearful trepidation accompanied by a certain creeping sensation that we made our way instinctively through several groups of patrons until we reached the pianoforte which was of the domestic upright type. Our fears were given substance as our disbelieving eyes fell upon a person who was standing adjacent to the pianoforte and singing terribly out of tune. He was dressed in a mid night blue suit underneath which he sported an ostentatious silver-toned finely woven silk waist-coat and ruched ripple shirt.

On this occasion his collar was not fastened by a necktie and orchidaceous purple stone of amethyst, but was open revealing his throat. Upon his shoulder, slipped to one side, was a black cape with a flamboyant blazing red silk lining. He also wore, albeit at a precarious angle to one side of his head, a slightly marked black silk top hat. He appeared to be in a delirious trance as he sang and his eyes rolled aimlessly in their sockets. He stood there flapping his elbows as though attempting to gain flight. Rather as a chicken might.

The person attempting to sing in tune was Lodge. And, had a glazed look in his eyes and seemed oblivious to not only us, but to his surrounds too, period. And it was with a grave expression upon his face, as he sang, which intimated to all around him that he may have sustained a catastrophic basic loss of sensibility or even dignity.

Jack may have been very astute in his prediction as to Lodge's re-action to the preceding events which had unfolded in the Royal Albert Music Hall earlier this evening. Lodge had indeed made his way to the

Waterman's Arms. As for me, I was transfixed at Lodge's apparent fall from grace and departure from his own defined unimpeachable standard of dignity.

Certainly, it was not his demeanor that was of concern to me. Nor indeed that of any God-fearing person with even a passing acknowledgement of decency or rudimentary appreciation if self respect. Rather it was the song that he was singing. And doing so in a vigorously manner and with inordinate enthusiasm devoid of any aspects of shame or even feelings of remorse. I turned my head and attempted to vacate the room. But I was unable to, as a direct result of the not inconsiderable crowd now surging forward towards Lodge and the pianoforte, to witness the song. A song [4] very rarely performed in public.

After some minutes Jack and I were able to effect an escape out of the Waterman's Arms Public House and the lascivious lyrics being sung by a distraught Lodge.

1 Originally called the Newcastle Arms and later run by Dan Farson (1927 – 1997), Marie Lloyd's biographer
2 A particularly volatile concoction of chloral hydrate and used in drink to induce rapid inebriation
3 Refer to the book, *Burlesque – The Endless Attempts.* Chapter 15
4 Reports of the occasion conflict and are fragmentary, but it seems the song sung by Lodge was a variation on a Gus Elen song.

Chapter 8

The Absurd Encounters

We had managed to quit the Waterman's Arms Public House in which Lodge had taken refuge as a result of the yet another débâcle regarding the performance of the Choral Anthem Symphony. Or rather its performance immediately after Muriel George's bawdy rendition of the Rat Catcher's Daughter, when in fact the symphony was listed to be performed after the long interval spent at the various Crush Bars ranged around the Music Hall. Consequently, the Choral Anthem Symphony could not be performed with any sense of *Noblesse oblige*, ethereal majesty or indeed, basic dignity. For the moment however, Jack and I were headed towards a rail road station operated by the London & Blackwall Rail Road Company in order to avail ourselves of a train back to central London.

Having entered the station precincts we approached the ticket office. But whilst I was purchasing the tickets a commotion erupted nearby. It was soon quelled as various servants of the rail road intervened between the arguing contestants. We then prevailed upon rail road *employé* standing upon the platform. He was dressed in his dark blue velveteen uniform complete with red piping and inquired of him from which platform, would the next the next train, to Fenchurch Street Rail Road Station, start. He did not know. So, we availed ourselves of another rail road servant standing nearby.

Jack put our inquiry to him. The rail road *employé* listened attentively with a polite demeanor and nodded his head at suitable intervals as though to indicate that he knew precisely the nature of our predicament. When Jack had completed his inquiry, the facial expression of the rail road servant changed suddenly, with a look of abject horror manifesting itself upon his face. Whereupon he looked at Jack with his rannine eyes bulging, as though in disbelief of what Jack had said. He then turned on his heels, and promptly marched off quickly down the platform to the far end leaving us with our mouths open and in total bewilderment.

"It seems nobody here," I said to Jack, "ever does know where a train is going to start from, or where a train when it does start is going to, or anything about it."

That rail road servant in the ticket office felt sure that the train would depart from Platform 5, while another rail road employé, with whom he discussed our inquiry, had heard a rumor that it would go from Platform 6. The Station Master, standing imperiously on his Platform, number 4, whom we had met previously, on our way to the ticket office, on the other hand, was convinced it would start from the rear end of Platform 3.

To put an end to the matter, we climbed some metal stairs and walked over a cast-iron trestle bridge straddling the rail road tracks. Having descended on to another platform we put our inquiry to the Superintendent of the Permanent Way, a rail road employé responsible for rail road traffic in his area including this rail road station.

"Surely he should know," I said to Jack.

But when we asked him, the Superintendent of the Permanent Way told us that he had just met a man, who said he had seen a train he thought might go to Fenchurch Street Rail Road Station standing at number 7 Platform. So Jack and I hurried over to Platform 7. However, on reaching Platform 7, the authorities there said that they rather thought that train was the 21-35 to Shoeburyness. That or else the express to the Empire Docks, located as they are, at Tilbury. But they were sure it was not the Fenchurch Street Rail Road Station train. Though why they were certain it was not, they simply could not say.

Then another rail road servant who had overheard us, pointing with his index finger at a stationary locomotive, proposed that must be it, there on platform 9; adding that he thought he knew the train. So we climbed some metal stairs and again walked over the cast-iron trestle bridge that traversed the rail road tracks below, to platform 9.

There we spoke with the driver of the large purple painted locomotive that was hissing steam fiercely. We asked him if he was going to London, specifically either to Fenchurch Street Rail Road Station or any rail road station in central London. His reply to us was he could not say for certain, of course. But on the other hand, maybe it could be that he was going to a rail road station in London. Aside of which, if his train was not the 21.15 for the Empire Docks located at Tilbury, then he was absolutely confident his train was the 22.55 for Enfield Town, or the 22-05 local for Southend-on-Sea, or somewhere in that direction. But then, we should all know when we got there; would we not?

"This absurdity could never happen on our Central Rail Road or even the Pennsylvania Rail Road operating out of New York," Jack remarked to me.

At length an express train of the London & Blackwall

Rail Road Company came thundering down the other side of the platform upon which we were standing. It was hauled by a huge green painted locomotive belching out thick black smoke from its smoke-stack and depositing smuts upon our over-coats. When it eventually juddered to a halt a voice announced it to be the 22-10 express train direct to London Waterloo Rail Road Station.

"That is near enough for me," said Jack, "let us do this thing."

Accordingly, we both duly climbed aboard into a vacant 1st. Class compartment. We made ourselves comfortable on the heavily patterned blue brocade upholstered seats. Which were divided by substantial armrests and complete with intricately designed white cotton antimacassar covers for head rests. It was agreeable to be sitting in comfort in a 1st. Class carriage in comparison to the one we had made earlier in that 3rd. Class parliamentary carriage operated by the London & Blackwall Rail Road Company.

Eventually after a whistle was heard, the train pulled away with the customary sharp jolts and glided down the platform and burst out from beneath the iron and glass canopy over the platforms in to the still pervasive fog. I was staring out from the window contemplating the events of the evening thus far and in particular about our experiences at both the Royal Albert Music Hall and the Waterman's Arms. Suddenly our corridor door opened and in walked a ticket inspector.

"Tickets please gentlemen!"

I instinctively reached into my inside pocket and produced with a flourish my leather wallet containing our 1st Class tickets, I had purchased. Without a second thought I handed them to the guard. I continued to stare out through the carriage window into opaque oblivion still absorbed with the events which had occurred earlier in the evening.

"Theo," I heard Jack say, "I think this gentleman wants your attention!"

"Thank you." I said expecting the return of our tickets duly perforated by the railway servant.

"Just a remark," said the guard in a distinctive Cockney accent, "but are you enjoying yourselves in this 1st Class carriage?"

I was somewhat taken aback by the inspector's somewhat confident, if impudent, inquiry.

It was Jack who replied.

"As it happens yeah, yeah we are..!"

"The reason I ask," interrupted the inspector, "is because these tickets are for 3rd. Class accommodation and not 1st Class. I am afraid these tickets do not entitle you to occupy this carriage. I must therefore ask you to vacate and remove yourself to the parliamentary carriage located at the end of this train. There you shall be accommodated in the style and dignity befitting the class of ticket you hold!"

At this juncture I intervened.

"There has clearly been a misunderstanding......"

"Not as far as I am concerned," interjected the inspector, "I hear gents such as you bemoaning the advent of the parliamentary train. Yet when persons as yourselves occupy a 1st. Class carriage with a 3rd. Class ticket I am somewhat compelled to force your immediate vacation from the carriage in all fairness."

"What are you talking about and just where...," I protested.

"I appreciate fully your concerns," the guard continued, stifling our protest, "and the lack of a cotton antimacassar covered headrest on your un-upholstered seats, but the timber benches are of sturdy English elm and will suffice for your needs.

"This is outrageous." I exclaimed.

"It may well be," said the inspector, "but it does not require much systematic reasoning, deductive or otherwise, to conclude that you are both occupying a carriage that you ought not to be doing. Or, I might add, in having a basic understanding of the information contained in that most excellent of pocket books – Bradshaw's Railway Guide, which I highly recommend you purchase, read and apply its uplifting and useful information! Availing yourselves of that useful book might help you appreciate the class of ticket that you hold and your correct location on a train and thus avoid being in embarrassing situations such as this one!"

And with that Parthian shot, he stepped out of the carriage and motioned us to follow him down to the parliamentary carriage for completion of our journey on this non-stop express train to London. Needless to say the embarrassment and ignominy of our being escorted by this velveteen uniformed supercilious ticket inspector through several packed carriages to the rear of the train. And then being consigned to a noisy smoke filled parliamentary carriage for the second time this evening, was one of the most thoroughly unpleasant experiences which I have ever had to endure. After an interminable slow journey we eventually steamed back into London to Waterloo Rail Road Station.

Chapter 9

The Escape from Eternity

The previous evening we had witnessed yet another débâcle surrounding the performance of the Choral Anthem Symphony at the Royal Albert Music Hall embedded in the East End of London. It would seem that on every occasion the symphony is performed. The high ideals and aspirations, upon which the symphony is structured, laudable as they may be, degenerate into pandäemonium or disrespect. One is therefore compelled to wonder just how long Lodge can tolerate such incidences of catastrophic failure; and on an all too regular basis. Our other experience last night included witnessing Lodge personal performance at the Waterman's Arms. And our miserable experiences in that parliamentary train. Accordingly I tried to strike, out of my mind, the memory of riding that train. Save for the injunction that would to God I should ever enter such a parliamentary carriage again.

Such concerns were of monumental indifference to Jack as he munched on his Brätwürst on rye whilst we took break-fast beneath chandeliers tinkling with cut glass in the elegantly appointed Grand Dining Room at the St Pancras Hotel in which we are still holed up. Looking through the quatrefoil window reveals of the Grand Dining Room. I could see that the acrid yellow fog

St. Pancras Hotel

suspended in the aëther outside was still with us and had not dissipated. The fact that the windows were still opaque bore testament to this disappointing fact.

I consulted the red tasselled menu in order to satisfy my hunger. I then looked at Jack, in order that I might satisfy my curiosity too regarding the events of yesterday evening; notably those which occurred in the Waterman's Arms Public House in Limehouse.

"Well Jack, do tell me. You obviously figured out that Lodge would repair to that Public House, the Waterman's Arms in the Limehouse district of the East End. How could you be certain that he would do so?" I asked.

"Pure deductive reasoning Theo, and also because as I said last night. Given the circumstances Loge found himself in. It would be reasonable to assume that he sure would not repeat his undignified performance such as we witnessed outside the Queen's Hall a few weeks back. No he would almost certainly go someplace else where his public notoriety and personality were safe. Where else in the vicinity but to the relatively nearby Waterman's Arms?" answered Jack.

'Pure deductive reasoning.' Where have I heard those words spoken previously? That is before Jack spoke them just now. I asked myself. Then it came to me. It was Lodge! It was he who spoke them whilst in the grip of chronic catachresis.[1] He was at the time endeavoring to describe his thought process in establishing a connection with synthesising the solution via *deductive* reasoning as opposed to *inductive* reasoning, resulting in systematic reasoning. And, whichever remains must be the correct conclusion by analysing the solution retrogressively from consequences to principle!

I looked impassively and replied.

"How do you explain his performance last night at that domestic upright pianoforte in the Waterman's Arms, singing such lascivious songs in the style of a costermonger, to the extent that he would have even put Gus Elen to shame?" I inquired.

Jack merely looked at his *'London Chronicle'* newspaper.

"Lodge did not in any way appear as a man beset with remorse or self doubt," I continued, "rather he seemed to be enjoying himself thoroughly, irrespective of the potential repercussions to his name and reputation. I do not begrudge the man enjoyment or happiness. But I do strike a line at such wanton behavior, and in public too, singing renditions of songs I thought could result in one being indicted by a Grand Jury and eventually finishing up in jail, certainly one would in New York City!

"Before I could quite get away from Lodge's singing,

due to the crowd surging to reach Lodge, and forcing me back in that direction. I was amazed to hear Lodge break into a song, with alternative lyrics; based on that scandalous play, performed by Olga Nethersole on the New York public stage, called 'Sapho.' That performance caused an outrage across Metropolitan New York led by such organisations as the New York Society for the Suppression of Vice, the New York Mother's Club and the Society for the Study of Life. All of whom considered the play to be degrading, indecent and an unadulterated and infectious concentration of filth!"

"In particular, some people were outraged by what they considered to be unacceptable language expressed on a public stage and the provocative costumes worn by the actors. As you and I know Jack. Such was the was the level of public outcry that the District Attorney for City of New York, name of Gardner, Asa Bird Gardiner, ordered the immediate arrest of main instigator Nethersole and members of her touring company with indictments handed down by a Grand Jury. Together with the police closing down Wallack's Theater on Broadway and 30th. Street.

"What surprises me here Jack. Is the fact that of all persons we know. Lodge should get in there and perform those songs, and with inordinate enthusiasm too. I find this hard to accept, especially, given his much vaunted highfalutin stance on certain moral issues, and his claim to be a virtuous person, operating only on, as he would say, 'dignity!' And Jack, as for your explanation of Lodge's resorting to the Waterman's Arms, merely as a way of dealing with the events of last night. With respect Jack, this comes over to me as an anæmic excuse as any that I have heard," I completed.

Jack was still engrossed in his 'London Chronicle'

newspaper to even look at me let alone reply to my verbal outrage. This concerned me.

I looked hard at Jack. Eventually he returned my gaze. At the same time he pointed with his fork to an article on the front page of the '*London Chronicle*' newspaper and the banner headline that had caught his attention and which had absorbed him.

New mysteries of the ill-fated R.M.S. *Titanic* revealed !

It proclaimed, in its report from an inquiry set up to look into the loss of the *Titanic* ocean liner.

"That ill-fated *Titanic* boat is destined to continue to cast its dark shadow over we the living," said Jack, in a delivered and pensive manner.

I had finished my break-fast. So I left Jack engrossed in his newspaper. I repaired to the Grand Salon and sat down on a green moiré silk covered sofa shaded by a ubiquitous palm tree rising out of a red glazed urn placed on top of a limestone jardinière. In front of me was a selection of English and American newspapers. I saw the name Pittsburgh mentioned in connection with the dreadful loss of the *Titanic*; and so resisted the urge to refrain and instead started to read from the newspaper.

It was the '*Daily Gazette,*' and from a cursory glance at the printed article realized it was reporting on the findings of the inquiry by the British Wreck Commissioners convened to investigate the loss of the so called, '*Ship of Dreams,*' the ill-fated R.M.S. *Titanic*.

The report in the '*Daily Gazette*' made for grim reading.

'Under the auspices of the Board of Trade, an Inquiry has
been set up to investigate the recent loss of the White Star

Liner, R.M.S. *Titanic* in the waters of the north Atlantic Ocean.

The Inquiry is to be headed by a judge of the High Court in the person of Lord Mersey, an experienced examiner in such marine matters. The Inquiry is charged with investigating the reason and particularly those responsible for the loss of over fifteen hundred souls including men women and children on that fateful April night.

The Inquiry heard evidence that the owner of the *Titanic* is a certain Mr. John Pierpont Morgan. A banker and head of the International Marine & Mercantile which in turn owns the White Star Line, operators of the *Titanic* boat. Mr. Bruce Ismay, the chairman of the White Star Line and survivor of the *Titanic* tragedy fielded several questions on behalf of JP Morgan, who was not in attendance. To one question asked by counsel representing the Board of Trade inferring a link between JP Morgan's IMM and the Pittsburgh steel barons Carnegie or Peacock. Ismay answered in the negative. In response counsel informed the Inquiry that there was in fact a link. In the year 1901, Morgan was responsible for merging Carnegie's iron works in Pittsburgh with other iron founders creating the largest industrial concern in the world; that of United States Steel Corporation.'

I sat back into my green moiré silk covered sofa. And thought about the ramifications of what I had just read in the *'Daily Gazette.'* Jack and I met with Alex Peacock. A very genial and hospitable man, when we performed at a private party in his lavish mansion called, Rowenlea. I remember the house very well, located as it is, in the fashionable and very wealthy neighborhood of East End located in Pittsburgh, Pennsylvania. Sure Peacock had become a multi millionaire as a result of Morgan buying out Carnegie steel works of which Peacock was director.

Rowenlea Mansion, Pittsburgh

I could not quite figure out what the *'Daily Gazette'* was trying to establish in its report from the inquiry. Other newspapers took up other aspects of the inquiry. In particular, so I read, in the *'Daily News.'* It was most virulent in its condemnation of Edward Smith, captain of the *Titanic* and Commodore of the White Star Line, owner and operator of the ill-fated *Titanic* boat.

> 'The Inquiry was informed by reliable witnesses who survived the *Titanic* disaster as to the velocity at which the boat was hurtled in to a well known and expected ice field by the captain of the ship, Edward Smith, Commodore of the White Star Line. At that speed of twenty-one knots, the Inquiry was told, one might reasonably expect to encounter, an iceberg, the size of St. Paul's Cathedral, floating down the Labrador Current into which the ill-fate *Titanic* was now inescapably and inexorably steaming, at speed.'

An iceberg the size of St. Paul's Cathedral, kind of brings home the enormity of the iceberg which collided with the *Titanic*. Now curious, I reached down and picked up another newspaper. It was the *'Chicago Tribune.'* It too was vociferous in its condemnation of certain persons involved in the tragedy. I glanced at the report on the front page. Their report of the findings promised to be equally astounding. Just what had the inquiry by the British Wreck Commissioners revealed? I asked myself.

'FROM OUR SPECIAL CORRESPONDENT AT THE INQUIRY.

The British Inquiry regarding the sinking of the US owned *Titanic* has revealed some basic navigational and maritime practices which need urgent revision. Notably the provision of adequate number of life boats for all passengers including those of steerage. More importantly are the lessons to be learned from this senseless and avoidable tragedy upon the high seas. Evidence emerging from the Inquiry suggests incidences of flawed marine practices and a sheer recklessness at best or a contemptible attitude to the lives of the passengers on the *Titanic*. Why, one asks oneself, did an experienced captain of thirty years' standing steam into an ice field at twenty-one knots. Such an action can only be interpreted as being nothing short irresponsible even reckless given the damage an iceberg can inflict on any large vessel. The Inquiry was also told that the look outs on the forward mast of the ship were not provided with field glasses. Had they been issued with glasses the look outs would have spotted the iceberg some distance away in front of them. And allowing time to steer the ship out of the path of the iceberg and avoid a catastrophic collision.'

However, it was not the article in the *'Chicago Tribune'* which absorbed me now. Rather it was a banner headline my eye had caught on the front page of a London newspaper called *'The Echo.'* I reached over and picked it up.

Titanic Subterfuge for Olympic Boat !

Sensational information emerged yesterday at the hearing regarding the collision iceberg and a ship of the line, the *Titanic* which sank with a loss of over fifteen hundred lives. It was suggested by a reliable witness from the US city of Pittsburgh at the hearing that the *Titanic* boat which sank was in fact the *Olympic* boat that was launched earlier in October 1910. Evidence had also been submitted establish irrefutably that the *Olympic* had not been a financial success and had spent a considerable amount of time in a dry dock being repaired. One such case being after a collision with a ship of His Majesty's navy called the *Hawke*. Other incidences recording the accident prone *Olympic* involved the boat shedding one of her triple screw propellers when she steamed in to something bigger than the *Hawke*; England!

The Inquiry was informed that the *Titanic*, launched in May 1911, was the second in a line of large ocean liners capable of carrying two thousand five hundred persons in abject luxury. The third boat being built is called the *Majestic*. Each of the boats is identical in their appearance. It would therefore, not be an insuperable impossibility to change such identifiable signs as burnished copper nameplates or architectural details of the construction of the *Titanic*, in order to replicate the *Olympic* in appearance. Thus giving the false impression that what sailed out on that April evening on her maiden voyage was the new *Titanic* and not the compromised or damaged *Olympic* boat. The opportunity to change the physical identities of the boats could have been facilitated whilst the damaged

Olympic was in the Thompson Graving Dock literally side by side the brand new *Titanic* boat being fitted out for her maiden voyage.

The *Olympic* boat was a prototype and accordingly a failed experiment in the creation of large ocean-going passenger liners. Lessons learned from these failings were later incorporated in to the later designs of the *Titanic*. No one could doubt the fact that the *Olympic* boat has been seriously damaged. Her hull and ability compromised to the extent the *Olympic* is now truly incapable of creating vital revenue and profit through passenger traffic from Europe to the New World.

The *Olympic* was a financial failure and draining resources from the profit conscious International Mercantile & Marine of which Mr J. P. Morgan is in total control. The easiest solution to this marine and profit liability was to sink the boat in mid Atlantic. The evidence suggests that is exactly what happened to the broken *Olympic* boat masquerading as the *Titanic*.'

At that point, so the article informed the reader. The inquiry by the British Wreck Commissioners decided to adjourn in order to consider this astounding revelation. Such an allegation is not so farfetched or preposterous as one might at first think. I do recall at the time of that dreadful sinking. Rumors that were making the circuit regarding an alternative explanation for what was quite an avoidable sinking, with the resultant appalling tragedy involving the loss of over fifteen hundred souls no less. [2]

Both the *Titanic* and the *Olympic* ships were identical in construction and shape and were often mistaken for each other even by their owners! The White Star Line, promoted its White Star Flag, as the preferred carrier of the rich and famous across the Atlantic. At the time enthused in the newspapers about the 'inter-changeability' of items in the boats. They mentioned especially their fittings, including all removable items, crockery, cutlery and linen which carried the name 'White Star Line' and the white star flag emblem, but never the name of a particular ship. The White Star Line , of course has a fleet of ships all the names of which end with the suffix, '*ic*' as in *Republic*, *Delphic*, *Oceanic* or even *Titanic*. Similarly, the Cunard Line style their ship with names ending in '*ia*' as *Lusitania*, *Carpathia*, *Mauritania* or *Aurania* &c.

The point here, the newspaper was inferring, is that the operators of these ocean going liners are anxious to represent the White Star Line or Cunard Line and not the particular ship one might find oneself sailing on. It therefore seems plausible that the removal of the one unique item on the boat, the burnished bronze name-plate bolted on to the stern of a ship, could allow the ship to be substituted for another!

Therefore, so the rumor proposed, it would be reasonable to suppose, that having removed or exchanged the burnished bronze name-plates, plus a few other minor details, including the transfer to other ships of certain members of the crew, one could effectively replace one ship with another. In this respect the new *Titanic* was exchanged for the impaired *Olympic* whilst adjacent to each other in the Thompson Graving Dock. Even the Inquiry had recognised this possibility.

I felt a vacuüm developing in my chest as I took in the enormity of the on-going saga and revelations surrounding the sinking of the ill-fated *Titanic*. Or should we now call it the ill-fated *Olympic*? But then, of course, Jack and I accompanied Lodge to England on the R.M.S. *Olympic* only a few months ago. [3]

I looked up at a person standing on the other side of the table in front of me. It was Jack, and looking unusually down. Even his smile was sad.

"As I said earlier Theo," said Jack, "the *Titanic* is still is able to cast a dark shadow over we the living. The effects of that dreadful sinking are still with us as new information is revealed about what happened on that fateful night. In particular, how Music Hall artistes responded to that dreadful event, which still haunts us."

"I agree with you. I am minded about our experience in the New Bedford Music Hall when Queenie unexpectedly addressed the audience in a truly remarkable manner that I have never witness in my thirty years of Vaudeville. I recall we were about to join the stampede to the Crush Bars, when all of a sudden a deathly hush descended over the auditorium. Then sporadic applause was heard coming from the stalls.

Gradually it developed into a sustained and tumultuous applause from all sections of the audience gathered in the New Bedford Music Hall. Rich or poor, crude or refined, drunk or sober, all were united in according Queenie great acclamation as she stepped into the golden lime light which created an ethereal elegance around her.

Eventually Queenie spoke.

'How many of us here have lost dear ones, friends or sweethearts when the ill-fated *Titanic* went down? And in so doing, the Titanic took with it, their souls and dreams as it plummeted to the depths of the Atlantic Ocean. Consigning their memories to a permanent, *Iron Mausoleum*, which the sunken *Titanic* has now become?' [4]

"Jack, within minutes Queenie had several people, including total strangers clinging to one another. Others, ranged around the auditorium related their personal stories. They did so with unashamed tears in their eyes to complete strangers sitting or standing nearby, regarding their loss as a result of the recent sinking of the *Titanic* Ocean liner.

What you and I witnessed in the New Bedford Music Hall that evening Jack, was not Music Hall. It was something I cannot even now define. It was not contrived, but natural. I think it was a sincere and spontaneous outpouring of profound grief which the loss of the *Titanic* was able to induce in ordinary people. Queenie merely released that reservoir of repressed sadness.

"Is there no escape from eternity?" Jack asked me.

"There is always that possibility," I replied, looking into the middle distance.

"Come on Theo," urged Jack, "Cinderella is in the foyer. And you know her. She will not be kept waiting! We need to go through our material before appearing with her this evening at the St. James's Theatre."

1 Incorrect use of words
2 Refer to book, *Iron Mausoleum – A case of Sherlock Holmes and the Titanic* Chapter 20
3 Refer to book, *Royal Aq.- Queen of Music Halls* Chapter 9
4 Refer to book, *Royal Aq.- Queen of Music Halls* Chapter 31

Chapter 10

The Incorrigible Cinderella

Following on from the disappointing, if partial performance of the Choral Anthem Symphony, in the Royal Albert Music Hall, Lodge had sought refuge, as a re-action, in a Public House called the Waterman's Arms. This Quality Wet, though located in Limehouse, on a place called, incongruously, the Isle of Dogs, a district in the East End of London. But this Public House, in fact, houses a small intimate auditorium, rather in the style of an early form of Music Hall, and in which Jack and I witnessed Lodge singing several bawdy renditions of songs of a risqué nature. That performance, no doubt, was not Lodge's début. However, since then, we have not seen him. In the mean time we are to meet with Cinderella in the foyer of our hotel and journey on to the St. James' Theater in order to rehearse and therefore perfect our début act, ready for this evening, with which we hope will sweep all before us.

Cinderella was not in the foyer. Neither was she in the bar. Rather she had abandoned those opulent places complete with heavy red flock velvet wallpaper punctuated raised designs in the form of golden fleur de lys and gothic pointed quatrefoil window reveals and arches supporting a decorated vaulted ceiling. Instead she had removed herself to a new location; that of sitting in an open top Clarence carriage in the Port Cochère. Or at least so the Concièrge informed us. We took his advice and indeed found Cinderella sitting in the bench in the Clarence carriage with her open white cotton parasol resting on her shoulder. She looked every part serenely elegant. Even the shrouds of swirling acrid yellow fog seemed powerless to obscure this ethereal vision of her.

The Clarence carriage was in the charge of a liveried coachman resplendent in his rather flamboyant, if ostentatious pale green tail-coat complete with gold braid emblazoned on the front and gold tasselled epaulettes to the shoulders. In addition, he wore a gray horsehair powered wig beneath a shiny black top hat with a blue rosette on one side. He appeared vaguely ridiculous wearing this rather extravagantly ornate uniform, the rank of which was indeterminate.

"Ah Jack, Theo," said Cinderella, as we climbed into her Clarence carriage.

"Cinderella," responded Jack, kissing her outstretched hand.

I followed suit.

"Where is the impresario Lodge, is he not with you?" asked Cinderella, with a look of concern upon her gentle facial features.

I explained what had happened at the Royal Albert Music Hall. And in particular, the premature performance of the Choral Anthem Symphony and its undignified ending, which led to only part of it being sung by the *Three Graces*, culminating in a débâcle organised by the costermongers.

"Oh well Lodge is by now, one would have thought, used to a débâcle attending any of the performances of that ridiculous choral extravaganza fit only to be sung at funerals," responded Cinderella.

Cinderella's remark produced a broad grin on Jack's face.

At the same time our extravagantly attired coachman whipped up his chestnuts horses and set us in motion for the St James's Theatre located in King Street, just down from Piccadilly. Presently, we pulled in to the Euston Road, dense with traffic.

The fog was particularly heavy and so we made our way cautiously along the Euston Road following the red tender lamps of other wagons in front of us.

After a few minutes travelling along the Euston Road, I could just make out in the fog, a now familiar and very elegant classical structure, which comprised a group of female statues, and known as the Caryatid Porch. This Porch is of course, a faithful imitation of part of a classical Greek temple, called the Erectheion which is one of several temples constructed on the Acropolis at Athens, Greece. This beautiful Caryatid Porch representing classical sculptures, seemed somewhat out of place, located as it is in the midst of a fog-bound Metropolis. Rather than being sited beneath an azure Aegean sky.

Several minutes later we were clattering down Upper Woburn Place and into Russell Square,

"This place brings back memories," I said to Cinderella, as we cantered into Russell Square and past the Hotel Russell. "Jack and I were involved in a carriageway accident whilst riding with Lodge in his Barouche carriage..."

"Who was the coachman driving the carriage?" interrupted Cinderella.

"Why it was Aloysius, then, man-servant to Lodge," I answered.

"That figures," said Cinderella, with a rueful smile on her soft pink lips.

The Erectheion Temple

"At the time," I continued, "Jack, Lodge and I were travelling south on our way to the Canterbury Music Hall. The ever pervasive fog had become noticeably thicker and more acrid. Made so, I guess, by the numerous chimney stacks ranged across the Metropolis pouring out their coal and wood smoke in to the stilled fog-laden aëther.

"As a consequence of this condition, visibility was down to just a few yards in front of us. And whilst our liveried carriage driver, Aloysius peered continually in front of him into the opaqueness created by the fog. His prudent action did not prevent our Barouche carriage becoming involved in a collision with an omnibus!"

"An omnibus," repeated Cinderella.

"Yes, an omnibus," I confirmed, "a green omnibus operated by the London & General Omnibus Company."

"Yeah, and we were then compelled to resort to riding a public tramcar in order to complete our journey. Imagine the ignominy if you will?" asked Jack.

We all sat in silence for a few minutes, during which we drove past a substantial building in Holborn, that I knew to be a Mausoleum to a great Victorian worthy who obviously wanted the world to know that he once had existed. Needless to say the building emanated, as much as one could determine in the swirling fog, a solemn and restrained dignity, if on a monumental scale. However, it still retained a mysterious and minatory look about it seemingly abandoned in its own grounds and splendid isolation, surrounded as it was by tall iron railings.

Continuing our journey, we eventually made our way towards Cambridge Circus en-route to Shaftesbury Avenue, '*Avenue of Theaters*,' as Cinderella reminded us. I was struck by one observation in a London street. This peculiarity I had noticed before. It involved the electric street lighting in certain London streets. Such lighting is provided by the Westinghouse Company out of Pittsburgh and is very effective at creating illumination in the vicinity around the electric street lamp.

However, the light streaming down from those incandescent lamps has an unusual, almost surreal effect on the faces of pedestrians making their way along the sidewalk. In that the light from the street lamps produces a hue which exaggerates the facial features of those passing pedestrians making their eyes look sunken and dark and their lips an unnatural purple in color, creating an almost grotesque facial apparition.

Mausoleum Building, London

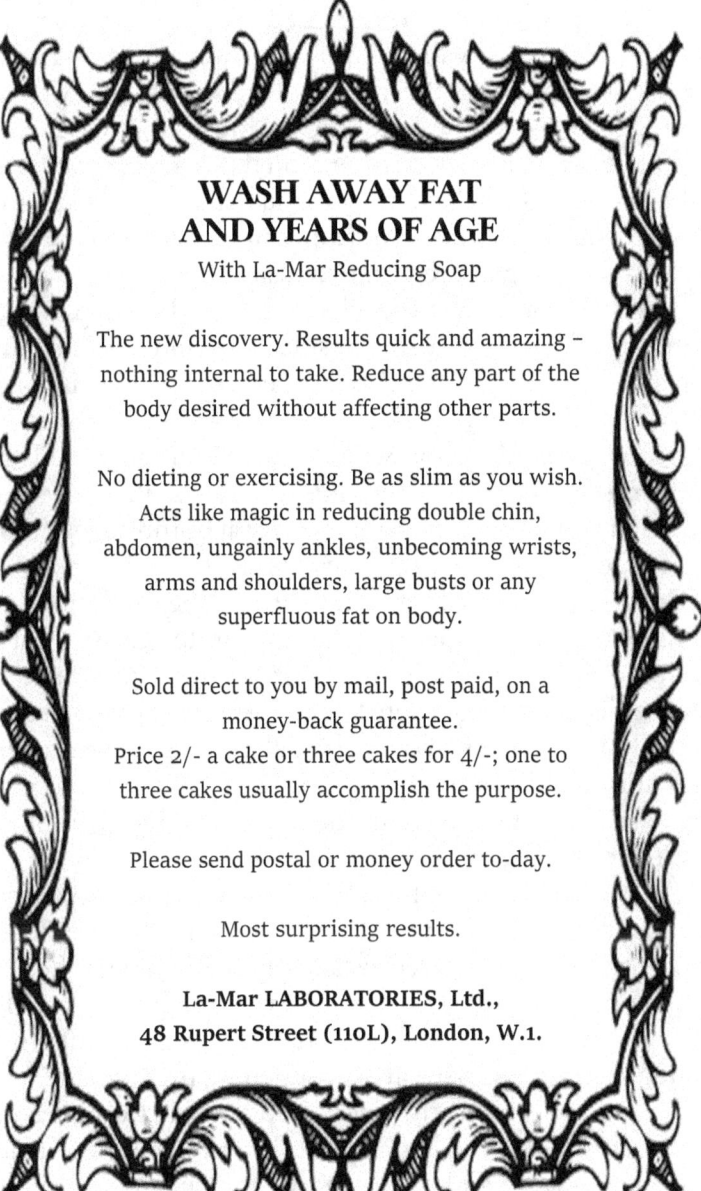

Later our Clarence carriage came to a standstill as a result of some altercation ahead of us. Jack was in the middle of a discussion about the rôle of Steinway Welte-Mignon player pianos in the creation of music today. Against Cinderella's well argued contention that such contraptions, she thought, facilitated cheating and the contrivances of *synthetic* music. I looked out from our carriage and on to an advertisement plastered on to a nearby wall.

I noted the poster proclaimed that the soap would produce, 'most surprising results.' I could well imagine this to be the case. And reminded myself that in New York City, such reckless and wanton display of unsubstantiated claims would almost certainly land the advertiser in the local penitentiary! I then realized the wall was in fact part of the Palace Theater at Cambridge Circus.

I recall Jack telling me some time back. That Cambridge Circus, which forms the junction of Shaftesbury Avenue and the Charing Cross Road, reminded him of Columbus Circus on Broadway and West 58th. back home in New York City. For myself I recall that the Crush Bar in the Palace Theater was a very luxurious and sumptuous space. The interior décor being equal in opulence to what one might find in the imperial splendor of ancient Rome.

Whilst we were stationary I looked up at the ornate and imposing front of the Palace Theater. The five storey red-brick banded curved façade of the building, reflected the curve of Cambridge Circus over which it looks. The impressive façade of the theater, still commands attention, even if partially shrouded by the fog.

The basics architecture reflected an early Romanesque style complete with arched windows forming enfilades to each floor, and culminating in triangular framed pediment, the apex to which supported a statue, and

Palace Theater, Cambridge Circus

rising from the attic, punctuated with a roundel forming a window reveal. The façade of the building was buttressed by two turrets rising up beyond the attic level and capped by domes upon which were affixed statues.

Cinderella broke off from her discussion with Jack to inform both Jack and me that the Palace Theater and the London Pavilion are the only island site theaters; in that the building are not connected to any other edifice.

In the next instance our Clarence carriage was on the move again progressing down Shaftesbury Avenue towards the London Pavilion and onwards into the Regent's Circus.[1]

Our coachman manœuvred his Clarence carriage in a stately fashion down the Shaftesbury Avenue and then reined his horses left around the island site of the London Pavilion. After waiting for a few moments, we continued into the Regent's Circus, located at the beginning of Piccadilly, eventually driving past Alfred Gilbert's newly erected aluminum sculptured statue of the Angel of Christian Charity.[2] At length we progressed by the Criterion Building which houses the Criterion Theater and the Criterion Restaurant. Both of which Jack and I have experienced.

"Memories of that Criterion Building, with its theater and restaurant, come flooding back into my mind like a spring time deluge rushing down the Appalachian

London Pavilion

Mountains," I remarked to Cinderella. "And not for the first time when travelling around in London do I feel as if I were walking in a Gustav Doré ink illustration of the Metropolis."

"As one becomes familiar with buildings in London," answered Cinderella, "even in this pea-souper,[3] they assume an inordinate importance because of the vivid recollections associated with them. There is scarcely a building here in the West End, including theaters, which do not hold fond memories because of failed acts on the stage. Or indeed, where one might have reached the apogée of recognition in some production or other!"

"I am beginning to understand that appreciation Cinderella," I replied, looking ruefully at the Criterion Building to our left not totally shrouded by the fog-bound aëther. "I myself with Jack have memories, though not necessarily fond ones, regarding our relationship with Judd. Judd, you may remember was an over loquacious wooden Ventriloquist's Dummy we used in our previously acts. That is until he got above himself on the Criterion stage. He did so by arguing very persuasively for his emancipation as a dummy from Jack and me. Indeed Judd managed to inveigle the audience very effectively against Jack and me. After such confidence exhibited by Judd, we dispensed with his services," I said.

"I know," replied Cinderella, "that is when I rescued him from the basement of the Criterion Theater, located in that Criterion Building!"

"You are right Cinderella; memories!" I responded.

Accordingly, I slipped into a reverie about the Criterion Building. The sumptuous façade to this five storey Criterion Building clad in grey Portland stone, was designed by Thomas Verity in the French Renaissance style with suggestions of Second Empire addressing the

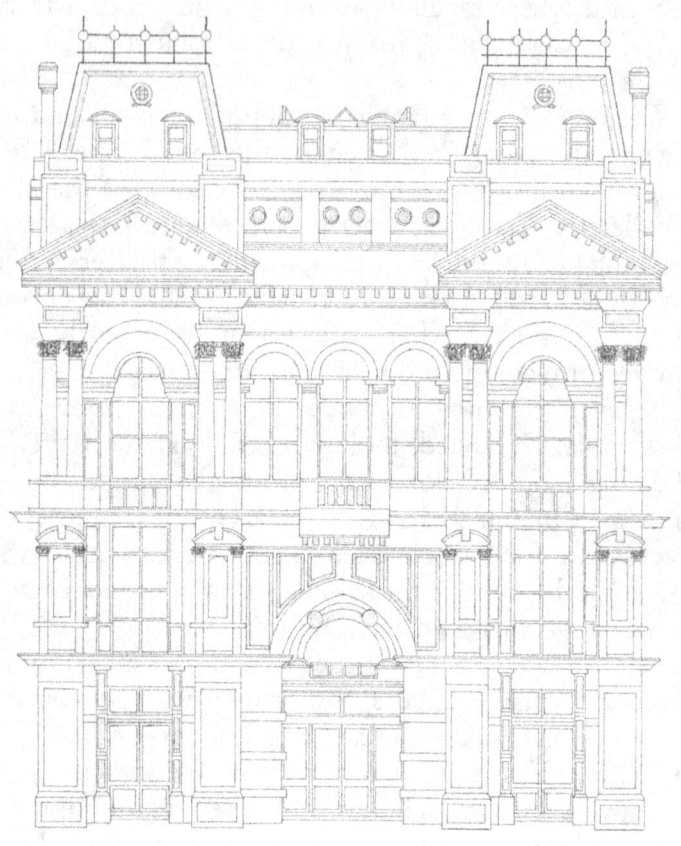

The Criterion Building

attic level. Complete with an ornate Mansard roof structure, that was punctuated with ornate lucarne window reveals and crowns of metal fencing. Traces of early Art Nouveau were evident, especially in the decorative detailing to the building's façade. Jack and I had, of course, been here before, whilst performing on the stage with Judd our Ventriloquist's Dummy.

"The Criterion was completed in 1870 and interior decoration carried out by Simpson & Sons to a very opulent and extravagantly ornate finish," Cinderella suddenly announced as if she had read my thoughts and the expression on my face as I looked at the building.

I looked at her.

"The Criterion is a veritable *Emporium of Tastes,*" continued Cinderella, "and has quite a history considering it was only constructed forty two years ago. Most of the entire theater and auditorium is below ground in the basement and even Dress Circle can only be attained by walking down stairs to it! Imagine! The rest of the building, of course, is above ground, and rises through five floors, and comprises the Ballroom on the fifth floor, a Marble Hall housing a salon, an a la carte restaurant and the Long Bar, which no doubt you and Jack have used!"

"We certainly have Cinderella. But speaking of buildings which can induce within us, memories of experiences past," I said, whilst pointing vaguely with my cane in the direction of the Regent's Street. "I am reminded of what Lodge had to say about a certain building called Vigo House, just up the road there. And, more interestingly, about the bizarre rituals which occurred there on an all too frequent basis. And the peculiar activities indulged by certain respectable individuals, which went on inside the circular domed structure on the roof. And they did so at the dead of night!

"Yes I am familiar with that story," Cinderella replied, "astonishing to think that such odd or even questionable behavior could be tolerated in the very midst of our Metropolis. When news of those activities was made public in the *'Daily News,'* I recall the whole of polite society in London, was devastated and truly shocked to

Vigo House, Regent's Street

the core on learning about the revelation of those bizarre and peculiar practices extant there.

"If you ever get to see Vigo House, in the absence of this acrid fog, the first thing that will become obvious to you, is the building's peculiar mannerism and presentation to the street. It is not just the design of its façade but rather the fact that the upper sections of the building retain the features of a masked human face!

"The design of the building is representative of a Neo-Classical motive with strong references to a repressive monumental style and expressed in the building's design. Especially in the entablature, progressing upward from the roof line architrave, extenuated by the horizontal deep recessed openings cut into the building's upper section. It was this pertinent fact, that of the building resembling a human face, which attracted several quite respectable individuals to it at night. They would meet there in the dome regularly and then commit the most bizarre of practices or outré diversions, rather than appreciate the intricacies of the designs in the façade of the building and its innate serious architecture!" Cinderella informed me.

By the time Cinderella had related her story, we were then proceeding along Piccadilly. At length we came to Fortnum & Mason's emporium and turned left in to Duke Street St. James's. We had only progresses a few yards down the street when Cinderella reached over and tapped the shoulder, covered with a gold tasselled epaulette, of our coachman with her white cotton parasol.

"My good man, please pull over. This will do," instructed Cinderella.

"But ma'am the St. James's Theater is farther down this street in King Street," responded our liveried coachman.

"If we are going to be singing for our supper this evening we might need some sustenance or fortification," continued Cinderella, handing the coachman a golden guinea.

"Ooh, thank you ma'am," re-acted the coachman, putting the guinea in between his teeth.

Jack and I exchanged glances. I consulted my steel case pocket watch, and noted that it was barely noon.

We alighted from our Clarence carriage in to a lane called Jermyn Street. Or so a road plate informed me.

"Follow me," invited Cinderella, slipping her arm under Jack's arm and doing the same to mine. Together arm in arm we marched down Jermyn Street to where I did not know. We walked in silence along the sidewalk paved with glistening York flagstone made wet by the fog condensing on them. Past Paxton & Whitfield's store from which the smell of cured bacon and fresh sage and onion stuffing emanated to the sombre sound of bells reverberating in fog laden aëther pealing out their message to the faithful.

"Here we are, "said Cinderella guiding us in to a street named for the Duke of York.

Moments later we all three of us were standing outside a Quality Wet called the Red Lion Public House. The exterior decoration addressing the ground floor was impressive and reminiscent of the Queen Anne period, but in keeping with Victorian concepts of opulence and ornate detailing expressed in the façade at every opportunity. Three doors led into the establishment two of which were framed by gilded pilasters supporting semi-circular sectioned fan windows.

The glazed panels set within the window reveals were acid etched with intricate designs and opaque areas. Through these windows shone an inviting soft red light which beckoned us to enter the comfortable interiors. We did not resist and following Cinderella, promptly marched towards one of the doors.

"So this is the place that you had in mind for us to derive sustenance or fortification?" inquired Jack eagerly.

"Absolutely," replied Cinderella, turning the brass fluted door handle and pushing open a particularly ornately carved and highly varnished Mahogany panelled door. The small glazed panels to which were also acid etched with exquisite designs.

Accordingly, we stepped off the sidewalk and made our way inside. The bar was large and illuminated gently with soft red lights emanating from several ostentatious acetylene gas-fuelled patterned opaque globe lanterns. And in particular, one large intricately fashioned chandelier with a least eighteen branches each supporting a flickering candle. Other chandeliers throughout the place were less ornate and comprised crystals tinkling with cut glass which augmented an array of extravagant and exuberant vernacular decoration. The décor and designs combined, very successfully, the Baroque and Queen Anne styles, built of highly polished mahogany woodwork with brass fittings, handrails, marble surfaces and decorative glazed panel openings in the internal timber partition walls.

The walls were covered with a heavy maroon flocked silk wallpaper with punctuated raised velvet designs in the form of with golden fleur de lys. Some of the walls were adorned with prints of paintings of Romanticized and sylvan scenes by members of the Pre-Raphælite Brotherhood. Set in between these gilt-framed paintings were wall-mounted appliqués in the form of angels holding forth in their hands firebrand-shaped torches at the end of which were opaque lantern globes radiating a weak light.

Complementing this style was the generous neo-Byzantine opulence of mirrors, glazed screen with acid etched designs and mosaics on various walls and surfaces. There were rich green and red brocade drapes, secured with golden colored twisted tassels, framing exquisitely engraved windows. The ornate stucco ceilings were of painted and gilded moulded plaster with patterns in the form of raised tracery and filigree geometrical designs tipped with gold leaf. Looking down on elaborately patterned silk broadloom carpets upon which were positioned several indoor palm trees rising out of green glazed urns.

The various bars ranged around the place were built of highly varnished mahogany with integral intricately carved designs complete with covered with opulent red *Rosa Collemandina* marble, upon which were huge gasogenes dispensing äerated water almost on an industrial scale. The effect of this luscious and opulent décor, was to create a ornately sumptuous, if meretricious Quality Wet of the highest accolade and extravagant ornamentation representing the best of Victorian red plush ambience of the vernacular type.

We had no sooner gotten ourselves to one such highly varnished mahogany bar. When we were distracted by a slightly dishevelled looking individual seated on a red damask covered sofa in the corner, beneath a palm tree seemingly growing out of a green glazed urn. He was clearly waving at us. Moments later he beckoned us over to join with him.

I looked at Cinderella for guidance as to how we should respond to the individual's invitation to join his company. But she was busy ordering a flagon [4] of dark stout for herself and two large whiskies; one for Jack and one for me.

"Oh let us go and join him," Cinderella suggested, "otherwise he will take umbrage at our not doing so."

1 Incorrectly called Piccadilly Circus.
2 The statue is of the Greek God Anteros and not that of Eros.
3 Particularly dense fog.
4 A vessel holding two pints.

Chapter 11

The Singular Narrative

En-route to the St. James's Theater in King Street, near Piccadilly, Cinderella had suggested that we call by the Red Lion Public House in the Duke of York Street ostensibly to derive some sustenance or fortification. Whilst waiting at the ornate bar. A person sitting some feet away from where we were standing, had beckoned us to come and join him at his table. Cinderella suggested that perhaps we ought to do so.

Accordingly, we made our way along the elaborately patterned silk broadloom carpet, past several patrons as we did so. Eventually, we arrived at the individual's table which was littered with glasses and empty bottles and an old edition of **VARIETY** magazine. He in turn withdrew from his silver-toned finely woven silk waist-coat pocket a heavy gold Albert chain at the end of which was a gold Hunter that he consulted before studying us. He then smiled from a somewhat lean, if not gaunt looking face which exuded indolence.

"We seem destined to be always finding you in Public Houses," said Jack.

"Quality Wet Jack," advised Lodge, slightly slurring his words, "Quality Wet."

"Is there a difference?" inquired Jack.

"Yes," replied Lodge, "in who they allow admittance."

"What, one rule for one and another for others?" asked Jack, with aspersion in his voice.

"Ah but what are rules; there only for the guidance of fools," proclaimed Lodge.

"I did not know that you were devoté of this establishment Michael," said Cinderella, rolling up her white cotton parasol.

"I am a devoté of all that is cultured and refined," replied Lodge, moving his arm in an arc and in an expansive gesture to indicate possession. And did so in an overtly thespian manner, worthy even of Oscar Wilde.

I noticed Jack roll his eyes upward, towards the heavily patterned ceiling with raised filigree designs, in a show of impending intolerance with Lodge, and his exaggerated presentment of inordinate confidence. A state invariably induced by a generous intake of alcohol, clearly evidenced by the array of upturned glasses and bottles adorning his green veined *Verde Acceglio* marble table top.

However, Jack then released his soul.

"Alright Loge, what are the goods on what happened in the Waterman's Arms yesterday evening? The last time we saw you. You were singing terribly out of tune at domestic upright pianoforte secreted in the back of that Public House or Quality Wet or whatever. You were attired, as usual, as a sybarite and, you still are, in that mid-night blue colored tail-coat and trousers, your black cape with its ostentatious blazing red silk lining and wearing a black silk top hat. And what has become of your necktie that was fastened by that orchidaceous purple stone of amethyst? Or is it de rigueur here in London to walk about only half dressed? Both Theo and I were aghast at your behavior, and in a public bar too. Have you no shame, no remorse, no feelings of culpability as to your actions last night?" asked Jack.

"None what so ever," replied Lodge, lifting his glass to his lips and from which he took a deep draught before banging it down on to the table, and breathing out noisily and smacking his purple lips. "As I have *intimidated* on numerous occasions; as an impresario, I have to be seen to be omnipresent. It is not enough that I am here; rather I have to be *seen* to be here!"

I noted with dismay Lodge's monotonous regularity for his innate propensity for catachreses with which he is afflicted. I suspect the word he meant to say was *intimated*.

"That would not surprise me Loge," continued Jack, "you appeared to be in a delirious trance and had a glazed look in your eyes as they rolled aimlessly in their sockets. At the same time you were attempting to sing songs of a contemptible and questionable nature. During which you were standing there next to the domestic upright pianoforte, moving your elbows as though flapping as a chicken might in an attempt to gain flight. Do you remember?"

"I most certainly do. Those improvised lyrics I sang can be quite a challenge and a tongue twister for all but the adept!" replied Lodge.

"Or those dispossessed of fortitude," countered Jack.

"Really Jack, "said Lodge, "by that specious argument, you would no doubt probably endorse murder?"

"Well as with most things, in moderation!" replied Jack, looking into his whisky.

Lodge merely looked at Jack.

"But answer me this inquiry. Why is it that you ...." asked Jack.

That question and indeed the answer, if one could be formulated by Lodge, would have to wait. For at the very moment in walked, in the midst of a commotion, the ebullient and loquacious Marie Lloyd, Queen of the Music Halls and former member of Lodge's *Three Graces*. On Her arm was Charles Morton, manager of Canterbury Music Hall.

"It cannot be so," said Morton to Lloyd, "it cannot be the impresario to end all impresarios!"

"You are quite, quite correct Charles," said Lodge, attempting to stagger up from his red damask upholstered seat, "it is me. Impresario and benefactor to dispossessed Music Hall artistes, especially given my unflinching generosity in..."

"To me you are neither!" interrupted Lloyd, before raising her fluted glass, over flowing with champagne, to her lips and having taken a deep draught, breathed out noisily.

"Ahh, that is better!" she rasped.

"Such vulgarity," said Lodge, looking at Lloyd whilst collapsing back on to his seat.

"As for your exaggerated claim of being a benefactor to dispossessed Music Hall artistes, you were never that to me. You Lodge, treated me shamefully and used me cruelly in the extreme," continued Lloyd, in an emotional outburst.

"One has to cruel to be kind," retorted Lodge, in a measured and deliberate tone.

"Or merely cruel for the sake of being cruel," insisted Lloyd.

"Devil take that Valkürian woman," hissed Lodge under his breath.

"But what else could one reasonably expect from a tyrant," retorted Lloyd, "who dragged poor Belle Elmore's corpse in a cortège around Highgate Cemetery. All in a futile search for a none existent limestone built Mausoleum, for which you had been inveigled to part with ready money and purchase from a charlatan who must have seen you coming, even in the fog-laden aëther!"

I moved forward in order to come to Lodge's defense in an attempt to say something which might lend some degree of verisimilitude to this encounter between Lodge and Lloyd. But was unable to do so because the arrival in our midst of Harry Lester followed by Mabel Green. Both, I noticed, had been drinking heavily.

It was Harry Lester who initiated the suggestion.

"Do tell us Lodge, what exactly happened at your much vaunted Titanic Benefit Concert in the Queen's Hall some time back and your rapid descent in to madness and despair?" [1] Asked Lester, innocently.

Both Jack and I looked instinctively at Mabel, who had made herself comfortable in a nearby Chippendale styled chair, the seat of which was covered in yellow and green striped moiré silk. She pretended not to have noticed our questioning looks at her. But instead she feigned innocence, while sipping genteelly, at her large fluted glass containing neat absinth and gin. Mabel had obviously put the word out on the street and the Music Halls about Lodge calamitous Titanic Benefit Concert.

It was Jack who took up Lester's suggestion in relating this singular narrative

"It was not all about insipid madness. Nor indeed an immediate decent into mental anguish or despair," said Jack.

These words had the effect of drawing others into the bar including Frank Coyne, Charles Tempest and Jack Lambert. All eager to be apprised about the sordid details of Lodge's decent into temporary insanity. Or at least so they had been told, probably by Mabel Green.

"It all started off innocently enough," continued Jack.

"Basically the stratagem was a ruse to cash in on the recent *Titanic* disaster and generate unprecedented Box Office receipts, about which he is infatuated. A monomania obsession and burning desire very close to Lodge's heart, as we all know. Things went wrong from the very start of the Titanic Benefit Concert because of the presence of a concentration of Nihilists, who are by way of being revolutionaries. And other heckling agitators secreted in the audience, notably in the stalls.

"It was during Mabel's vigorous singing of the sublime hymnal, '*Abide with Me.*' Along with members of the audience, whom she had invited to join in with her, that a commotion erupted. Sure enough several Nihilists and other hecklers embedded in the audience, but mainly in the cheap seats in the stalls, were now standing up, in plain sight of God and man, and disrupting the concert by shouting out their shrill unequivocal and outrageous demands to redress perceived inequality of wealth distribution in society.

"Though it must be said, Mabel here stood her ground and continued to sing, '*Abide with Me,*' undeterred by the action of the Nihilists. And on at least one occasion, she confronted two of the Nihilists attempting to gain the stage!"

At this point Mabel stood up and curtsied to the assembled listeners at the bar, which gained her scattered applause.

"A few minutes later, Robert Newman, the General Manager of the Queen's Hall entered the auditorium at the head of cohort of tough-looking ushers resplendent in their black morning-coats with red piping. Eventually they restored order and the concert continued with Mabel eventually ceding the stage to Vesta Tilley.

"Vesta stood there motionless. She was dressed in a

152

long, fitted, fawn colored coat beneath which she wore striped trousers. Her shirt was white and with a high stiff collar fastened with a stone of some indeterminate origin. Her slender pointed boots were black and highly varnished. Upon her head was a black silk top hat and in her right hand she carried what looked like a riding crop.

"I recall she sang a song called, *'Burlington Bertie,'* which totally took David Moody, the orchestra conductor by surprise, because according to the concert program, she was billed at this stage to sing an anthem called, *'Above Us the Waves.'* None the less, Vesta discarded the anthem and instead sang her song out without the orchestra. Vesta had barely gotten to the last line of the third verse from, *'Burlington Bertie,' 'He's wealthy and foolish, but if you want pluck,'* when another commotion by the Nihilists erupted again. But this time it came from a different section of the stalls.

"The first and now that second disruption were clearly part of a concerted plan formulated by the Nihilist to wreck Lodge's concert..." said Jack.

"And, they were succeeding," interrupted Vesta Tilley who had just entered the bar in which we were drinking, "had it not been for my timely intervention. Those Nihilists may well have disrupted the concert earlier."

Vesta Tilley was dressed, as usual, in the garb of a gentleman, resplendent in her black tail-coat and tight fitting trousers with a silk stripe down each side. Her white shirt was starched, and the high stiff collar of which, was fastened with a stone of radiant amethyst. Placed on her head, at an angle, was an impeccably brushed black silk top hat. She stood in a pair of highly varnished patent black leather boots and in her hands she held a fluted glass in one and a bottle of Pierre Jouet champagne in the other.

"She is better dressed than most toffs or swells which one sees strolling down the Strand or Piccadilly," Carrie Laurie was overheard saying to Sabrina Passley and Charlie Edwards.

"Not for the first time," continued Jack, "did Robert Newman reënter the auditorium at the Queen's Hall during the Titanic Benefit Concert. Leading his well rehearsed phalanx of ushers, still resplendent in their black morning-coats. Back into the thick of the mêlée in his endeavors to reëstablish order in his Queen's Hall. But by now of course, well dressed respectable people, some in silk gowns, were abandoning their plush red velvet seats.

"It was all Robert Newman and his ushers could do to contain the Nihilists. Eventually the concert disintegrated into pandäemonium and in to a disaster that people were saying, as they left the auditorium, was equal in magnitude to that of the actual sinking of the stricken ill-fated *Titanic* itself. For which the benefit concert had been organized by Lodge in his desperate and speculative attempt to increase his precious Box Office receipts. Minutes later the Titanic Benefit Concert was abandoned altogether. Alongside with Lodge's hopes of achieving hitherto undreamt of profits!"

It was this massive blow, this monumental disappointment to Lodge which unhinged him, causing him to lose that tenuous grip on his sanity. Subsequently he contracted brain fever which caused his unstoppable and inescapable deterioration into insanity.

"Evidence of Lodge's rapid descent into madness was furnished when Mabel here, escorted him, unannounced, to our break-fast table in the Grand Dining Room at the St Pancras Hotel," said Jack.

"Were you at any time fearful for Lodge's mental state

of mind?" Inquired Charles Coborn, whilst adding äerated water to his whisky from a huge gasogenes adorning the bar.

"No," answered Jack decisively.

"A few of us were concerned Jack," said Cinderella. "It was a very noble gesture by Michael here to put on a concert for the now helpless dependents of those victims who perish in that dread-filled sinking of the *Titanic* boat."

"As I mentioned," continued Jack, "Theo and I were enjoying break-fast in the Grand Dining Room in our hotel the following morning after the financially catastrophic concert. All of a sudden, Lodge, supported by Mabel, walked, or rather, staggered into the Grand Dining Room. A few moments later Mabel appeared at our table with Lodge clutching her arm for dear life, or so it seemed to us. He then collapsed in to a nearby Chippendale chair.

"He looked drawn and dishevelled and agitated and his hands twitched constantly as though he were afflicted with St. Vitus's Dance disease. As..." said Jack.

"What, rather dishevelled as he is looking now?" Interrupted Walter Norman, whilst attempting to light his Trichinopoly cigar.

"Theo and I were aghast at his state of decline. From being a man of affairs and exuding inordinate confidence only the day before to being reduced to this twitching wreck a former shadow of himself. Even after Mabel had handed to him a cup of coffee in an endeavor to calm his nerves. Lodge was so nervous that he succeeded only in spilling the coffee on to Grand Dining Room's green silk broadloom carpet with integral gold-colored fleur de lys designs woven into the pattern!" said Jack.

Queenie Leighton then walked into the bar and immediately came up to me.

"Theo," she whispered in my ear, "I have just been to the St James's Theater in order to rehearse my act involving humorous arias from Ottorino Respighi's doom-laden opera, '*La Campana Somersa*.'[2] But the stage door man told me that there was, at the moment, more impromptu Music Hall at the Red Lion Public House in the Duke of York Street, than anywhere in the West End. Theo, just what is happening?"

"See for yourself Queenie," I replied, "Jack is regaling everybody with his *interpretation* of the catastrophic events leading up to Lodge's mental collapse as a result of the financially disastrous Titanic Benefit Concert. Which Lodge thought would solve his financial desires. Instead, at the time it was possible that the concert may well have bankrupted him!"

"Well Lodge appears oblivious to Jack's interpretation of events. He appears, even with that blank cherubic look upon his face, as though he has relinquished that essential control of his person which is necessary if one is to maintain a modicum of dignity!" said Queenie.

"I agree. And to be honest Queenie, at times, I swear, Lodge actually nodded his head and smiling, as though he were concurring with Jack description of event!" I offered.

Jack had, in the meantime, paused in order to replenish his whisky which was done by an obliging Jeff Vendome.

"I did not know you were on the bill at the St. James's Theater tonight Queenie?"

"I was not," Queenie replied, "a last minute substitution. Kate Paradise was down to sing the rôle of the heroine, Rautendelein in '*La Campana Somersa*,' but is indisposed due to influenza. So the theater management asked if I could step in and sing some jaunty arias based on that opera."

"I do not think that I have heard of it. [3] By an Italian composer called Ottorino Respighi you say?" I asked.

"The libretto for the opera is convoluted to say the least Theo. It is a well that I am just singing a selection of arias! The doom-laden plot would consign Wagner's grand opera *'Götterdämmerung'* [4] to the realm of light operetta by comparison. The opera is over four acts with the libretto by Claudio Guastalla, which was based on the German author Gerhart Hauptmann's fairy-tale play called, *'Die Versunkene Glocke.'*[5]

"The opera, being based on fantasy, allowed Respighi to create a lavish operatic score punctuated with serenity and sonorous chords. And given the fact the anti-hero in the opera is a bell maker. The music throughout echoes the ethereal chiming and ringing of the sunken bell. You would enjoy it Theo!" advised Queenie.

Replenished with whisky and a Trichinopoly cigar, Jack continued his interesting narrative.

"Our greatest fear," Jack started in, "was Lodge's inane ramblings and mutterings of his being ruined and destitute. And become that of which his worst fears are comprised; being literally relegated to the ranks of the *Undeserving Poor.* And who exist only in the twilight. Lodge had repeatedly these words through his thin purple lips before they trailed off into a series of incoherent mumbling sounds, whilst at the same time wringing his hands anxiously as though in total desperation.

"Lodge then pulled himself together, albeit momentarily, and went on to relate to Mabel, Theo and me, his innate reckless generosity which, or so he claimed, knew no bounds. Then in the depths of his despair, had the temerity to wish a pestilence upon the fool, who uttered that reckless exhortation,

'…if I can help someone as I go along; then my living shall not be in vain.'

"But then promised us all, sitting around the break-fast table, that in future, he would never ever again succumb to such rash conspicuous altruism or abandonment of financial sense!"

Queenie was giggling quietly to herself. As indeed others gathered in the bar of the Red Lion in the Duke of York Street, were too smiling ruefully. Jack had his audience enthralled by his narration of the story. I have, over the years of knowing Jack, always realized his innate ability to tell stories. Even stories which by their very nature could be described as boring, become of intense interest when related by Jack. In this respect Jack can infuse a fascination even in to the mundane or moribund.

At that moment there was a commotion in another adjacent bar. Moments later Lottie Lennox, Harriet Vernon and Florrie Forde stepped in to our bar demanding to know where the floor show was. Most pointed to Jack. Some to Lodge, still recumbent on the red damask covered sofa in the corner, shaded by a ubiquitous palm tree rising out of a green glazed urn. Lodge appeared content in his own world; because, at the moment, he was certainly not of this one.

After people had settled down again and broken glasses picked up from the elaborately patterned silk broadloom carpet, Jack continued with his singular narrative.

"As I said before, Theo and I were taking break-fast in the St. Pancras Hotel, when Lodge, clinging to Mabel's arm, arrived at our table in the Grand Dining Room. Having collapsed in to a nearby Chippendale chair, Lodge then informed us of a few intentions he had made. Including abandoning London! Well only for a few days, he later qualified.

The Abbey Grange

"It was Lodge's intention to impose his person on Sir Augustus Harris. Impresario and manager of the Theater Royal in Drury Lane by repairing to Harris's country retreat, the Abbey Grange, at Chalfont St. Giles in Buckinghamshire. In order that Lodge might be afforded an opportunity to recover his dignity and self esteem. And attempt to put that previous evening's calamitous affair behind him. And that Theo and I should join him.

"Oh yes" continued Jack, "Lodge had invited, and I quote, 'that Cinderella woman, as she may yet prove to be useful as a housemaid or in some other servile capacity to wait upon us and attend to our every whim or fad, during our prolonged sojourn at the Abbey Grange!'

"Our journeying to the Abbey Grange, Lodge informed Theo and me, meant in effect our travelling from Marylebone Rail Road Station. And from there avail ourselves of a steam train of the Great Central Rail Road to convey us to a rail road station, at a place called Beaconsfield and thence make our way by carriage to the Abbey Grange at Chalfont St. Giles.

"It was while we were sitting in the rail road carriage travelling to Chalfont St. Giles that Lodge acute fragile state of mind manifested itself in an alarming manner. At the time we were steaming through the outer neighborhoods of the Metropolis.

"It was Cinderella who pointed, with her white cotton lace parasol, at a partially assembled structure of steel girders rising above the misty fields resembling the beginning of a tower. And informed us that it was in fact the construction of a tower to rival in size and height that of the Eiffel Tower in Paris, France. And was the dream of Sir Edward Watkins, the Chairman of the Great Central Rail Road, along the permanent way of which we were travelling."

"At the time I asked Cinderella why would the chairman of a rail road company, desire to construct a metal tower to rival that of Eiffel's in Paris, France. However, up until then Lodge had been silent and morose whilst sitting in the corner of the rail road carriage, wearing an expression of pure indolence upon his face. But then he spoke.

"'Because,' Lodge informed us, 'Watkins thinks it will become a place of interest and attract visitors who will use his Metropolitan Rail Road, of which he is also chairman, operating out of Baker Street Metropolitan Station in order to visit the tower. One could only envy Watkins's success in generating profits, which would appear easier to achieve with rail road passengers than with the occasional visitor to a Music Hall. It is quite possible that Watkins may corner the international tourist market and create undreamt of profit. Well at least he

Baker Street Metropolitan Station

does not have a concentration of Nihilists, hecklers, revolutionaries or ungrateful audiences to contend with all of whom are intent on my financial and moral destruction!'" said Jack, quoting Lodge.

A deathly hush had now descended on those gathered in a bar of the Red Lion Public House in the Duke of York Street.

"An innocent comment and no doubt made by a disturbed mind," said Jack, "and we of us sitting in that rail road carriage paid it no great attention, but Lodge had not quite finished.

'Would that I ran a rail road,' Lodge suddenly declared, 'then truly I should indeed become master of the world!'"

This frightening assertion by Lodge of his desire to run a rail road in order that he might truly become master of the world, created look of horror on all the faces of those assembled in the bar of the Red Lion. And the fact people drained their glasses in one go, only bore unequivocal testament to that potential nightmare. Some people, I noticed turned their heads away from viewing Lodge. Even Lottie Lennox, was so overcome, that she had to be helped down into a nearby chair.

"I remember at the time, sitting in that closed rail road carriage, hurtling along the tracks, when Lodge first proclaim that desire. The sentiment caused a creeping sensation in my body," I remarked to Queenie, who looked visibly distraught at the prospect of Lodge becoming master of the world.

It was Cinderella who stepped into the fray in support of Lodge. As usual, I am always intrigued by Cinderella and her ability on the stage to control effectively the costers with an iron fist in a pink silk glove, as it were! And now, here in the Red Lion Public House she was effectively doing the same in Lodge's defense.

"Ladies and gentlemen," announced Cinderella, "that was a re-action by Michael some time ago. I am sure that we can all appreciate the terrible pressure, which the collapse of that laudable and well intended Titanic Benefit Concert, imposed upon him."

Her remark elicited low but spontaneous applause. To which Cinderella responded with a curtsey. Even Lodge appeared to be making a rapid recovery from his semi dormant state, and even demanded a drink from Arthur Pearl who just happened to be passing by him.

I was waiting at the bar trying to get drinks for Queenie and myself and surrounded by eager Music Hall artistes, all of whom were attempting to do the same. When I saw the anæmic and intense Anna Pavlova come tip toeing up to near where I was standing whilst looking around expectantly for a savior to buy her a drink.

Eventually George Lashwood felt obligated to. I remember Pavlova at Lodge's Bacchanalian reception at his town house in the Bergen Avenue some time ago. There everybody was committed to indulging themselves in debauchery and excess. Not Pavlova, who engaged me in a preposterous conversation about aspects of her mental health. I could well sympathize with Lashwood, who was now subjected to the full blast of her inner most thoughts regarding her sanity.

She did not disappoint and she immediately launched into some interminable nonsense about feelings of pain or isolation especially each time she contemplated doing something, such as making a cup of mint tea, whilst in fit of pique or in the grip of chronic ennui. Or perhaps whilst one explored regular episodes of feelings of rejection and mental pain every time one did something thoroughly despicable? I overheard her ask this of Lashwood, who by now was regretting coming to her rescue at the bar. He looked, for all of us at the bar to see, as though he was the fated one in an inescapable grip of chronic ennui. That, or structural boredom from which there could be no escape.

I rejoined Queenie suitably armed with our drinks.

"Jack seems to have stolen the show with his relating the story of Lodge's decline into insanity! Look. He has several Music Hall artistes slapping his back," said Queenie.

Indeed, Jack was in the middle of several Music Hall artistes all eager to hear more from him.

"Decline into insanity," I said to Queenie, "it was not quite that bad. And I do not think Lodge heard half of what Jack said. Had he done so, I feel confident he would have rebutted Jack's assertions!"

"Still, he looks happy enough engaged in as he is in some discussion with Hetty King and Sabrina Passley, who was holding her new baby daughter, Ch'i-Amour.

A few moments later Lodge detached himself from them and abandoned himself into blowing exaggerated kisses from his lips into the aëther with open fingers. Seconds later he intercepted and embraced Marie Löhr.

He then escorted her over to where Queenie and I were standing.

Ignoring Queenie, Lodge introduced Marie Löhr to me. I in turn, introduced Queenie to her.

"Marie has just had a good run with, *"Tantalizing Tommy,"* written by Paul Gavault and Michael Morton which attracted excellent reviews," informed Lodge.

"I am delighted to hear this good news," said Queenie, shaking Marie's hand.

"Do you remember Theo, my mentioning the fact that I knew Gustav Mahler who assisted me in some small way, in creating the Choral Anthem Symphony? Well when we worked on the symphony, Mahler was actually staying in London and accompanied by his friend Friedrich Löhr. Well this charming young lady is related to that Friedrich Löhr!" said Lodge, pulling out his red leather cigar case, and offering a Trichinopoly cigar to her.

"Only as a distant cousin," interjected Marie Löhr, "I have never actually met with the man," she said, whilst pulling out two cigars from the cigar case. One of which she handed to Queenie.

"Well the co-incidence does not stop there," continued Lodge, "by chance I introduced, in the Criterion Restaurant [6] some time back. Mahler and your distant relation Friedrich Löhr, to a good friend of mine, the renowned artist Walter Sickert, a prominent member of the acclaimed Camden Town Group.

Sickert, Mahler and Friedrich Löhr got on extremely well and during the course of luncheon, Sickert actually drew an image of Mahler, which I still retain.

"You say the Camden Town Group of which Sickert was a member. Just what was the Camden Town Group, a neighborhood association or something?" Asked Marie Löhr.

Gustav Mahler

Lodge seemed slightly surprised by this inquiry. But none the less answered Löhr.

"Walter Sickert, in about 1905 I believe," said Lodge, "set up an art studio in Fitzroy Street in Bloomsbury, near Euston. The studio has now become a popular meeting place for younger artist such as Spencer Frederick Gore, Harold Gilman, Lucien Pissarro, the son of the more famous Impressionist painter Camille Pissarro.

"These artists are influenced by the likes of van Gogh and Gauguin in representing strong decorative coloration depicting real contemporary scenes especially, to be found in the Music Hall. In order to give a more identifiable aspect to their view on art they have formed, with others, the Camden Town Group, based in Mornington Crescent in Camden Town. The Group has become even more popular and attracts other artists, such as Wyndham Lewis and Augustus John.

"Sickert in particular is instrumental in depicting scenes

and impressions from various Music Halls, notably the New Bedford Music Hall in nearby Camden High Street. His paintings depict realistic scenes of the auditorium together with the re-action of the audience being entertained by Music Hall artistes performing on the stage. The New Bedford Music Hall, naturally enough is patronized by the Camden Town Group in providing inspiration for their paintings. Indeed Walter Sickert has immortalized one of my *Three Graces* in one of his paintings called, '*Little Dot Hetherington at the Old Bedford*'," completed Lodge.

"Going back to your image of Mahler by Sickert," responded Marie Löhr, "I did not know that he drew sketches. I always associate Sickert with brilliantly evocative images in his prolific paintings of Music Halls; those and French pastoral scenes or townscapes?"

"Nor did I," responded Lodge, "like you I always thought of Sickert as a painter of large canvasses depicting the interiors of auditoria or street scenes. But his exquisite image of Mahler is a drawing that I treasure!"

At that very moment Eleonora Duse, arrived in the bar as though she were on a state visit. Lodge tactfully withdrew with Marie Löhr. [7] After looking around she reclined on to a nearby banquette [8] upholstered in red striped moiré silk and swooning as she did so. As though reprising her rôle of, '*La Dame aux Camèlias,*' [9] in her eternal vigil. I really was truly pleased to see her.

She had a very profound effect upon me when Jack and I visited with her in the company of Lodge some weeks ago. I was fond of her, and especially liked her unequivocal, if contentious statements about art; or at least what art should be. Typically, she had asserted at the time.

'If I had my will, I would live in a ship on the sea and never come nearer to humanity than that!'

'The playwright creates in his mind a scenario, but it

New Bedford Music Hall

is the actress who converts that dream into a reality using the theater as the medium to give meaning and life.

'To save the theater, the theater itself must be destroyed; the actors and actresses must all die of the plague. They poison the aëther, they make art impossible. It is not drama that they play, but pieces for the theater.'

'We should return to the Greek way and play theater in the open; the drama dies in the stalls and private boxes and evening dress, and people who come to digest dinner.'

'The weaker partner in a marriage, is the one who loves the most; as much as sorrow is the real cost of love.'

'Evidently to where destiny leads my weary soul,' she had replied to an inquiry put to her by Jack.

At the time of our visit Jack posed a question to her. 'Can this be the brave Eleonora I know of, who dispatches fear to oblivion and courage to the frightened?'

To which she responded. 'Fear is my nearest relation; with courage being but a distant cousin and curiosity a recent in-law.'

'It is the province of the actress, not the creator, to interpret the rôle of the character. A writer confined to his garret in the attic producing one work after another is not in a position to understand how that work will translate onstage in front of an audience. We the actresses do understand; it is what acting is all about. We portray the character.'

I retain very fond memories of that Villa Dusa, located in Avenue Road, St John's Wood. And recall that the building was, if anything, of a very modern design. Reflecting a cubic style of architecture, reminiscent of the *Jugendstil* [10] movement which I believe is prevalent in Vienna.

In keeping with modern designs, the villa has white painted walls, the façade of one housing the front door, which was framed in a projecting concrete surround. Also punctuating this flat regular façade was a series of unarticulated windows reveals. Above which was a coffered soffit beneath a cornice surmounted by a flat roof. Inside Eleonora's villa was palatial and a fine

Villa Dusa

example of a combination of understated elegance and visual delight.

I recollect a very amusing incident at the Villa Dusa involving Eleonora and Lodge over a misunderstanding about the rôle of the Metropolitan Board of Works. A statutory public body here in London charged with the task of building deep level brick-lined sewers, for which, incidentally according to Lodge, they are without rival, and eminently suited for. But in addition, they are also charged with regulating the conduct of Music Halls. Needless to say, they remain the bane of Lodge's life as he sees them as interfering bureaucrats with little else to do except make his life, as an impresario, difficult.

Lodge was trying to explain this dichotomy to Eleonora. On the one hand building sewers and on the other regulating Music Halls. However, Eleonora, being fiercely Italian, was involved in trying to explain to Lodge the power of life itself. Indeed the flame of life!

Typically, in order to augment this statement and add emphasis, she said. 'If the sight of blue skies fills you with joy, if a blade of grass springing up in the fields has power to move you, if the simple things of nature have a message that you understand, rejoice, for your soul is alive!'

Lodge continued with his description of the somewhat mundane sewer duties of the Metropolitan Board of Works, but was interrupted by Eleonora.

'They build deep level brick-lined sewers; this Metropolitan Board of Works? They are in charge of opera in London? I am talking about the flame of life; not deep level sewers,' Eleonora had responded.

I wanted to make her acquaintance again. Accordingly Queenie and I went up to her.

"Queenie, what a pleasant surprise to see you and too my friend, Theo who knows Pittsburgh in America," she said, holding out her hand in red satin glove for me to kiss.

"You know Theo from New York?" reminded Queenie.

"Of course, and Jack too," responded Eleonora, "for who could forget two charming gentlemen who know Pittsburgh, and not only its famous Duquesne Club on 6th. Avenue where they have performed. But also my good friend Alexander Peacock and his beautiful mansion he has named Rowenlea."

True to form and before I had even sat down on the banquette next o Eleonora. She launched into her abject horror of the cult of the personality becoming more pervasive in the arts. Queenie enthusiastically agreed with her.

"That cult of the personality is still extant in the arts," informed Eleonora, "and the glorification of the person often is emphasized at the expense of the art. This of course is a trait of the bourgeoisie, which will always defeat their endeavors to rise in social standing, because of this endorsement of the cult of the personality, which is destructive to art and artistic creation.

Duquesne Club, Pittsburgh

"Endeavoring to gain access into the class immediately above them is perforce their undoing. The bourgeoisie can never change to become that which is beyond them. What they do instead is to infiltrate aspects of the upper classes' domain, especially in England; Ascot Races, Henley Regatta, Wimbledon, hunting or even the opera at Covent Garden. Rather than adapting, which they cannot, they try to impose their mediocre values, including their cult of the personality.

"In so doing they destroy the very thing they desire! The only thing they achieve is to shunt upwards that class above them, who of course, will find refuge in alternative interests and pastimes. The bourgeois class will, yet again find themselves with only a Pyrrhic victory resounding in hollowness as they survey the deserted rationale of their endeavors and so-called apparent achievement.

"And yet the reason is simply; rather than dwell on the importance of music – its structure, its sublime beauty, its ability to inflame one's passions, release one's soul or ignite one's imagination; they concentrate on the performing musician to the exclusion of the music.

"And, rather than consider the depths of the painting, its composition, its fine representational detailing, its ability to excite one's imagination or invoke our power of comparison. The bourgeois class will applaud the painter only and relegate the artwork to irrelevance. This is how their minds work, in their consuming inordinate adoration of the cult of the personality and not the art form. Irrespective of profound talent or ability, because of that pervasive adulation of the *persona*, cult of the personality, at the expense of the art form often accompanied by a manifestation of being ego-centric and sybarite!

"How many of us here sitting here in this Public House have seen where culture has been acquired by the yard or ton, especially in the homes of the newly enfranchised bourgeoisie? Libraries filled with shelves of un-cut books written by famous writers. Bronze or porcelain figurines by famous sculptures or other wonderful creations by acclaimed designers positioned badly in a room, or oil paintings by well-known artists exposed to direct sunlight?

"No! It is because wealth allows the bourgeoisie the ability to acquire instantly the accoutrements of success without any concept of appreciation of the works by those creators. They know the cost of everything; but the value of nothing. It is similar to demanding that a Haydn string quartet be played merely to fill the vacuüm of silence. But in so doing, they reveal their real philistine distain and contempt for the arts of which, in reality, they know very little," said Eleonora Duse, baring her soul on this matter.

Before either Queenie or I could formulate a response. A lone voice at the bar called out.

"Theo, hey Theo do tell us about the time you were locked in Wilton's Music Hall during the mid hour at night and endured a series unexplained nocturnal experiences?" said the anonymous voice. [11]

People at the bar looked at me and then began to congregate around where I was standing.

"Yes do tell us Theo," said Queenie enthusiastically, whilst taking my arm.

---

1 For a fuller account refer to *Vaudeville – The Struggle Continues*, Chapter 27

2 *The Sunken Bell*

3 The opera was premiered in November, 1927 in Hamburg.

4 Twilight of the Gods

5 *The Sunken Clock*

6 For a fuller account of this meeting refer to book *The Première*, Chapter 24

7 Lodge had a falling out with Duse as described in *Vaudeville – The Struggle Continues*, Chapter 17

8 An upholstered bench along a wall

9 *The Lady of the Camellias*, a novel by Alexandre Dumas

10 A German interpretation of Art Nouveau

11 Sir George Robey, known as the *'Prime Minister of Mirth.'*

Chapter 12

The Silent Performers

Jack, having been invited by Harry Lester, had related the singular story regarding Lodge's mental re-action to his failed Titanic Benefit Concert. Now someone, out of sight, but embedded at the bar of the Red Lion Public House, in which we were unexpectedly holed up, had asked me to relate my experiences of being locked in Wilton's Music Hall over night. With Queenie at my side and holding a large whisky in my hand, I commenced my narrative, as invited to do so by that lone anonymous voice at the bar.

"Jack and I had just arrived in London as guests of the impresario, Michael Lodge." I said, pointing to an incumbent Lodge, seated nearby. "We were strangers to your city having spent all our stage life working the Vaudeville theaters in New York, Chicago and other cities especially those along the Eastern seaboard.

"At Lodge's instigation we had arrived at Wilton's,[1]the oldest Music Hall in London to enjoy, or endure, the turns and acts extant on the stage there that evening. Certainly, the act involving the so-called Dumb Mute was impressive and it was clearly a favorite with the audience. However, our primarily purpose in attending Wilton's Music Hall that evening, was to observe the peculiarities of English Music Hall traditions in comparison to

Wilton's Music Hall

American Vaudeville. And there are some major differences.

"Notably, as Jack and I have now learned, that Vaudeville in America is certainly not the same as Music Hall in England. And what in England might be considered Burlesque would, in America, be termed Vaudeville! However, none of these establishments would be considered to be of equal ranking with the emerging red plush Theaters of Varieties and their..." I said.

"I can vouch for that," interrupted Marie Lloyd, [2] after which she curtsied to those assembled around the bar.

"Unfortunately," I continued, "on that particular evening I had contracted a stomach ache and so decided to leave the Music Hall and make my way back to the St. Pancras Hotel, where we are holed up, and attempt to gain sleep. Before leaving however, it was my intention to pay my respects to the Music Hall manager, name of Clay, Thomas E. Clay with whom Jack and I had been

St. Pancras Hotel

introduced to earlier and, also to thank him for his hospitality.

"Accordingly, I went in search of his office which I knew to be located in the basement of the Music Hall. Setting out, I made my way down a carpeted flight of stairs from the foyer and descended a second set this time made of stone. These steps took me into the depths of the Music Hall, and onwards to a narrow corridor at the end of which I felt confident was located the manager's office.

"It may have been that the gas mantles had been turned down, leaving the corridor in subdued lighting or, the fact that I was not concentrating on where I was walking. Somehow though, I lost my footing and fell down a flight of stone steps at the end of which I then toppled over a low parapet wall and down to the floor below it! Picking myself up in a daze and uncertain as to my whereabouts or condition, I leaned against the wall for support. At that instant, the wall gave way, causing me to fall into a room. I looked about me in a half-bewildered state.

"Imperceptibly at first, my senses did return, but only partially, as I was still very much shaken and confused. Gradually I realized that I was in a room, a chamber of a kind the walls of which were made of iron, rusting iron. I knew the door leading into the room, that I had leaned against, had slammed shut behind me. I did though, in my delirium, notice scratch marks, intense scratch marks on the iron walls of the chamber, as if a tormented soul had been in forced confinement there. I then felt a sickness as my head began to swim and my vision became blurred. I instinctively knew that I had concussion and then blacked out whilst collapsing to the floor.

"Gradually I came to; regaining my senses and found myself at the point of reëmerging back into consciousness. But I then realized something. I was, not in the chamber, but rather outside in a white painted brick hallway, slumped in a wicker chair. I do not recall leaving the chamber, even as a somnambulist! [3]

"I decided to rejoin Jack and Lodge and abandon my accident prone search for Thomas Clay's office. Accordingly, I consulted my steel case pocket watch. It showed me that it was the mid-hour at night! I was at a loss to understand just how this could be. Surely I had not been unconscious for a period of just under four hours. And yet my reliable pocket watch indicated that I must have been so!

"Pulling myself together, more out of feelings of repressed panic, I searched for a way out of my predicament. The corridor I found myself in was illuminated but only partially with gas mantles in the form of wall mounted appliqués. I staggered down the dimly lit corridor unsure as to quite where the passageway would lead me.

"Then I heard it. The noise was only faint at first, but did have the effect of making me stop momentarily transfixed by the surprising sound. I continued on down the corridor but only hesitantly for some reason. Nor could I fail to notice that this ethereal and singular sound was becoming louder with each step that I took towards it. The sonorous sound, I could hear becoming louder, was being produced by a pianoforte! I was unsure how to re-act to this unexpected event at first, but figured obviously, that at least one other person was also in the theater practicing their pianoforte scales, even at the mid hour at night!

"At length I came across a partially opened highly varnished mahogany door leading into the room from whence the music emanated. I opened the door further and looked inside the room expecting to see the pianist playing at the pianoforte. Neither happened and the arpeggios continued to tinkle, rather like a cascade of diamonds ricocheting off a marble surface. What I saw momentarily unnerved me probably as a result of my concussion I had sustained earlier..."

"Hi Theo, hi Queenie!" interrupted Little Bo Peep, as she curtsied her way to a chair at a table a few feet away from where I was standing delivering my singular tale.

Several at the bar responded by blowing her kisses.

"Am I missing something?" she continued, whilst looking about her, and taking a deep draught from her large glass of whisky. "I just popped in to avail myself of a quick libation before performing at the St James' Theater this evening. My, the Red Lion is busy this afternoon!"

When Little Bo Peep had settled down, I continued my narrative.

"Having arrived at the room in which a pianoforte was being played. I looked in expecting to see someone playing the pianoforte. The sight in the room that I beheld caused me to momentarily panic, creating a feeling of dryness in my throat. The pianoforte glistened with its heavy black varnish reflecting the weak light in the room. Resting on the front sound board of the pianoforte was an ornate brass music rack.

"Placed upon this rack, were several dog-eared and torn pianoforte music sheets, on which the print was faded. They were illuminated by the only source of light in the room that came from two bronze candelabras, affixed to the front panel of the pianoforte. Each candelabrum held four cracked yellow candles which were lit and their flame flickering, as though caught in a draught.

"There was no pianist at the pianoforte playing; instead it was a player piano, of the type which we all know to be called an Aëolian pianola. The sight of this Aëolian pianola playing sonorous arpeggios to itself contentedly slightly unnerved me. Not least in knowing that someone had obviously set the Aëolian pianola in motion. In addition to having applied a flame to the candles. And, which showed clear signs of having only just been lit. This fact was evident to me because the tops of the candle sticks still retained their apex tips and pointed as in a pyramid. The candles were now illuminating the keys, being mechanically operated up and down, on the keyboard. And surely not, I thought, for the benefit of the Aëolian pianola itself, that was functioning automatically as an automaton. Therefore, I concluded, the candles were lit for the benefit of a pianist to see and therefore read the sheet music, if not to actually play the keyboard. This realization caused a consternation in me and then induced a sensation of a vacuüm being created in my chest. I immediately abandoned the room with its Aëolian pianola playing to itself."

There was a deathly hush at the bar in the Red Lion as people hung on to every word I uttered, broken only by Queenie then urging me to continue to relate my singular experiences whilst in Wilton's Music Hall during the mid-hour at night.

I complied with her wishes.

"Unlike perhaps some of you artistes gathered here. I was not familiar with the layout of Wilton's Music Hall and my searching for a way out of the theater was hampered by the fact the building was in twilight. But somehow I came across a staircase and so elected to ascend the stairs to where? I did not know. However, at length I eventually emerged into what I took to be the Upper Circle at the top of the auditorium. It was deserted and a deathly screaming silence pervaded the space. Indeed, I had now figured out, the entire Music Hall was in fact deserted.

"I was still feeling weak as a result of my previous fall and subsequent blackout and so decided to sit in one of the plush red velvet seats and gather my strength. I looked down in to the empty auditorium, in which the red plush seats were barely visible in the subdued light. I could however; just make out some props and scenery on the stage, but again the subdued light was very poor and provided very little light to illuminate anything.

"Then, despite the subdued light, something vague did catch my attention. It was imperceptible at first and thought that I was dreaming. So I dismissed the notion. A few moments later it continued. This time I was not imagining things, but witnessing an event unfolding before my very eyes. What I thought had happened, was in fact happening and continuing to do so as I stared down onto the stage through the gloom. What I was now witnessing involved a large section of backdrop scenery being lowered down, very slowly, from the stage attic by an unseen hand!

"My heart's action froze as my mouth instantly dried up whilst I slipped into a paroxysm of abject fear. At the same time I slumped back into my seat in an attempt to make myself invisible to anybody out there in the darkness, operating the backdrop. However, imperceptibly at first, but gradually becoming visible, was a dull yellow light that appeared to emanate from the wings, stage left.

"What I now found even more unnerving, was another curious event unfolding on the stage, and before my very eyes. Part of the stage backdrop scenery was being lowered by an unknown hand and in so doing revealed a hidden scene painted upon it. I got the distinct impression that this stage scenery had long been forgotten or abandoned; because as it was lowered, dust cascaded down from the unfurling shrouds during its descent!

"The scene was illuminated only by that faint yellow light emanating from the stage wing. The scene on the backdrop depicted an image of a temple, a large classical temple, which I remembered was the Schauspielhaus in Berlin with its representation of a double Parthenon.

"Then my ears detected a faint sound, a distant sound of the tinkling of musical arpeggios, emanating from a pianoforte, being played in one of the wings of the stage, but out of sight. The sound of the musical arpeggios that I had heard earlier, created by that Aëolian pianola, in the depths of the theater, was not the same as the music now drifting across the stage.

"The flat tones of the music which I was presently listening to, indicated to me that they emanated not from an Aëolian pianola, but rather from a functioning pianoforte. The style of playing was decidedly different, almost mournful and the sound created was of a translucent quality, weak, almost anæmic. As though the pianist had not the strength to depress the piano keys to create or sustain a chord.

"Notwithstanding this fact, the sound of the sonorous and sublime tinkling arpeggios was in fact becoming louder and now more intense. Again I recognized the music. It was that of the Abbé, Franz Liszt's pianoforte transcription of *Bénédiction de Dieu dans la solitude* from his acclaimed *Harmonies Poétiques et Religieuses*. But on this occasion the music was being played with an indescribable intensity and manic interpretation, as though the player were seeking release from torment or redemption from his condition. Whoever, or whatever was playing. Certainly had at their command an ability to manipulate the keyboard enabling the player to create a melodic progression based on a slow tempo inducing an exquisite and profound sound by the use of minor seventh and major seventh chord changes.

"I became momentarily transfixed; listening to the music but also began to experience another sensation not of my choosing. This ethereal combination of sensual musical arpeggio technique and of my being in a state of anxiety combined with a repressed fear, induced in me a growing feeling to panic. Moments later, I felt and would have done so, were it not for another singular event which unfolded before my very eyes.

"The stage scenery depicted a large classical building. I recognised the building as being that of the Schauspielhaus in Berlin, in Prussia. The structure comprised several windows both to the front and side façades. In front of the building was a flight of wide steps leading up to a colonnade comprising fluted Ionic columns supporting a triangular pediment.

"Behind that pediment was another temple structure, the columns of which were square and rebated into the façade. And upon which a second pediment rested. On top of this pediment, addressing the apex, was an equestrian statuary group, comprising two bronze horses. They were hauling a chariot being driven by some Valkürian warrior holding a wreathe of laurel leaves in one hand and the reins in the other. On various parts of this classical temple, were placed statues upon plinths.

Schauspielhaus, Berlin

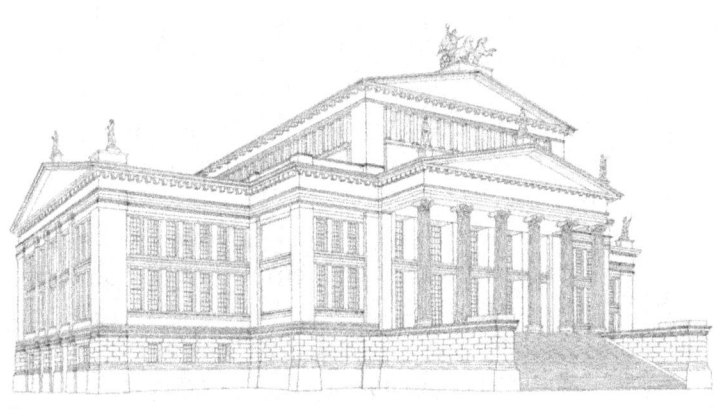

"It was not the architecture of the building depicted upon the stage scene, but rather the fact that there was a light flickering behind the backdrop. The light was in the form of a fire brand and it was being held high. The fire brand was being held by a little girl dressed in a long flowing white cotton gown. My heart momentarily skipped several beats, as I looked transfixed by fear, upon this apparition.

"The child was making her way along the back of the scene. From my stage left to right, and in so doing, illuminating each of the window reveals as she progressed along the ground floor, as it were, of the temple. When her ghostly form, made visible by the firebrand in her hand, reached the end of the scene, she appeared to rise up to the *piano-nobile*, of the temple, whereupon she commenced her walk from stage right to left along this first floor, and again illuminating each window reveal as she passed by it.

"This went on for several minutes and all to the accompanying sound of the pianoforte, which was now being played with a sustained manic intensity, as the sound of the arpeggios increased, to an almost deafening level. By now the apparition had made its way to the upper levels of the building, and in fact, the light from the fire brand was seen to flit in and out between the square rebated columns which addressed the upper levels of the temple. It was as though she was entering one room after another as she progressed in her ascension through the building.

"The child, dressed in white flowing gown, was making her way to the very top of the temple, and I could only watch her progress, whilst in the grip of a paroxysm of fear. Such was my state of nervous anxiety at being transfixed by what I was experiencing, that I found it difficult to breathe or move and thus attempt to leave. The girl then appeared to have climbed on to the roof of the temple and was walking on top of the east wing behind a low parapet wall towards a vacant plinth constructed on the apex of that roof. On reaching it she climbed up on to the top of the plinth. There she stood motionless, but held up high, before her face, the firebrand which continued to blaze, and radiate out its incandescent illumination.

"Gradually the blazing light from the fire brand began to diminish in its intensity, as though burning itself out. The music too, being created on the pianoforte, was approaching its closing section of the Abbé Franz Liszt's intense pianoforte transcription of the *Bénédiction de Dieu dans la solitude*. Eventually, the music progressed on to the inevitable tempestuous crescendo of the finalé. As the music died away so did the light from the firebrand held by the child. The decreased light from the flaming torch had returned the stage and auditorium back into twilight.

"However, the diminished light from the fire brand did not return the stage into total darkness. Nor was it so dark as to prevent me from witnessing what had happened to the child standing motionless on the plinth set upon the roof. Along with other statues standing on the various roofs of the temple; the child in white had become petrified.[4] She too had become immortalized as a statue and was now adorning the temple for eternity!

"This visual realization in front of my very eyes unnerved me to the extent I felt myself losing consciousness. Within a few moments I had slumped back into my seat as darkness took over my mind. I do not know how long I had been unconscious, but when later I did eventually come to, my attention was focused on a peculiar movement on the stage.

"Imperceptibly at first, but taking on form almost as

the seconds went by was an apparition on the stage. I was a vision of a man, a tall man made more so by the fact he was wearing a tall stove-back top hat and black voluminous trousers. I could not quite make out his face; for the simple reason, it lacked definition or any pronounced features. The black cape he wore over his attire was lined with blazing red shimmering silk, that looked as though it were on fire.

"His slim black shoes were highly glazed and with cavalier buckles of brass. His whole sartorial ensemble seemed to sway as though in a breeze. Indeed he almost glided across the stage floorboards as if he lacked any bodily form or definite substance, as if translucent.

"His moving form was as though he were a black shadow fleeting across a blackened stage. He moved, or rather, glided around the stage, in a manner to suggest he was involved in an intense conversation with someone or, perhaps even with himself, as a Monologist might do.

"Then it happened. My worst fears took on a real form as quite distinctly something or someone brushed by me. The immediate shock to my shattered sensibilities manifested itself in the form of an electrical charge forming around my tongue. I instantly recoiled back in horror and in so doing; my legs gave way as I slid out of my Upper Circle seat and on to the floor.

"I was now hidden, behind a row of seats, from the person on stage who had presumably heard my muffled fall. I picked myself up and peered over the scarlet velvet seat in front of me. However, the noise of my fall had the effect of making him looked about the auditorium to ascertain the source of the commotion, which I had caused. My heart nearly stopped when he glided to the front of the stage and peered into the gloom of the auditorium and then specifically in my direction.

"His face was now visible to me and it was deathly white and pock-marked. He looked towards me for a few anxious moments. All of a sudden, he seemed to avert his gaze from my direction, and instead, raised his eyes up, within their blackened sockets. He then, lifted his head up and looked upwards above himself. His facial features and countenance changed abruptly, as though he were in total despair and terrified of something.

"Then a look of abject horror crossed his face, that he tried to shield with his arms, which he threw around his head. Again, the enormity of what I was now experiencing, and the attendant shock it was causing to my wrought nerves, caused me to lapse into another blackout, brought on by my continued nervous anxiety.

"Again, I eventually came to, but instead of staggering around I decided to stay where I was and try to sleep until dawn and hopefully release from being locked in Wilton's Music Hall during the mid hour at night. I did fall off into a fitful sleep but was rudely awakened by a squeaking noise. At first I thought they were rats foraging around for scraps of food left by the audience from the previous evening.

"Then I realized that the noise was coming, not from the seating areas. Instead, it was definitely coming from the direction of the stage. I uncurled myself, and then, very tentatively, looked over the row of red velvet seats immediately in front of mine, and from behind which I was reposing. The vision I beheld of the stage confused me. Was I dreaming, I asked myself?

"There in front of the familiar stage back-drop of the temple, were two individuals; a man and a woman. Again, like the gentlemen wearing the stove-pipe top hat and the cape with a blazing red silk lining. These two had an almost ethereal look about them too, as though very loosed jointed and almost swaying as though in a breeze. Of the two, the gentleman wore a dark purple fez made of felt with a gold tassel to one side. In addition he wore greying voluminous trousers which tapered at the ankles. His shirt was of flaming red in color over which he wore a purple waist-coat, with gold piping, that matched his fez.

"His companion, a rather diminutive woman, wore an ostentatious dress, resembling a layered petticoat, above a pair of exposed horizontally differently colored striped knickerbockers. She too wore a flaming red shirt and a purple waist-coat with gold piping. But upon hers, silver sequins had been sown into the fabric. What made this double act peculiar was the fact that both were blindfolded and she was tied to the revolving Katherine Wheel!

"It was from the wheel, as it revolved, that I had heard the squeaking sound. In the meantime the fez-wearing gentleman, was holding in his left hand, five sharpened knives glinting in the subdued light. The final destination of those knives was evident to me, and would no doubt be thrown at the woman! The fez-wearing individual, still swaying, poised himself in readiness to perform his death-defying feat. In the next instant he had thrown all five knives in rapid succession whilst still blindfolded.

"But then to my horror, in the gloom of the auditorium and stage, I had come to realized something. The squeaking noise from the Katherine Wheel, that had awakened me, was now audible no more, and in fact had ceased. Subsequently, the Katherine Wheel, upon which the woman was tied, had stopped revolving altogether. Then to my unfolding horror, it dawned upon me. The Katherine Wheel upon which the woman was lashed, had not been able to revolve in sequence, to her erstwhile partner's knife throwing act. Consequently, because the Katherine Wheel had ceased to revolve, she had remained motionless, and thus unable to avoid receiving all five sharpened knives straight into her chest, each one piercing her heart!

"I fell back into my seat in total despair unable to think clearly let alone appreciate the torment and despondency searing through my mind. Was I dreaming or experiencing a series of nightmarish scenarios being played out in the confines of my mind as a result of my concussion. I did not care to determine such a question and resolved there and then to deal with my situation and pull myself together and quit this place of torment.

"That was it. I was out of here at whatever cost to my sanity. My resolved paid off because after wandering around in the Music Hall in the twilight and with a repressed panic in me. I succeeded in locating the Grand Foyer of the Dress Circle, on the *piano-nobile*. Eventually, at long last I found the grand staircase which led down to the ground floor foyer.

"On reaching this floor I stumbled across the Mahogany Bar and knew then my release was imminent and physically not far away from the front doors of the Music Hall. Irrespective of this fact, I felt sorely tempted to help myself to a bottle of whisky as some kind of compensation for my nocturnal ordeal. A minute or so later, I succeeded in locating a set of highly varnished mahogany doors leading into Grace's Alley and escape from the confines of Wilton's Music Hall.

"The doors, I found upon closer inspection, were securely fastened, but this in no way impeded my resolve to gain egress from the building. My determination paid off and having burst through these double set of highly varnished mahogany doors, I found myself outside in

Grace's Alley, albeit shrouded in fog, but at least free from the confines of Wilton's Music Hall! At the same moment an indescribable feeling of euphoria gripped my heart on knowing that I was free of that mental torment!

"I later learned that my experiences were not exactly hallucinatory and in fact could have been based on real facts. All the persons who appeared in my delirium were in fact real people. And indeed at least two persons actually now in this Public House had previously mentioned to me the fact that Wilton's Music Hall has a history of sadness. In particular a young girl who tragically fell to her death from the Dress Circle. A Monologist, the life in whom, was crushed out of him, when a cast iron beam supporting the back drop scenery depicting a classical temple, collapsed on to his person. And a blind-folded knife-throwing double act going horribly wrong and resulting in the death of the female artiste!" I completed.

There was a stunned silence before the assembled persons at the bar erupted into ecstatic applause led by Queenie and Little Bo Peep.

Instant offers of whisky to replenish my empty glass were made by several people and all of them were eagerly accepted. Charles Morton came over and shook my hand.

"You know where the Canterbury Music Hall is Theo. There is always room for you there," he said, pressing his Carte de Visite.[5] into my hand.

Jack came marching over with Marie Lloyd.

"My God Theo. In the years I have known you. I did not know you had such a talent!" said Jack, shaking my hand vigorously.

I did not know Lodge was standing behind me until he slapped my back.

"Good story Theo. Well narrated," he said.

"I know one of those experiences I had involved someone close to you and..." I offered.

"That was some time ago Theo" interrupted Lodge, "I am glad that happiness can be brought to those who listen to the story," replied Lodge, pensively.

My enjoyment of the moment was all too short, because at that very moment the perverse Flora Miller pushed her way into the bar. The Red Lion being a Victorian Quality Wet meant that there would invariably be a pianoforte in the establishment. There was, in the next bar and it was to this instrument that Miller instinctively headed. My heart dropped at the prospect of having to witness Miller cavorting lasciviously at the piano with her overt and suggestive danseuse act. She did in fact eventually gain the pianoforte. And to my searing disappointment, her doing so elicited a spontaneous, if muted applause.[6]

On this occasion Miller was dressed in a flowing, iridescent, pale green moiré silk gown with white lace trim around the neck so as to engender a look of angelic innocence about her presence. My experience of her would indicate that she was nothing of the like. Indeed that contrived look of naïve innocence evaporated almost the moment Miller opened her mouth and began singing whilst playing the pianoforte.

Jack and I had seen her perform before at the Hungerford Music Hall at Charing Cross and the Oxford Music Hall in Oxford Street. But on those occasions she usually performed on stage with an elaborate brass plated Aëolian pianola, lavishly decorated with intricate raised designs, which she would stoke tenderly in a highly overtly provocative and suggestive manner.

"The pianoforte she was at the moment engaged in playing was not so elaborately decorated but rather was

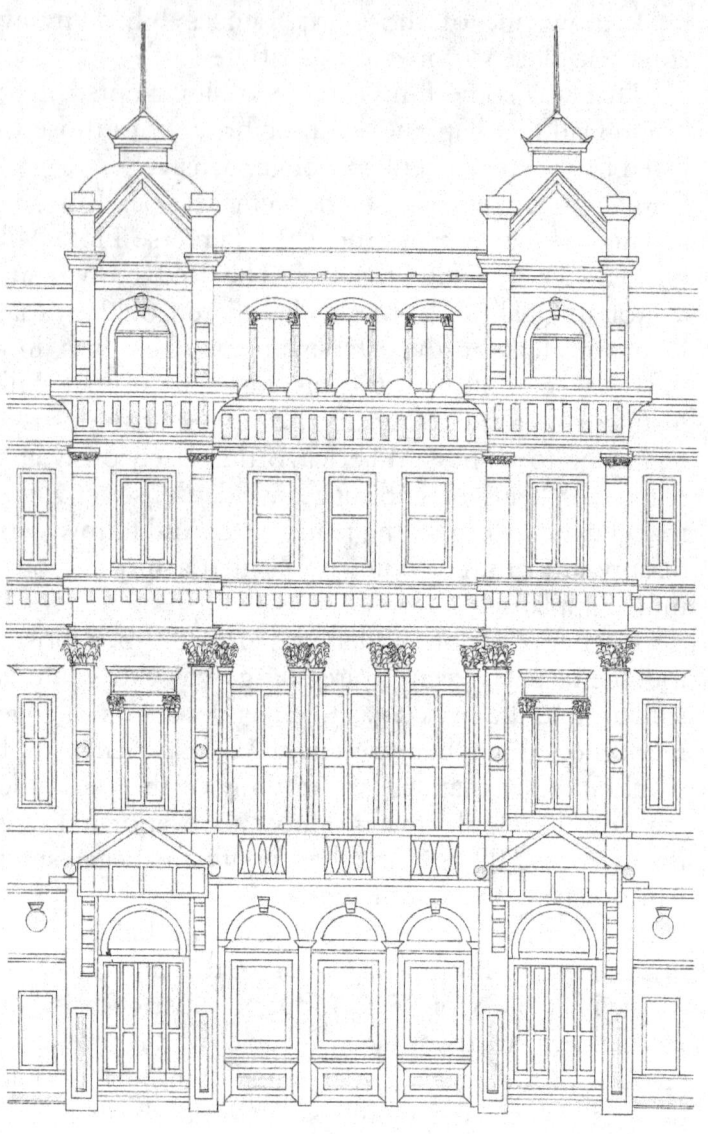

Oxford Music Hall

of the plain domestic upright variety, constructed of plain elm panels. This utilitarian aspect of the pianoforte in no way impeded her enthusiastic rendition of song about being in the garden shed looking out amongst the cabbages and peas, to the accompaniment of the sublime tinkling of arpeggios and triple A's.

"Theo, did we not meet when you were working the Majestic Theater during the World's Columbian Exposition in Chicago a while back?"

I turned around to answer the inquiry and came face to face with Billie Burke.

"Billie! How are you doing?" I replied, "Billie, this is Queenie Leighton. Queenie, this is Billie Burke, a dear friend from our early Vaudeville days back home in the States. And yes, we played the Majestic Theater on West Monroe Street in Chicago during the Chicago World Fair."

Queenie extricated herself from my arm in order to go to the bar.

"Theo," continued Burke, "I have not seen either Jack or yourself since you quit Chicago and that Castle Hotel on West 63rd. Street in the Englewood neighborhood of the city, near Jackson Park. We all of us read later in the *Chicago Tribune*, about the dreadful series of murders

World's Columbian Exposition - ticket

which had taken place there.[7] When you and Jack failed to turn up to perform at the Majestic, well, we assumed the worst and thought that the both of you had been done in by that murderous individual, name of Mudgett, Herman Webster Mudgett, A fraudster who styled himself as Doctor Holmes. He ran that Castle Hotel ostensibly for visitors to the nearby Chicago World Fair; but really he operated the place as a murder mansion.

"Take it from me, you both are very fortunate and lucky to be alive. And I am not referring to the outbreak of smallpox or indeed the conflagration which engulfed the World's Columbian Exposition buildings. Nor am I referring to the civil disorder which broke out leading to serious riots and even an assassination of the mayor of Chicago. No, you both lucky not to have been done in by that murderous Doc Holmes as you slept in your hotel beds!"

"Tell me about it Billie; tell me about Holmes, this Doc Holmes. Given you have been in Chicago since Jack and I were there," I responded.

"Apparently the Chicago Police Department were tipped off, by an indicted informant, as to the murderous activities of Holmes the hotel proprietor. Doc Holmes, it transpired, designed and built the Castle Hotel for himself specifically with murder in mind. He used several constructors separately and all at different times. Some builders doing just a part of the building, so no one constructor or persons had any idea of the overall plan or lay out of the hotel, except Doc Holmes.

"His victims could be gassed whilst locked in sound-proof chambers or were left to suffocate in a sealed bank vault located in the basement. Their corpses would then be cremated in an adjacent concealed crematorium in the foundations of the hotel! Nor was Holmes above placing dead bodies in lime pits in addition to acid baths. Poisons were a favorite of the good doctor, and often he administered them to recalcitrant hotel guests.

"Well Theo, I am truly pleased to see that you and Jack are alive and well and survived that hotel of death." scompleted Burke, with a smile on her lips.

"I remember the odd lay out of the hotel," I responded, "which comprised over a hundred rooms, most of them were without windows! In some hotel rooms, the doors only opened on to brick walls. Some doors could only be opened from the outside the room and not from within! The place was a labyrinthine maze of corridors and hallways some built at odd angles or stairways leading nowhere. I remember too that there was a strong musty odor that occasionally drifted down the hallways.

"It makes my flesh creep, even now Billie, on realizing that the smell drifting down the corridors, was in fact, the odor of death! I read later in the *New York Times* that Doc Holmes confessed to at least twenty-seven other murders. Though the police in fact believe the figure could be in excess of two hundred!" I remarked, then taking a deep draught of whisky from my glass, which I needed having just related my ghastly experience to Billie.

"It may just be rumor Theo," continued Billie Burke, "I do not know. But I read an article in the *Chicago Tribune* which alleged that the proprietor of the hotel, Herman Webster Mudgett, masquerading as Doc Holmes. Used the heat generated by the burning corpses in the crematorium to provide central heat and hot washing water to every hotel room; an amazing innovation at the time!"

Speaking of murder, our attention was taken by the performance at the piano of Flora Miller who too was in the process of committing first degree homicide on musical harmony. I found her verses and suggestive manner embarrassing. Especially, since I was standing next to Billie Burke. And given Billie's refined sensibilities, coming as she does from out of D.C., even more so, I thought.

I looked at Billie then at Miller then again at Billie to apologise visually with my facial features for Miller's performance and questionable behavior at the pianoforte. Billie seemed thoroughly entertained by Miller's singing and cavorting at the pianoforte. Rather as that Rachel D'Arcy does with her ukulele when she performs on the stage, as we saw at Daly's Music Hall recently. Miller then suddenly invited those standing at the bar to join in the singing.

"Altogether now," Miller exhorted those at the bar, with her outstretched arms and closing her fingers on to her hands.

Accordingly, and without hesitation, those patrons at the bar took up her suggestion. And did so with a unified and perfectly synchronized response to Flora Miller's verses which were laced with covert vulgarity and lascivious innuendo, quite clearly audible over everybody else's rendition of the normally accepted verses!

1 For a fuller account refer to *Royal Aq. Queen of Music Halls,* Chapter 20
2 Lloyd was banned from appearing at a Royal Command Performance at the Palace Theater due to her risqué singing
3 A person who walks in their sleep
4 To be turned into stone.
5 An Early form of business card containing a facial image.
6 For a fuller account see *Vaudeville – The Struggle Continues* Chapter 10

Chapter 13

The Fateful Meeting

Cinderella, Jack and I were supposedly en-route to the St. James's Theater. But we had decided to call in on the Red Lion Public House in Duke of York Street. In so doing we had inadvertently come across a dishevelled Lodge at the bar. In addition, other Music Hall artistes, all of whom were scheduled to do their turns at the St. James's Theater that very evening, had also decided to repair to the bar. Not unexpectedly, where there is a gathering of Music Hall artiste with access to alcohol, the place had turned into an impromptu Music Hall with Jack and me relating our experiences and observations whilst in London to a captivated audience.

"Here you Theo, one large whisky and you deserve it," said Charles Morton, manager of the Canterbury Music Hall.

"You know Billie Burke, out of Washington?" I inquired,

"No, I do not; but I do now," replied Morton, shaking Billie's outstretched hand.

"I appreciate Lodge is guiding you around the Music Halls of London and no better man to do so, but do tell me, how did you meet him?" asked Morton.

"We were working the Majestic Theater in West Monroe Street in Chicago," I replied," as indeed so was

Billie here. But we, and other artistes, were continually being heckled by hecklers and concentrations of Nihilists intent on disrupting any or all Vaudeville acts on stage every evening. However, during one particular night, we, and Heywood Broun, a seasoned Improvising Monologist [1] had suffered badly at the hands of a bunch of particularly vociferous hecklers. To the extent that we abandoned our act on the stage and instead repaired to a bar on North Michigan Avenue next to the famous gigantic, if ornate, Gothic Water Tower which dominates the avenue. And which was only one of the few buildings to survive the Great Chicago Fire of 1871.

"Well, we were just bemoaning our fate on the stage by the hacklers, when suddenly, a suave looking person wearing a black silk coat with a collar of luxuriant Astrakhan fur and black silk top hat, approached us at the bar. [2]

'Are you two the double act known as Mitchell and Houston, out of New York?' he had inquired.

"I replied that we were and introduced my stage partner Jack Mitchell.

"He had gone on to say that he saw our act earlier at the Majestic and was sorry that the Nihilists had ruined it. And that the hecklers appeared to be getting quite above themselves and wrecking everybody's enjoyment at the theater. I had agreed with him and his kind offer of a drink for Jack and me.

"It was Jack who had asked the stranger for his name. And I remember the response from the stranger who informed us that his name was Lodge, Michael W. Lodge. And then he handed to each us, one of his expensive, if orchidaceous, carte de visite, upon which was a flamboyant daguerreotype of his image.

"After several rounds, which he funded, from a wallet

that showed no signs of fatigue. He came to the point of why he wanted to meet with us. He confided in Jack and me and said that he was looking for new talent to perform in various Music Halls in London which he was associated with. Jack was sceptical and was resistant to Lodge's offer. For myself, I was interested in his proposal.

"The crowds attending the World's Columbian Exposition were thinning out as the World Fair was winding down. I figured that within a few days we would have to make our way back to New York. Or did we? Here was an opportunity to check out a different place, such as London. After all we had come to Chicago, albeit to entertain the huge crowds attending the Exposition, so why not London.

"We did not agree there and then and instead arranged to meet with Lodge at the Auditorium Hotel the next day. But then Lodge informed us that after our meeting, he was leaving Chicago the next day aboard the *Iron City Express* via Pittsburgh bound for New York, with or without us.

"Lodge then gave us both a searching glance, finished his drink and sailed out of the bar with his cape flapping like a gigantic bird of prey.

"I had then told Jack that we should accept Lodge's offer especially if the if the *Iron City Express* was going to New York's Pennsylvania Rail Road Station. If nothing else Lodge was offering to pay for our train journey back to New York. Jack was still not convinced and even less enthusiastic. Indeed he was more prepared to dismiss Lodge, typically as a stranger one occasionally might meet at a bar. However, the next day Jack and I did meet with Lodge at the Auditorium Hotel. Needless to say, we did in fact accompany Lodge back to New York. A couple

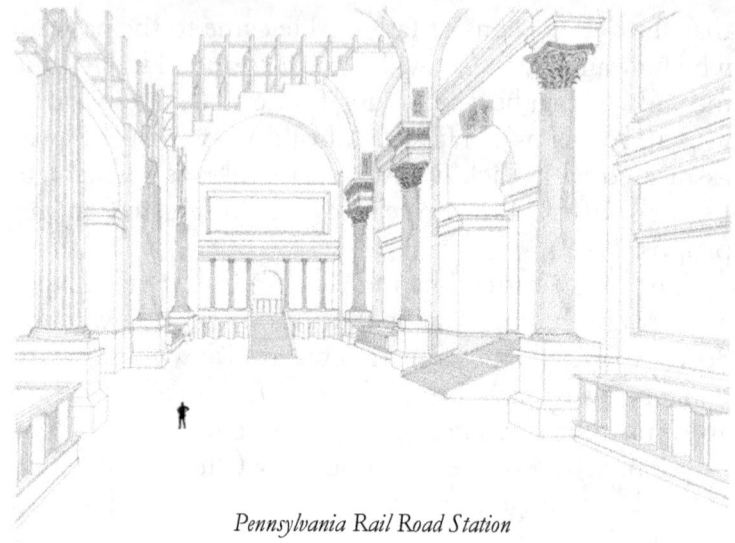

Pennsylvania Rail Road Station

of days later we took ship, or rather the R.M.S. *Olympic*, sister ship to the sunken R.M.S. *Titanic*! And here we are as Lodge's protégées!"

"Well for myself Theo, I am glad you took Lodge's offer and joined us here in London," said Charles Morton.

"I liked Jack's story about Lodge's re-action to the Titanic Benefit Concert," said Mabel Green, offering us a whelk from a plate she was carrying, whilst walking past us. Morton and Billie took one. I desisted. It was a plate of warm whelks, eaten at Gatti's Restaurant, in Villiers Street, Charing Cross that was responsible for causing me the stomach ache which led to the dreadful events I experienced at Wilton's Music Hall during the mid hour at night.

"What have been your most lasting impressions of English Music Hall Theo? I am particularly interested to learn what Vaudeville artistes out of America think about our acts or turns," inquired Morton.

"Without a doubt the Dumb Mute's act [3] that Jack and I witnessed at ironically, Wilton's Music Hall. I liked the fact that he was positioned on the steps leading up to the front door of a large dwelling wherein a recent death of the master of the house had taken place. The Dumb Mute's exaggerated mannerism was of interest to me and reflected such pathos and also extreme agitation, suggesting that he may be in the process of suffering from profound mourning at the recent loss of a person. I also liked the way the Dumb Mute portrayed desperation as he kept clutching at his throat, with both hands, as if gasping for breath. His face was stretched upward, as though in an agonizing desperate manner, whilst trying to gain the aëther, as his eyes rolled aimlessly around inside their blackened sockets, seemingly oblivious to vision," I replied.

"But then," offered Charles Morton, "the sole function of the Dumb Mute, employed professionally at an astounding rate of six pennies each hour. Was to position himself on the steps next to the front door of the house. And there re-live the agonies of dying and imitate the death scene, all for the benefit of those members of the family and friends who were unfortunate enough to miss the actual recent death of the master of the household. And this tradition, it is still customary in the East End of London and regarded as a necessary optional extra to any funereal proceedings!"

"The other memorable experience was that of the St. Vitus's Dancer [4] I saw at the infamous Empire Music Hall in Leicester Square. Both the Dumb Mute and the St. Vitus's Dancer are just so English and in fact brilliant portrayals of Victorian characters. I doubt they would be understood properly in Vaudeville, Burlesque or indeed any type of theater in the United States. In this respect they remain so rooted in English mannerism, as to prevent their effective transfer to America.

"I particularly liked the portrayal of the St. Vitus's Dancer and his narration of his life which had been punctuated with melodrama and tragedy. In particular when the St. Vitus's Dancer informed the audience, that as a child he had contracted cholera, then typhoid and quickly followed by scarlet fever. Before he was but four years of age and told how his mother, to avoid contagion, put him into a wicker basket. A basket which she then shoved out into the out-going tide at Wapping Reaches on the Thames!

"The St. Vitus's Dancer then related his story. Whilst doing so, he was shaking quite uncontrollably. And, to an alarmingly extent, brought on no doubt, by his having gotten the St. Vitus's Dance disease. He told us how the wicker basket, began to leak, when out on the river and in which he began to drown, but for the swift selfless action of a kindly nearby tosser [5] who, at the time, was wading through the shore tide. The figure then chanted with an intense sadness about missing his home, and told how he had spent his life searching the Reaches of Wapping on the Thames, for his mother and still continues to do so to this day.

"Of how he was put into living bondage, because of his scarred face, and forced to work as a grave digger. And was only fed just enough whelks from the nearby river Thames to enable him to labor continuously. But, when he asked for a pay rise of only one farthing a year, so it could continue to search for its mother, his employer tried to bury him alive, in the very grave it was digging for another corpse! Such is my memory of the St. Vitus's Dancer when I saw him perform at the Empire Music Hall," I completed.

"Interesting you say that Theo, because in my experience, such acts are more popular with the costermongers and tossers than with audiences which might frequent say theaters of varieties, such as the London Pavilion," retorted Morton, slowly as his, Billie's and then my attention were caught inadvertently overhearing a loud conversation between to Jolly John Nash,[6] and Virginia Francis. It was Francis who was talking whilst at the time was wagging her index finger as she did so.

Empire Music Hall

"The last time I saw you was at poor Belle Elmore's Wake of remembrance at the Vaudeville Music Hall and you were obnoxious then as indeed you are now," said Virginia Francis to Jolly John Nash, offering freely her considered opinion of him.

"What I remembered of you at that wake," countered Nash, who was having none of it, "was less than dignified and quite, quite consistent with your atrocious behavior earlier at Belle Elmore's funeral at Highgate Cemetery. I recall quite vividly they had not lifted Belle's coffin off the catafalque outside Funereal Chapel before you led an undignified scramble as you pushed and shoved your way to a prime position in the pews in the chapel.

"And madam, that deepest black regalia you were dressed in from head to foot, especially wearing that hat, which elicited from more than one person, comments to the effect that in its own right merited some kind of architectural recognition. For such was its inordinate size and ostentatious, if orchidaceous, construction! Others assembled were more accurate in their comments which included such phrases regarding your head dress as, 'could only attract derision and scorn,' or 'ridiculous on a woman of her advanced age.' Good day madam," said Nash, before repairing back to the bar from whence he had come. There he stuck up a more amicable conversation, or rather so it sounded, with a person I recognised as being Jerry Driscoll.

In the meantime, at the bar in the Red Lion Public House, Flora Miller's questionable recital at the pianoforte was brought to an abrupt end. It was done so, to my great relief, by the fortuitous arrival of Wilkie Bard, who insisted on singing the well known song, '*She Sells Sea Shells by the Seashore*,' which is guaranteed to confound the most accomplished of singers. On this

Vaudeville Music Hall

occasion, he was accompanied at the pianoforte by played by Flora Miller, who refused to abandon the instrument.

That song was followed by, '*I Want to Sing in Opera*,' as Morton informed Billie and me that he had tried to book Wilkie Bard for a production of, '*Puss in Boots*, at the Canterbury Music Hall. But Bard had been persuaded by Augustus Harris to appear, in women's clothes in a pantomime revolving around, 'Dick Whittington and his Cat,' at his Theater Royal in Drury Lane.'

Presently a fellow came over to me and shook my hand.

"Very interesting story you related to us about Wilton's Music Hall, very atmospheric. Oh, my name is Tribune, Dean Tribune. I am pleased to make your acquaintance."

"This is Billie Burke and Charles Morton," I responded

"How long have you known Lodge?" he then asked.

"Just a few months really," I replied.

"Do you know Tom Holmes?" Tribune then asked me, as another fellow joined our small group.

"I do not believe that I do," I replied, shaking his hand, "but could you in fact be related to Sherlock Holmes, the famous Pinkerton detective out of 221 Baker Street, here in London?"

"Alas, I am not," replied Holmes, "but I wish that I were. My notoriety would be limitless were I to be so!"

"Are you then in fact related to the infamous Doc Holmes out of Chicago?" inquired Billie Burke with a rue smile playing upon her lips.

"I do not think that I am. Why, is he a renowned physician? Should I know him?"

"I think he obtained a medical degree of sorts out of Michigan University. But he gave up that vocation to run the Castle Hotel on West 63rd. Street in the Englewood neighborhood of the city, near Jackson Park,"

Tom Holmes seamed fascinated at the prospect of having a relation in Chicago and was about to enunciate an inquiry directed at Billie. But at that juncture in the conversation, Hetty King walked past us. She was wearing, in keeping with her style, a particularly loud Prince of Wales style checked patterned suit and spats on her highly varnished boots. Hetty looked very much as if she were en-route to a race course.

221.b. Baker Street.

The next minute I found myself face to face with Maxine Elliott out of Rockland, Maine. After a few pleasantries were exchanged between us she suddenly made an announcement in hushed tones to me.

"Theo," she continued, "I know the Stanley Theater in Jersey City and feel confident that I saw that Lodge fellow there some years back. But for the life of me I cannot figure out just in what capacity. I simply cannot remember. Though, come to think of it I had no idea you and Jack were in England. Are you working the Music Halls here in London?"

"We are indeed Maxine and have performed in a number of central London Music Halls already since we arrived here some weeks back," I replied.

"How are you finding it?" asked Maxine.

"Good fun, interesting and very different to Vaudeville back home. In fact I was just discussing with Charles Morton and Queenie..." I answered,

"Is that *the* Charles Morton, manager of the Canterbury Music Hall?" interrupted Maxine.

"Yes," I replied.

"Theo, do introduce me to him. I feel confident he could use my talents on his stage at the Canterbury," implored Maxine.

"Sure Maxine," I continued, "I will be pleased to do that. But as I was saying, whilst talking with Charles Morton, that watching certain acts on the stage in London Music Halls such as that of the St. Vitus's Dancer or the Dumb Mute both of which are just so English and brilliant portrayals of Victorian characters. To the extent Maxine I doubt they would be understood properly in Vaudeville, Burlesque or indeed any type of theater in the United States. I just do not think we have the history to understand their evolvement. But do tell me Maxine.

Stanley Theater, Jersey City

What brings you to London? I did not think you would venture way out east as far as London?"

"I am here to see Elsie Janis out of Delaware in her new show which is to open next week. And lend her moral support, as it were or at the very least bring verisimilitude to the proceedings! But as I said to Theo, whilst here in London, I should like to tread the floorboards at some Music Halls," replied Maxine.

My heart sank at the prospect of meeting Elsie Janis, or Elsie Bierbower her real name. Or, 'Beerbarrow,' as we have nicknamed her for obvious reasons reflecting her loud ebullient character. But then took comfort on learning from Maxine Elliott that Janis had been unexpectedly delayed in rehearsals and would not be joining her friend Maxine here at this bar today.

Then the unbelievably young Constance Talmadge,[7] a child prodigy of the Vaudeville theaters in Brooklyn, rushed by us as though on a mission, being escorted by Lily Elsie, the well known stage beauty. It was a pity she

Empress Theater, Kansas City

seemed to be in a hurry; as I should have liked to have spoken with Lily. But then, who would not have?

Her meteoric rise to fame with the public was based on a series of successes on the stage, including, her staring rôle in Franz Lehár's, *"The Merry Widow,"* premièred in 1907. In addition, so the rumor has it. She remains the most photographed stage beauty of the era. She, of course, is even more famous now because of a pervasive advertisement for a preparation called, 'Phosferine,' which regularly appears in the popular newspapers and on the walls of buildings and rail road station platforms.

I was pondering this concern, when Jack arrived with Maud Jeffries on his arm accompanied by Little Ganty and Daisy James.

"Hi Theo," she said, "how are you doing? I am delighted to meet with Jack and now you too, here in this quaint English Public House! The last time we met with each other was back stage at the Empress Theater in Kansas City?"

"I remember you Maud, out of Coahoma County, Mississippi?" I inquired.

"You have a very good memory Theo," she said, smiling.

"Good experiences are easy to remember!" I responded.

It was my earnest intention to escort Maxine Elliott out of Rockland, so that I might introduce her to the legendary Charles Morton. However, as sometimes in the case when Music Hall artistes are gathered for whatever reason, a peculiar thing happened almost spontaneously. Suddenly and without any pre-ordained signal, prompting or exhorting by anyone, those Music Hall artistes, assembled at the bar in the Red Lion Public House, drained their drinks whilst others gathered up their scattered possessions.

Maud, Jack and I followed suit and finished our drinks. Breathing out noisily when we had done so. I in the company of others join the fray as we all then marched out of the opulent and comfortable bar into a fog bound Duke of York Street. Moments later we all of us were staggering down the street, led by Cinderella.

"Follow me," said Cinderella, holding up her white cotton parasol above her head for all to see, "I know the way!"

We all of us fell in eagerly with her suggestion. We did so, in order that we might be in a position later to entertain the great Music Hall going public, some of whom were now hopefully taking their seats in the red plush auditorium of the St. James's Theater located somewhere in this fog-bound vicinity of Piccadilly.

1 A person who relates sarcastically and continuously, without pause, a series of events or observations
2 An interesting account can be found *in Royal Aq - Queen of Music Halls* Chapter 4
3 For a fuller account refer to *Royal Aq. Queen of Music Halls,* Chapter 21
4 An interesting account can be found in, *Vaudeville - The Struggle Continues,* Chapter 31
5 A person who searches the Thames shore for washed up valuables
6 Jolly John Nash Died in 1901
7 Born in 1897 in Brooklyn

Chapter 14

The St. James's Theater

Our laudable intention to get some rehearsal in with Cinderella, in her stage guise as Marmeduke, before our début at the St. James' Theater in King Street, had effectively been sabotaged en-route by our repairing to a Quality Wet. Rather than going through our routine and polishing it to perfection, we had instead joined with Lodge who we found there drowning his sorrows there. And several other Music Hall artistes, all of whom were engaged to perform at the St. James' Theater that very evening, and for that matter, so were we.

After a few minutes groping around in the acrid fog following Cinderella through St James's Square. We were rather like the crayfish; making progress backwards. But eventually, we and a host of other Music Hall artistes arrived at the impressive façade forming the front of the St. James' Theater complete with a series of white opaque globes, pouring out their powerful light. But instead of entering through the illuminated main entrance in King Street. Cinderella wisely escorted us to the Artistes' Entrance located in the more secluded alleyway adjacent to another Public House. This one, I noticed was called the Golden Lion. We desisted just, the temptation to enter. And instead went on into the rear of the theater as a noisy pantechnicon went lumbering by.

An employé of the theater manning the Stage Door seemed more relieved at our appearance, even if we looked a little dishevelled. He directed us to a flight of stone steps leading down to a corridor in the basement along which various changing rooms were located.

Eventually and after some misunderstanding with an usher wearing a pink tail-coat with blue piping, we located our dressing room. Jack immediately helped himself to a plate of whelks and a bottle of warm beer put there by the ever thoughtful theater management.

"Well Theo, we are in good company for our début this evening at this St James's Theater," said Jack, handing me a hand bill with the various acts and turns printed upon it. "We are not the only act having our début here tonight. There is a Monologist, name of Clancy, having his too.

We are on after that Vesta Tilley. My heart dropped. For we both of us knew that following on after such an artiste as Vesta Tilley, is a hard act to follow. I reached for another bottle of beer but resisted the temptation to help myself to a whelk. I simply do not trust this species of the Buccinidæ or gastropod mollusc, having experienced my nightmarish ordeal in Wilton's Music Hall. No doubt brought on previously, as a result of eating some at Gatti's Restaurant in Villiers Street at Charing Cross.

From our dressing room we could hear the roar and laughter coming from the audience who seemed to be in fine fettle and responsive.

After Jack had finished his whelks and drained the last dregs of his beer we elected to go upstairs to the stage wings and view the audience in the auditorium. From that vantage point we could gauge the audience and finesse our act accordingly.

Peering through the red velvet side curtain I could see that the auditorium was filled to the rafters. Occupying the front rows of the stalls was the usual contingent of costermongers. Each wore an unforgiving stern countenance upon their face in reaction to a comedian doing his turn on the stage. Some were disposed to making quite audible facetious remarks.

"Ladies and gentlemen, attend me," the comedian continued, whilst pointing to the back of the auditorium with his cane, "if during a coal pit tragedy a coal miner were to be flattened by the collapse of a coal mine. In what musical key would one compose a funeral march, dirge, for the victim?"

This question stunned the audience into silence, though not submission.

"Why of course the key would have to be in *A flat minor*" informed the comedian, whilst giving a shallow bow and leaning on his cane. "Likewise, if one were to accidently step on a bumble bee. In what key would its funeral march be composed in?"

A look, not of expectancy, but rather one of incredulity, emanated from the audience.

"Quite simple the key would be in *B flat,*" said the comedian.

"For those of you who have taken the king's shilling – or not. If one were to compose a military march dedicated to our favorite sergeant-major in what key should it be composed in?" asked the loquacious raconteur.

After an agonising length of time the comedian relented.

"In the key of, *A sharp major,* of course!"

"Conversely, were one to take an ocean voyage, and become sea sick as a result of rough seas. Again in what key would one compose the music to mark this unpleasantness?" asked the artiste, moving around the stage in a zig-zag pattern and holding his cane behind his neck with both hands.

No reply was forthcoming from the audience or even the now subdued costermongers.

An atmosphere of lethal expectation pervaded the auditorium.

"Simplicity itself; the key perforce would be in *C sharp,*" answered the comedian.

The audience soon recovered its nerve and confidence as was evidenced by a rising crescendo of murmurs of disapproval. And in fact one of the more bolder of the costers, was moved to ad lib a remark.

"And by the same token," said the costermonger, "as we all now know, the *Titanic* boat sinking recently in a dead flat calm sea: no doubt the music score commemorating that disaster would then be composed in the key of *C flat.*"

This remark brought a spontaneous eruption of applause from all sections of the audience. From those occupying red plush private boxes to the *Undeserving Poor* seated in the rear of the auditorium on hard elm benches. The costers were now in their element clapping audaciously for that costermonger who had displayed ingenuity in extemporizing on the comedian's line of humorous anecdotes.

Undaunted, but clearly put out by this interruption to his act, the comedian continued his stage act.

"Two Australians talking in a bar in Sydney, New South Wales," informed the stage artiste.

'I am taking the wife to England to see the coronation,' says one fellow to the other."

'Oh you do not want to go there; England is where all those criminals they send out here come from!'"

Some of the costers looked decidedly uncomfortable at the comedian's joke and showed this by refusing to applaud.

"What is the difference between words unlawful or illegal?" asked the comedian of no one in particular.

After a suitable period of awkward silence had elapsed, he put the stunned audience out of their collective misery.

"The difference between unlawful and illegal," he repeated, "is that the word, unlawful means against the law. Whilst the word, illegal describes a sick bird!"

Clearly the costermongers were in a belligerent mood and minded to enjoy themselves at the expense of us artistes performing on stage for their apparent delectation.

At length the hapless artiste abandoned the stage to the sound of desultory applause.

"I really do wish to God, Jack we could commence our act now after his dismal performance. Instead we are to follow Vesta Tilley. What bad luck."

"Do not worry Theo," said Jack, "if that comedian is typical of the acts being performed here tonight. Then we have nothing to be scared about. We could only improve upon the situation!"

I concurred with him, though reservedly, just as Lodge appeared at our side.

"I assumed you had elected to stay in the Red Lion Public House," said Jack.

"Not at all," replied Lodge, "for it remains a pleasure for me to come to this here St. James' Theater. After all, this was the place where my very dear close acquaintance, Oscar Wilde, had his play, '*The Importance of Being Earnest – A Trivial Comedy for Serious People*,' first performed in 1895 and, to great acclaim too. But then, the St James's Theater has an illustrious history. The mere fact of its

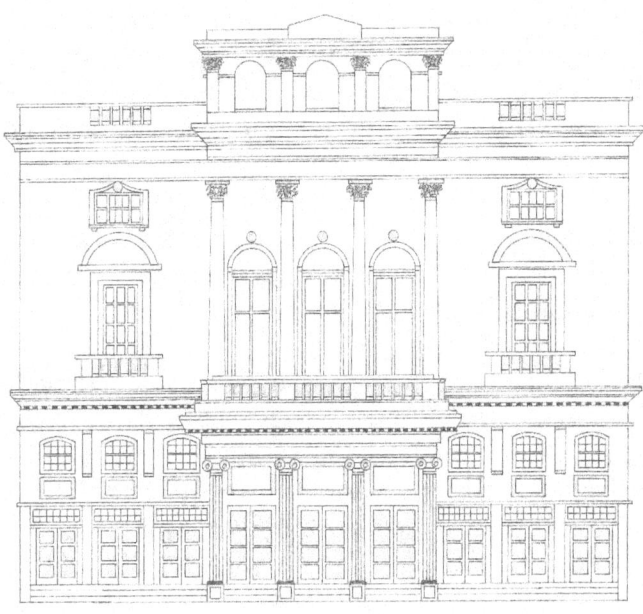

St. James's Theater

being located in King Street, in the St James' neighborhood of Piccadilly is indicative of its prestigious origin. Accordingly, it was designed in the classical style by Samuel Beazley for the impresario and tenor John Branham."

"Really," reposted Jack.

"And the theater was constructed by Peto & Grissell in 1835 with the interior décor, in the style of Louis Quatorze, carried out by the accomplished firm of FredK. Crace & Son out of Wigmore Street. The elaborately appointed auditorium can hold upwards of twelve hundred people. And is covered by an equally ornately decorated ceiling supported by arches the bases of which are in the form of classical Caryatides anchored to gilded plinths, And, from this ceiling is suspended a large intricately formed chandelier carved from gilded copper which illuminates the auditorium with a myriad of light and hues," informed Lodge, pointing with his gold capped ebony cane in to the auditorium.

"When we arrived earlier, I noticed the front of the building, what I could make out in the fog, is decorated with rich ancient Greek and Roman decorative motifs," I responded to Lodge's architectural discourse.

"Rather," continued Lodge, now in full loquacious mode "the façade, of the theater is adorned with a projecting portico, addressing the street level. Comprising four fluted Ionic columns supporting a stone balustrade from which a further four Corinthian styled columns, creating an ornate loggia, continue up to an elaborately decorated cornicing. The three niches which punctuate the embellished upper entablature also reflect a less exuberant Corinthian style, but remain no less impressive. The theater for some inexplicable reason, in 1840 changed its name to the Prince's Theater; but in 1842, reverted back to the St. James' Theater. However, the theater underwent several changes to its name; the Royal, then the Royal St. James' Theater. But after another reconstruction it became again, the St. James' Theater..."

All of a sudden Lodge's discourse was interrupted by the sound of a loud rapturous applause erupting as a performer made her way onto the stage.

It was Cinderella dressed in a white bellowing taffeta and wearing outsized hob-nailed pit-boots with steel studs on the soles. The first thing she did on entering the stage was to insult the costermongers assembled in the stalls below her. Some seemed quite taken aback by this unprovoked overt demonstration of inordinate confidence by Cinderella. Irrespective of the costermongers' reaction, she then proceeded to execute a most tasteful dance set to the accompaniment of one of Tschaikowsky's lyrical, if haunting melodies, generated in the music from his ballet, '*The Nutcracker.*' A ballet based on a fantasy by the acclaimed jurist ETA Hoffmann. [1]

The completion of her *danse entrée* elicited an ovation from the audience in general and a slightly confused set of costermongers in particular.

But before they could gather their wits and respond, a hushed engulfed the auditorium. I pushed my face forward through the red velvet curtains to ascertain the reason for this spontaneous quietude.

It was Jack who pointed out with his index finger the reason why a hush had descended upon the audience. I followed the direction of Jack's finger which was pointing to a red plush private box located in the Dress Circle. Four persons had just entered it and were taking their seats. I recognised them immediately. As indeed so did the audience who by now were staring at the private box.

It was our old friends; their graces the Duke of Teck and his Duchess with whom he is besotted. And the Duke of Cambridge and his lady, the former Music Hall artiste, Sarah Fairbrother, who used to work the Theater Royal Drury Lane.

Cinderella was having none of this distraction whilst she was performing on stage.

"This is what we call an alternative Command Performance" she declared, pointing to their graces with her parasol, "because it is, quite a performance!"

That remarked elicited a sustained applause, especially from the costers in the front row. Though I doubt their graces realized that Cinderella's facetious remark was aimed specifically at them. As they were too busy making themselves comfortable in their plush red velvet upholstered seats.

In the next instance Cinderella was joined by the Corp de Ballet, this time in the form of the *Inexhaustible Cremorne Belles,* of which, Mabel Green used to be one. And upon their entering the stage, executed a series of well coördinated and precise manœuvres. The type of which, really only the Cremornes can dance in perfect synchrony with the music and do so vigorously and faultlessly. And in so doing, have made, unquestionably their own.

After a few minutes of watching this impressive balletic spectacle involving the *Cremorne Belles,* Cinderella, wearing her hob-nailed outsized boots, marched up to the footlights fronting the stage.

"Right," she announced, clearly having some sway with the costers and at the same time twirling her open white cotton parasol on her shoulder. Looking every much the picture of refinement and innocence, "we are going to attempt to sing, in unison, the authorized and unexpurgated version of, '*Abide with Me.*' with the *Cremorne Belles* singing the harmonies. Not you the

Theater Royal Drury Lane

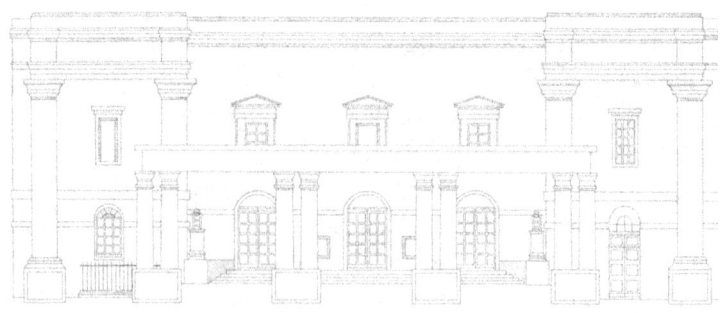

costermongers. You will restrict yourselves to singing faultlessly and in perfect harmony even, the lyrics to this serene melody of which the hymn is comprised.

Several members of the audience cleared their throats in readiness for this momentous occasion. Some even removed their cloth caps.

"All Together now," she exhorted the audience, who took Cinderella up on her kind offer. Some of the costers were even moved to stagger up on to their feet in order to deliver, enthusiastically, their rendition.

We had not gotten in to commencing the second verse of this solemn hymn however. When the most appalling cacophony erupted from the stalls, as the costermongers vied with one another in order to out sing each other. It was like Wagner's opera, *'Tannhäuser und der Sängekrieg auf Wartburg,'* [2] all over again. I looked at Lodge for some kind of explanation.

"Was this a typical English thing; to abuse a hymn?" I inquired.

He did not bother to reply. He seemed more preoccupied with his innate monomaniac condition. An affliction manifested in his obsession for looking over both his shoulders for no discernable reason.

However, I had gotten to know Lodge. And knew this reaction was indicative of a deeper malaise; one of an irrational fear of the unknown; a presentiment, as it were. Clearly Lodge was expecting the unexpected to happen in this Music Hall this very night. Though why he should be concerned, kind of intrigued me and I got to thinking, since he was neither the manager of this Music Hall, nor was he performing on stage. That dubious pleasure remained with Jack and me.

Irrespective of this concern by Lodge, the costermongers continued enthusiastically with their interpretation of this sacred hymnal. Quite what the costers did with the words, albeit led by Cinderella in the penultimate verse, '*Where is death's sting? Where, grave, thy victory?*' I will not chronicle here. Save that I hope to God that I never hear it again! And, indeed Cinderella's behavior was not itself entirely above reproach. Still, this is Music Hall, I thought.

Irrespective of the questionable behavior of the audience when they sang, '*Abide with Me.*' Together with the *Inexhaustible Cremorne Belles* providing the sublime harmonies whilst dancing. The costermongers neither exhibited remorse or embarrassment. But indeed completed the final verse to the accompaniment of a sustained and loud crescendo, followed by a thunderous and rapturous applause for Cinderella, the *Inexhaustible Cremorne Belles* and of course, themselves.

When the applause eventually ceased, Cinderella curtsied several times to a euphoric audience. Whilst being bathed in a single shaft of pale limelight from an arc lamp trained on her person. She then abandoned the stage with her entourage of the *Cremorne Belles*. Some of whom threw themselves enthusiastically into the aëther above the stage in a series of graceful arcs and pas de deux.

Vesta Tilley then pushed past me and strode on to the stage wearing the clothes of a toff, or swell, as we call them in New York City. She raised her shiny top hat and started chatting to the audience. I decided to go back to my dressing room and indulge in a quick bottle of beer and maybe even a whelk or two. Alas Jack and I were on stage immediately after her.

Having done precisely that, several minutes later, I returned to the side of the stage in an apprehensive mood. And just in time to witness a commotion on the stage. It involved Little Bo Peep, and she was in her element interrupting Vesta Tilley's song and dance act. Even from where I was standing. I could discern quite easily the undisguised look of concentrated malevolence in Tilley's facial features at the sight of Little Bo Peep's unscheduled appearance on the stage. Wearing a cute cotton smock and holding her shepherdess' crook. Whilst performing her lame act. Complete with her lamb that was wondering around the stage un-tethered and bleating loudly.

Eventually Little Bo Peep reclaimed her errant lamb and left the stage. However, it was difficult for Tilley to regain total control of the audience's attention, for such was the effective interruption, caused by Little Bo Peep who has successfully disrupted Tilley's act, which was now mortally compromised! The audience were not interested in Tilley, who remained on stage for just a few more minutes. Clearly this audience would rather have watched Little Bo Peep cavorting around the stage instead.

Cinderella in the guise of Little Bo Peep had deliberately gone on stage to sabotage Tilley's act. In so doing of course she had made our entrance on stage all the more easier! Following an accomplished act as Tilley is difficult. But can be made easier especially if that previous turn on stage is effectively sabotaged, resulting in its total degeneration into chaos or better still, pandäemonium!

Eventually Jack and I were introduced by the Compière and accordingly we marched on to the stage. Our performing several songs, surprisingly went down well with the audience. About half an hour later we were joined, on cue, by Marmeduke to commence our triple act. Once on stage, we executed our act reasonably well.

To the extent that when we abandoned the stage at the end of our song and dance routine with Jack playing an upright pianoforte we received loud applause. More, I suspect, generated by Marmeduke's joining our act than just for Jack or me. But at least our turn did not deteriorate into a farce unlike that of Tilley's! Irrespective though, I have to admit, whenever we perform with Marmeduke our act is a roaring success. And typically, our performance this evening was no exception.

In the next instant, the red velvet stage curtain began its slow decent; and in so doing triggered a mass stampede of biblical proportions to the various Crush Bars ranged strategically about the St. James's Theater. Within minutes, the auditorium was deserted. Jack and I looked at each other and then made our own exit from the side wings of the stage. A few moments later we arrived at a nearby Crush Bar. Aptly named; for it was teeming with patrons demanding drinks from weary looking bar-tenders dressed in their white jackets and checked trousers.

It did not take us long to find Lodge who was in the act of waving his gold capped ebony stick at one of the bar-tenders. He succeeded in getting his attention. He then saw Jack and me.

"Ah Jack, Theo; please do come and join me," Lodge said, in a contrived manner, indicative of the way he thinks. That is to say, having arrived at a most propitious or inconvenient time, just as he was about to order a drink. He obviously incorporated us into his generous offer. Because clearly, he could hardly not do so!

"A large whisky," announced Jack, "and the same for my long standing Vaudeville partner Theo Houston. Minutes went by but eventually our drinks arrived.

"You seemed to be a little nervous there Loge, "said

Jack, raising the whisky glass to his lips, "not your usually ebullient, if suave self brimming over with self esteem, the reserves from which are immense."

"You are prescient Jack," replied Lodge, "I am rather apprehensive of the inordinate number of costermongers assembled here this evening..."

"Being a performer on the stage," interrupted Jack, "I find the costermongers, in general, to be the life and soul of the audience in a Music Hall. Without their enthusiastic involvement, the essential Music Hall experience could only be diminished. And, I would venture to say..."

However that pearl of wisdom was destined to remain unspoken. Because at that very moment, a loud commotion was heard coming from just outside the Crush Bar. In the next instance the *'Queen of the Matinée,'* came in through the open double-leaf mahogany doors leading in to the Crush Bar. She then came marching up to where we were standing. She was of course, Millie Hylton and both Jack and I instantly recognised her. Especially with her Medusa-like facial features which could, without any difficulty, turn immediately one into stone. I looked into her face, as it was, of such repellent aspect, and felt myself turning cold, if not into stone.

She brushed past Jack and immediately launched into a tirade at Lodge. Perhaps this was the factor that had clearly unnerved Lodge and brought on his monomania affliction of looking over both shoulders as though anticipating a presentiment. Perhaps, I conjectured, he had seen Hylton making her way through the St James's Theater earlier. I also noticed Jack order two more whiskies at the bar. Clearly the Music Hall stage had come to this humble Crush Bar!

"Do you not think Lodge, that you owe me an apology,

"demanded Hylton, "for your earlier cavalier treatment of me a while back when you used me cruelly?"

"Madam, it is my belief that I owe you nothing of the like. Nor did I use you cruelly," replied Lodge, albeit nervously.

"You said to me that I could have a rôle in that Titanic Benefit Concert of yours. Or did the amount of alcohol coursing through your blood make you forget that rash promise to me?" continued Hylton.

"I have no recollection of promising you a rôle, rash or otherwise. That you allude to mistakenly," countered Lodge, looking inquisitively into his glass of whisky, as though it were of more relevance than Hylton's allegation.

"Well you do owe me an apology; because you did renege on your promise to me. But I forgive you! Yes I really do. My career as an accomplished Music Hall singer could never have withstood the ignominy and assault upon my reputation as those which emanated out of that disastrous performance of that hackneyed Cholera Anthem Symphony. When it was performed during the doomed Titanic Benefit Concert, at the Queen's Hall.

"Informed people, in all sincerity, are saying, that the concert deteriorated into a calamity. And as such was on a scale that it made the actual tragedy of the sinking of the Titanic boat, in comparison, look as though it had been nothing more than a capsized rowing boat on the Serpentine Lake in Hyde Park.

"In this respect you did me a favor Lodge. I am much indebted to you," she said, whilst patting Lodge's cheek with her black velvet gloved hand. Hylton then curtsied and marched off out of the Crush Bar. Millie Hylton did so in very much in the same fashion as she had previously entered; noisily and with a generated attendant commotion.

"The Impertinence of that accursed woman, that Valkürian woman, would that the Gods turned her into stone as she has done to others with that Medusan face of hers," said Lodge, only when Hylton had gone through the open double-leaf mahogany doors and was out of range of his words,

Jack and I exchanged glances.

"Still," Lodge continued, clearly more confident in the absence of Millie Hylton, "let us not condemn the ideal for a couple of glitches! And, as I have said on numerous occasions my favorite axiom; the public be damned; Box Office receipts come first. And in retrospect it would have been highly unlikely that orchidaceous, if Medusan woman, could not have made, by her presence on the stage, a significant contribution to those essential Box Office receipts. That is why I subsequently cut that incorrigible woman, with her repulsive nature, from the program."

He then drained the last drop of drink from his glass and having done so breathed out noisily, looking at Jack, in an appealing manner.

It was Franklyn Smith, who took up the challenge as he joined our group.

"Bar-tender," he yelled at the bar, "four large neat whiskies."

This Franklyn Smith, was of course Mabel Green impersonating a male. From my hazy recollections of Lodge's reception a while back at his town house in the Bergen Avenue. I recall that this so called Franklyn Smith introduced himself to Lodge. The occasion was memorable.[3] Because ironically when Smith came up to Lodge, we were in the throes of discussing why some persons like dressing up in clothes of the opposite gender. Typically Vesta Tilley or Hetty King impersonating men;

House in the Bergen Avenue

whilst Bothwell Browne though born Walter Bothwell Bruhn prefers to adorn himself in fashionable clothes appertaining to woman.

Both Jack and I knew this Franklyn Smith was in fact Mabel Green moonlighting as a man. Only Lodge, seemed then, in his town house, and still does, oblivious to this fact, and accordingly, to be totally unaware of Mabel's sartorial preferences or male identity when she impersonates. I remember the absurdity as Lodge addressed this so called Franklyn Smith in tones of absolute sincerity as he informed Smith, Jack and I, that he found it surprising that people would even consider getting into the clothes usually worn by members of the opposite gender.

He asked us to consider the indignity that could only attend such a reckless sartorial preference, together with the shame, the humiliation, and the scorn or ridicule one would to endure. Along with the vicious whispers including having to wear a large hat to cover one's eyes! He added that in his thirty five years in the Music Halls business, he had yet to meet such an unfortunate a person afflicted with such a debilitating social condition.

Franklyn was then asked did he hold any *views* on this matter. His reply was pure Vaudeville.

'A person who feel compelled to dress as though they were of the opposite gender, he answered, 'as it were, I find utterly remarkable and can only assume they suffer from a particular *idée fixe*, which propels their monomaniac condition to undertake such an extreme conduct. What could possibly drive a person to such drastic, or indeed, draconian lengths, one can only ask?'

'Money!' Jack had answered.

As Lodge studied Franklyn, now collecting our whiskies at the bar, Jack and I exchanged glances and smiles. We both of us could not quite believe Lodge's incredulity in not realizing that Franklyn was Mabel Green in the garb of a gentleman. Again, I was reminded of the fact that there is invariably more profound Vaudeville and entertainment enacted in the Crush Bars of Music Hall; than on the actual stage itself. And we were now experiencing such a luscious occasion.

"Well how are you doing Mr. Lodge?" inquired Smith, whilst handing out the whiskies.

The directness of Franklyn's unexpected polite, if simple inquiry, momentarily caught Lodge off-guard; but in characteristic fashion, he soon recovered his suave composure, and that certain self assurance, which he retained in droves. But then Lodge responded to Franklyn's question by correcting it.

"No, no. This will not do Franklyn," said Lodge, "my close acquaintances called me Loge in honor of the only noble character in Rickard Wagner's grand opera, '*Das Rheingold*.' [4]

Irrespective of the origin of Lodge's sobriquet, our attention was drawn to another impromptu performance nearby. From what I could see and hear, it involved Marie Tempest [5] and Maude Adams. And their discussion, which had been going on for some minutes, was now deteriorating rapidly into quite a heated argument. Both were trying to establish the merits or demerits accordingly of the music of an Austro-Hungarian composer, name of, Dvořák, Antonín Dvořák.

I was interested to hear what the protagonists had to say. Because just hearing this composer's name being said brought memories flooding back into my mind like a river in full torrent of biblical proportions. So I detached myself from my group, and made my way slowly towards the contestants. I have fond recollections of the music

World's Columbian Exposition

composed by this Dvořák fellow. In particular when Jack and I were in Chicago working the Majestic Theater during the World Columbian Exhibition. It was in Chicago, at a bar in North Michigan Avenue that we met with Lodge and had been subsequently invited to accompany him back to London to work the Music Halls there as his protégées.

Before accepting his invitation and as our farewell to Chicago, then the, *'City of Dreams,'* Jack and I had decided to attend the gigantic Orchestral Hall, largest concert hall in the world, contained in the Auditorium Building located in between South Michigan and Wabash. A beautiful building designed by Louis Sullivan in 1889, the ornate façade of which incorporates a series of arched window reveals in enfilade.

That afternoon the concert featured the Chicago Symphony Society Orchestra, performing a work composed by Dvořák, his Symphony No. 9 in E minor, and called *'From the New World.'* It was written especially to commemorate that Chicago World Exposition.

Having arrived at the impressive Auditorium Building

Jack and I made our way through the red plush interior and took our seats in the Dress Circle in the Orchestral Hall. My eyes took in the ornate interior of the auditorium, complete with its very pronounced and decorated ribbed barrel vaulted ceiling; which is an acoustic innovation, so the concert program informed me.

Presently, the concert opened with another work written by Dvořák; but it was not his Ninth Symphony, and nor was it in the concert schedule. It was, alas his *Opus 98*, the Suite in A major and called, '*The American*', which having been performed, was concluded to thunderous applause from a delighted, if unsuspecting, audience for this musical treat.

The orchestra and audience then settled down to the main item on the concert schedule. Dvořák's Ninth Symphony in E-minor. It opened with a slow but rising crescendo, inviting the listener on a journey through various musical landscapes. The power of the music portrayed in the minor idiom is immediately obvious to any trained musical ear. It promises to be the precursor of a monumental harmonic journey of discovery. Analogous with the discovery of America by Columbus – the rationale for the World's Columbian Exposition. 6

As the symphony developed, the ideas and concepts encapsulated within this musical work, I felt, were being expressed very succinctly. Including those hopes, aspirations, dreams or optimism which Jack and I had also experienced whilst walking amongst the masonry pavilions and exhibits on show and which comprised the World's Columbian Exposition at Chicago.

Among the musical abilities radiating from Dvořák is a characteristic, yet unexpected, harmonic development, together with the fresh and vital application of orchestral forces in expressing a coherent melodic progression which, in so doing, achieves a rich intensity of feeling. The concert was a resounding success and the symphony played to great applause. I was especially pleased to be able to witness Antonin Dvořák's E-minor Symphony, especially in this mighty Orchestral Hall.

It was therefore with blinding curiosity that I made my way towards Marie Tempest and Maude Adams. I did so in order that I might hear at firsthand what indeed they had to impart to each other, with such vehemence, concerning their thoughts about Antonin Dvořák! With my back to them, I gave the impression of being absorbed by a framed image of the Royal Princess's Theater affixed to a nearby wall.

Ironically, it was in that Royal Princess's Theater, with its ornate façade incorporating a loggia in the form a balcony overlooking Oxford Street. In which Jack and I had witnessed a performance of dance pantomime by Franz Schreker. And called *Der Geburtstag der Infantin,*' [7] based on a work,' by Oscar Wilde, of the same title.

Also Queenie had related to me the fact she had first met Lodge, professionally about twenty years ago at the Royal Princess's Theater when he returned to London after some years working Vaudeville in New York in the 1880's. Indeed a theater full of history, I thought. However, my immediate concern was to over hear what Maud Adams and Marie Tempest had to say. Or at least exchange with each other!

Maude Adams, I knew from the early Vaudeville days. And I always retain a light-hearted affection for her. Though quite a feisty girl, she is in fact out of Salt Lake City, Utah and was, she confided in me, born with the name Maud Kiskadden. What she might have to say about Dvořák would be of intrigue to me.

Royal Princess's Theater

However, both were too busy arguing to notice my presence. But rather than risk inhibiting their unbounded confidence in expressing their ideas to each other. I moved to the other side of a ubiquitous limestone jardinière supporting a palm tree rising out of a polished green urn. I was now not therefore immediately visible to them. And indeed I was now standing next to a purple silk flocked wallpaper covered wall punctuated with brass appliqués in the form of cherubic faces set in between more drawings of Music Halls.

One such gilt framed encased drawing, in front of which I standing. Allowed me to feigned an inordinate interest and absorption in its fine representation of the Lusby's Music Hall And thus listen without impeding the flow of invectives from Marie Tempest or Maude Adams, the likes of which I thought did not form part of the vocabulary of a lady; Music Hall artistes or not.

"I know my weakness less than you know your strength!" Tempest was overheard to inform Adams, who responded immediately.

"If you are implying that I am of the stature of a Vulcana.[8] Then madam, I suggest you revise your ill-informed opinion of me," said Maude Adams, reaching for her nearby bottle of champagne from which she replenished her empty fluted glass.

"As with everything appertaining to me," replied Marie Tempest, lighting her Trichinopoly cigar, "I am the soul of discretion and moderation in all that I do, practice or say."

"To me, my dearest of friends," countered Maude Adams, "you are none of these things, for alas those laudable qualities to which you allude. And, it pains me to have to say this. But in the opinion of most members of the *Arbiter elegantiarum*, [9] you remain, most certainly, an object of derision, if not of scorn!"

Lusby's Music Hall

Despite the last bell being sounded as a signal to return to the auditorium, I elected to stay and enjoy this performance. Clearly the majority of patrons at the Crush Bar agreed with me. All tried to look nonchalantly at the contestants; as though their argument was of little interest to them. Both Tempest and Adams had dispensed with their discussion of Dvořák's symphonic style, in preference for a more personal exchange of insults and remarks. All of which were as far remove from musical analysis or appreciation as could be.

1 A Jurist is a legal theorist researching Jurisprudence
2 *Tannhäuser and the Singers' Contest at Wartburg Castle.*
3 For a fuller account, refer to '*Vaudeville – The Struggle Continues'* Chapter 40
4 In reality, Loge in the opera is portrayed as being a venal and scheming character
5 Marie Tempest was born Mary Susan Etherington
6 The World's Columbian Exhibition was held in Chicago 1893
7 The Birthday of the Princess,
8 Vulcana is the leading, Strong Woman of the time
9 Leaders of artistic taste and style

Chapter 15

The Impromptu Performance

A most peculiar of days thus far; in that we had started out earlier in the afternoon with the intention of arriving at the St. James' Theater to rehearse a variation on our act with Cinderella in the guise of Marmeduke. But we had become embroiled in an unscheduled drinking session in the nearby Red Lion Public House in the Duke of York Street just off Piccadilly. Along with other Music Hall artistes all of whom would be performing on the stage at sometime during the evening. Jack and I had done our turn on the stage earlier, and to decent applause. However, we were now witness to another kind of Music Hall drama; that which is often performed at the Crush Bar. Indulging in a frank and mutual exchange of opinions and feelings, to the repressed delight of those at the Crush Bar this evening, were Marie Tempest and Maude Adams, between whom no love was ever lost.

"My dear, I am very sorry to say," said Marie Tempest, "but you are deluding yourself. Perhaps this condition could be as a result of your slow but, inescapable decline as a minor Music Hall artiste and..."

"Are we speaking from personal experience here?" interrupted Maude Adams. "Perhaps we are getting above ourselves and letting what little fame you derived from that play, *'Mary Goes First,'* [1] to go to one's inordinately small head. Let me remind you, about the absurdity and idiotic plot for which the play or pantomime is infamous and indeed notorious. Or is it too painful to relate?"

"There is very little that goes to my head, small or otherwise, including champagne or fame. For I am used to both," replied Tempest, "and being educated at the Convent des Ursulines, in Belgium, and later studying music in Paris and at the Royal Academy of Music here in London, you can believe this to be so. Consequently, my dear Maud, at least I can sing, as an accomplished soprano, for my supper. Having be taught to do so by the great Spanish singer Manuel Garcia, who, I will have you know, tutored the accomplished Letty Lind."

Interesting I thought to myself. Such an impressive list of achievements must be difficult to respond to. Maud did so.

"Perhaps, but I refer you back to your minor singing rôle in, *Mary Goes First.'* The plot of which is equal to the most banal of pantomimes, complete with an inherent indignity several levels below that of farce. What with local robber barons building, from their own private funds, hospitals and sanatoria for the local townspeople and wishing to be ennobled for his conspicuous, if contrived generosity. Do tell me? Are people still bothered about obtaining knighthoods, and thus a perceived position in society?" inquired Maud Adams, and then drawing deeply upon her Trichinopoly cigar.

Unfortunate Tempest was unable to answer this seemingly innocent question. Not because it confounded her. But rather as a result of the intervention of Lodge, who was now standing on the other side of the limestone jardinière supporting a palm tree rising out of a polished green urn in front of a gilt framed image of an ethereal vision of classical structures.

Vision of Classical Structures

"Did I hear the word knighthood being offered about with such reckless abandon? There is, after all, none more deserving than I. If I may be so modest as to suggest; since I remain a model example of what humility is, or at least ought to be."

The person offering this information was Lodge. Consequently, I moved around the limestone jardinière and made my presence known.

"How are you doing Maud?" I inquired on making eye contact with Maud Adams.

"I am doing just fine Theo, just fine. I saw you and Jack earlier on the stage. You were, as usual, a treat to watch. How is Jack?" she asked.

I noticed that Maud positioned herself deliberately next to me. As Lodge manœuvred himself, unwittingly perhaps, in between the unmovable Marie Tempest and the equally immovable ubiquitous limestone jardinière supporting a polished green urn out of which rose a resplendent palm tree. Whatever, Lodge was now trapped!

"Do tell me Lodge, what is the...?" asked Tempest.

"Not for the first time this evening, in this very Crush Bar," interrupted Lodge, "have I been compelled to advise the person talking with me that the name is Loge, especially to my close acquaintances."

"The question I was about to ask you Lodge was, what as an impresario do you think of the hugely successful play, '*Mary Goes First*,' in which I am the only star?

"Well Marie, I have not..." replied Lodge.

"Would you like my autograph Lodge?" butted in Tempest.

This question slightly put out Lodge. We could see this. Because his monomania returned with a vengeance as he started to look over his shoulders.

"Madam," insisted Lodge, "I am not used to people addressing me in such a confident manner and asking, whether I seek their autograph, especially when I do not know the person. The answer madam that I was going to furnish to your question about that play called, '*Mary Goes First.*' Is no, I have not seen it. And have no desire to sit in a theater and watch it. And madam, do not get out your press clippings. Theater reviews can be bought, as much as vegetables in a cabbages and frock street market for ready money!"

"How dare you, how dare you talk to me, as if I were some nondescript. That play in which I have the honor to be the leading lady. And a rôle for which I am eminently suited, has been hailed as a..." responded Tempest.

"I treat you madam in the way that I do because you are so," interrupted Lodge, "and my as rôle as impresario enables me to make such valued judgements. Including the preposterous plot of that play involving as it does farcical political intrigue based on outmoded notions which evaporated with onset of the Age of Enlightenment."

By now other patrons at the Crush Bar were migrating to our group. During which I overheard one well dressed gentleman say to his companion. "Could this impresario Lodge actually know something about the Age of Enlightenment?" [2]

Irrespective of this philosophical inquiry, Tempest continued her onslaught on Lodge.

"Impresario? Word on the street has it you are nothing more than a failed Vaudeville schmuck. That is why you over play your importance. And this is why your reputation is one of exploitation and exacting harshness on we performing artistes," replied Tempest, working herself up in to an emotional state, for which she is justly renowned; and as suggested by her surname.

"If that is a compliment; then I accept it gracefully, informed Lodge, tapping his black silk top hat with his gold capped ebony cane.

Tempest finally let go her feelings and verbally exploded in a tirade of invectives and allegations including one of his being a tyrant.

It was Jack who intervened.

"No, no," said Jack, "I have known Loge now for some weeks past. And I cannot stand here in all righteousness and let that remark, of Lodge being a tyrant, go unchallenged. You my dear Maria have not worked for Tony Pastor in his 14th Street Theater in New York City. He was much worse!"

"Perhaps we would all benefit if we had a drink, "suggested Cinderella, "rather than becoming emotionally embroiled with each other."

Tempest's reaction was simply to gather her mink coat, close it on to her chest and walked off out of the Crush Bar with her head held high.

"Good," said Maud Adams, "the drinks are on me, bar-tender!"

Having gotten our drinks, I was standing near Lodge and looking at Cinderella who was in deep conversation with Maud Adams. Both of them looked conspiratorial; as if planning some outrage or other outlandish event.

"Mr Lodge is it sir?" inquired voice emanating between Lodge and myself.

I looked at Lodge and together we both turned our heads to the source of the voice. I assumed it to be one of the theater ushers, for such was the deferential tone of the voice. Not so. The voice came from a face of such repellent aspect, for it was severely pocked-marked and blotched. His dark brown eyes, which twitched constantly, were set deeply beneath a bulbous forehead. His hair, though thick, was greasy and unkempt. He was tall and shuffled as he stood there as though afflicted with St. Vitus' Dance.

"Good God man, can that be you? What are you doing here? Come to beg for your old position back as man-servant to me eh?" asked a surprised Lodge.

"Nothing of the like, I have just come in here to avail myself of some light refreshment of aërated water and absinthe before I go on," replied the person.

This was of course the loquacious Aloysius, Lodge's former man-servant. And who deserted Lodge during the reception at Lodge's town house a while back. He did so after a monumental argument involving Lodge, Sir Augustus Harris and other Music Hall artistes attending that now infamous Bacchanalian party held at Lodge's town house in the Bergen Avenue.

"Go on, go on what?" inquired Lodge.

"Go on the stage," replied Aloysius.

"Go on the stage as what? Are you a stage hand or even a call boy here at the St. James's Theater or an usher?" asked an increasingly curious Lodge.

"Do I look like a stage hand, call boy or usher?" asked Aloysius.

Good question, I thought. Indeed I remember this over confident Aloysius when he was Lodge's man-servant. And especially the time when Aloysius was serving luncheon to the late Cora Bella Elmore, Jack and myself whilst guests at Lodge's town house in the Bergen Avenue.[3] There Aloysius displayed an extraordinary and deep contempt for Lodge who was supposed to be his lord and master. I also remember at the time thinking does this man-servant retain a hold over Lodge? Certainly his unchecked confidence knew no bounds. And facilitated a visible mounting disrespect and not just to Lodge himself, including his guests, but indeed for all and sundry irrespective of rank, title or position.

Aloysius' confident manner was evident from the moment we arrived at Lodge's town house in the Bergen Avenue.

Jack had knocked on the front door of the town house. Eventually after some considerable time the door was opened by Aloysius.

'What do you want?' Was his opening remark on first meeting Jack. He then later followed in with other words. 'Well; what do you want?'

His manner, personality and character were less than one would expect from a servant of the household, in the door way of which we found ourselves as personal guests of his master. That encounter at the front door lasted all but eight seconds! Finally Aloysius, on seeing Lodge approach the commotion at the front door, abruptly changed his attitude.

For the sole benefit of Lodge, Aloysius qualified his previous refrain to Jack with the words,

'Certainly sir, if you would just wait a moment.'

He then promptly closed the door in our faces!

His innate rudeness was in no way limited to his actions at the front door.

Before luncheon was served, we all of us were seated around the Dining Room table. Typically Aloysius shuffled over to me and quite impertinently asked me a question.

'Good day sir; and will you be taking luncheon per chance?' he had asked of me.

Astounded at his audacity, I had replied to him.

'That question is rather a ridiculous one it would seem

to me; since I am quite clearly sitting at the dining table as a luncheon guest of your master. Do tell me? For what other possible reason would I be seated at this table?'

'Why Sir, any number of excuses, how could I know?' he had answered with such characteristic unbridled rudeness, 'it is possible you might want to play cards or even poker or indeed any other immoral past-time whilst seated at the table.'

I have been entertained in houses across the States. And in such places, any flunky of the household, be they a humble housemaid, or senior butler, paid unceasing deference and unfailing politeness to their masters and guests in demonstrating respect and obedience. Clearly in the case of this man-servant Aloysius, unerring deference was but a theoretical concept to him.

That was then, I reminisced. I now attended the events unfolding at the Crush Bar in the St. James's Theater with regard to the arrival of Aloysius.

"Well what are you doing on the stage? Do not tell me you are performing?" inquired Lodge, repressing a slight laugh.

"I am that. And as a Monologist," answered Aloysius.

Lodge was not the only person surprised by that revelation. Indeed I should not have been surprised. For I do recall the fact that Aloysius was intelligent and that his intellect could never be in doubt. That he possessed inherent humility or politeness certainly could. His ability to return wit, instantly and succinctly with unerring and devastating accuracy was remarkable to say the least. And, in my experience of over thirty years treading the floorboards on the stage and working Vaudeville. Could, earn him an enviable reputation in Vaudeville or indeed in any English Music Hall as a Monologist or in some other similar rôle.

"Clancy, good to see you again, how are you doing?" inquired Jack, as he shook hands with Aloysius.

"Jack, this is Aloysius, previously Lodge's man-servant," I said.

"No Theo, this is Clancy, the Monologist," informed Jack.

"Well how do you know that?" I asked.

"Because the hand bill I gave you in our dressing room earlier informed me that there was a Monologist, name of Clancy, doing his début this evening at the St. James' Theater," replied Jack.

I offered my hand to Clancy.

"Good to see you too Mr. Houston, sir," said Clancy, deferentially.

In the next instant a call boy came into the Crush Bar.

"Clancy, Clancy you are up in ten," the call boy said, with a sense of urgency and wearing a manic expression upon his face.

Clancy immediately downed his large glass of aërated water with absinthe and followed the call boy out of the Crush Bar and up to the back of stage, ready to be called upon to perform his début.

We all looked at each other for a few moments. And then spontaneously and with no pre-ordained signal we all of us threw the contents of our glasses down our throats. And for the first time in my life I, together with Cinderella, Jack, Lodge and Franklyn Smith, stampeded *out* of the Crush Bar and made our way into the auditorium to witness Clancy's début on stage!

1 By Henry Jones and produced at the Playhouse in 1913
2 An 18th. Century intellectual movement expressing liberalization of ideas and philosophy
3 For a fascinating account of this encounter refer to *Music Hall – The Saga Goes on*, Chapter 3

Index